I0652965

ALSO BY RYAN J HAMSHAW

Keepers of the Crossing series:

The Dark Friars
The Handsel Witches

PRAISE FOR THE DARK FRIARS

KEEPERS OF THE CROSSING

THE DARK
FRIARS

Nominated for 7 Indieverse Awards including Book of the Year and Best YA Novel.

"What an absolutely brilliant, fun and addictive YA book! It's not my usual genre at all but I LOVED this one. I fell in love with all the main characters and had a giggle and a smile at some of the cheesy lines, pop culture references and old school movie stuff. I need more. Is this a series? I freaking hope so!"
— Jessica Huntley, Bestselling Author of Horrible Husband

"Good god, Tariq! My new book boyfriend and I am prepared to fight ANYONE who gets in my way. I found myself itching to pick the book back up any time that I wasn't reading it. The easiest 5 stars I've given for a while, and I am left SALIVATING for book two! I need more!"
— Ryan, Empire of Books

"This book is a MUST! So good! Great characters. Great Magic. Great plot. And it's only BOOK 1!! I cannot wait for more Keepers of the Crossing! I really hope Ryan Hamshaw gets this picked up by a big publisher one day. It's too good!"
— Justin Hall, Book Aficionado

"A new contender in Modern Fantasy has emerged. Mixing the real with the fantastical... a little magic, a dash of demons, and a generous helping of slow burning, well navigated queer romance."
— Jayce T, Goodreads Reviewer

"Hamshaw has created a world I want to dive right into and that I'll never feel ready to come back up for air from. Perfectly captures what a good fantasy book should, with great world building that isn't over complicated or boring. The magic system is unique and was truly a joy to read. Hamshaw's voice is so clear... this is just brilliant. Perfectly paced too, so important in a fantasy novel."
— Lorna, Goodreads Reviewer

"This was the kind of fantasy story I was after! Buffy the Vampire Slayer 2.0 with a male lead—and he's gay!!!!!! As a boy growing up on Buffy and Charmed, this is the type of story I used to long for. The lore of the Keepers is rich and perfectly explained, the romance with Tariq gave me everything—tension, fake dating, protector trope! Liam is such a relatable protagonist, hiding his identity like a true superhero. In a time where fantasy books are in abundance, this book shines like a diamond. I am sooo invested!"
— Anthony John Parody

RYAN J HAMSHAW

Chalk Stream Books

Ryan J Hamshaw asserts his moral right to
be identified as the author of this book.

Copyright © 2025 Ryan J Hamshaw
ryanjhamshaw.co.uk

Published in partnership with Chalk Stream Books
chalkstreambooks.com

ISBN (Paperback): 978-1-917056-58-8
ISBN (Hardback): 978-1-917056-59-5

This is a work of fiction. Names, characters, businesses,
places, events, and incidents are either the products
of the author's imagination or used in a fictitious
manner. Any resemblance to actual persons, living
or dead, or actual events is purely coincidental.

All rights reserved. No part of this publication may be
reproduced, distributed, or transmitted in any form or by
any means, including photocopying, recording, or other
electronic or mechanical methods, without the prior
written permission of the publisher, except in the case of
brief quotations embodied in critical reviews and certain
other non-commercial uses permitted by copyright law.

For permission requests, write to the publisher,
addressed "Attention: Permissions Coordinator",
at contact@chalkstreambooks.com

Printed and bound in the UK.

Cover design: Jamie Flack
www.catandcrown.com

FOR MY BEAUTIFUL SISTER, PAIGE,
WHO LOVES A BIT OF MAGIC
JUST AS MUCH AS I DO...

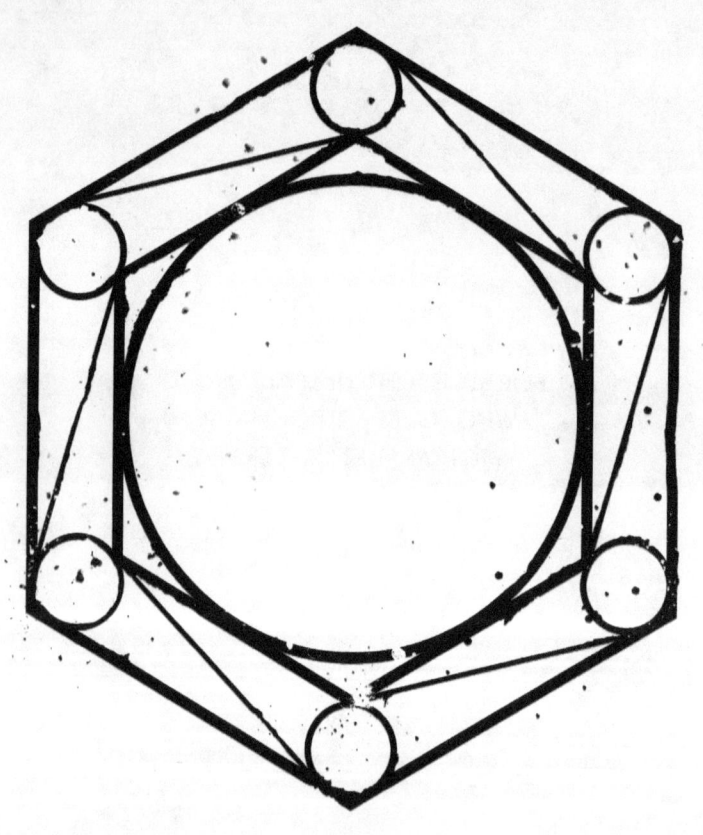

PART I

ONE

THE CLOAKER

Any one of these mannequins could be trying to kill me. Their stillness in the dark is unnerving. They all seem to be watching me as I slowly weave through them, like silent guards ready to strike if I make a wrong move. I step over one lying across the floor, its arm reaching up as if trying to grab me.

Something clatters somewhere in the boarded-up shop. It could be Tariq. Or it could be the Cloaker.

We've been tracking this shapeshifter most of the evening. According to Tariq, Cloakers are demons that take on the form of the humans they've killed. This one is currently masquerading as Bob, the security guard.

This shop is huge, spanning two levels, so Tariq and I split up to cover more ground.

I hold up my phone, its weak torch beam slicing through the oppressive darkness.

Tariq's by a customer service counter, bending down to examine a charity pot that's just spilled coins across the floor. He flashes me an awkward smile.

I thought I was the clumsy one.

The shop has been closed for months, and the air is thick with dust. Every breath tickles the back of my throat.

I'd rather be anywhere but here right now. In fact, I want to be at Leonardo's, scoffing a pizza with Tariq, enjoying our first date. But no. Instead of experiencing romantic candlelight and overly attentive waiters, we're stuck hunting down a shapeshifting demon.

It's been like this for weeks. Ever since the Festive Fling got cancelled because of a gas leak, Tariq and I have been trying to have a real date – something that doesn't involve our Keeper duties and all the blood and guts that come with it. Something normal. Like a fancy restaurant with all the cheese imaginable.

My stomach rumbles.

Why is this my life?

A piercing scream erupts from somewhere in the shop, freezing me in place.

The mannequins' blank stares seem to follow me. My grip tightens on my phone.

I strain to listen, hoping my enhanced hearing will kick in. It's one of the abilities I've been trying to work on – with Nathaniel's help, of course – but he's been as elusive as the shapeshifter these last couple of months.

Footsteps echo from the floor above. Dust falls as the ceiling vibrates.

Tariq appears from around the corner. He follows my gaze up.

'Cloaker?' I ask, shielding my eyes.

Tariq listens for a moment. 'That, or a really big rat.'

He heads for the motionless escalators, and I follow.

We take the metal steps slowly. Cloakers have super-hearing too, but their vision is practically non-existent.

When we reach the top, a foul smell hangs in the air. It's like rotting flesh. Bob the security guard, or at least what's left of him, is piled on the floor. His skin and clothes are discarded like an empty costume, his gold name badge glinting as my phone's beam hits it.

'Poor Bob.'

'Cloakers don't like to stay in their natural form for long,' Tariq whispers, scanning the area. 'It'll be looking for its next disguise.'

And that next disguise could be me or Tariq. I don't know about him, but I'm not interested in giving up my skin anytime soon.

'You hear anything?' He moves past Bob's remains.

I focus, trying to sharpen my hearing. My ears warm as I tune in. My heartbeat, and Tariq's. His breath is steady. Somewhere outside, a bus rumbles past the shop. But there's no sign of the Cloaker.

'Nothing,' I say.

But then something lands on the floor between us. It's sloppy. I shine the beam down, and it's… more of Bob's skin. But how…

Tariq's eyes meet mine.

The lizard-like creature clings to the ceiling. My phone's torch barely illuminates it before it drops down, screeching like a giant cat. Tariq and I throw ourselves out of the way as it lands between us, on all fours. This thing no longer resembles Bob. His skin has peeled away completely, revealing the green, slime-covered demon underneath.

It bares its needle-sharp teeth at me as I scramble to my feet, but Tariq is already armed with flames in both hands. He throws them toward the Cloaker, fire filling the air. But the demon is too quick. It springs off the ground, propelling itself out of Tariq's burning reach.

It disappears into the darkness of the shop.

'Speedy little shit, isn't it?'

'Come on,' Tariq says, heading off after the Cloaker.

It doesn't take us long to find it. The Cloaker is hurling itself at every window, desperately searching for an escape route.

'We can't let it get outside,' Tariq says.

Darting through empty clothing racks, I rush toward it, but the Cloaker spots me. It spins, its scaled tail whipping me aside. I'm flung across the floor, crashing into a cardboard cutout of a cartoon Santa Claus.

I recover quickly, but Tariq already has the demon trapped in a ring of fire. Its screeching reaches a fever pitch.

With both hands, Tariq slowly tightens the ring, the flames inching closer to the demon.

Suddenly, the room flashes with white lightning. Tariq's eyes flicker in the brightness. His concentration falters, and the flames fizzle out. Thunder booms.

The Cloaker's slitted eyes lock onto mine, and it leaps.

Tariq shouts my name, but the demon is already on me. The force of its attack sends us crashing through the walls of the changing rooms, plasterboard splintering around us as we hit the floor.

The Cloaker writhes on top of me, my arm the only thing holding it back.

Tariq tries to pull it off, but the creature knocks him backward.

It snaps at my face, desperately trying to force its way inside, to wear my skin.

But not today.

My hands find its sticky head, and as soon as I get a good grip, I pull hard. The Cloaker's head twists, its neck cracking. It goes limp on top of me.

'You okay?' Tariq asks, panicked, as he pushes the demon off me.

'Think so.' I rub the demon slime off, onto my shirt.

'Nice kill.'

The Cloaker is lifeless beside me. 'Thanks.' I try to pick myself up, but there's a shudder and movement beneath me. 'What's that?'

Tariq's gaze follows a crack in the floor, disappearing underneath us. 'Crap,' he says, and the floor gives way.

I fall, and Tariq falls with me. Debris rains down around us as my back hits the counter on the ground floor below. Tariq lands on top of me, shielding me from chunks of wall and floor. A cloud of dust wafts up around us.

There's a stillness as we wait for the air to clear.

'You think Leonardo's is still open?' I ask.

He laughs. 'Somehow, I don't think they'd let us in, even if they were.'

I reach for his hair, picking a piece of plasterboard from a curl dangling over his emerald eyes. Even covered in all this muck, he still looks ridiculously handsome.

'Thanks,' he says, then leans in. His lips press against mine, and suddenly, all the aching in my body melts away.

My stomach rumbles again. He pulls back, glancing down at me.

We laugh.

'How about we grab some chips and take a late-night stroll around the park?' He caresses my chin.

'That sounds—'

Lightning flashes again. The sky outside explodes, and, as if on cue, rain begins battering the shop windows.

We both sigh and clamber off the counter.

'I feel like the universe doesn't want us to happen,' I say, brushing myself off.

There's now a giant hole in the ceiling.

'I should call the clean-up team at the Guild,' he says, pulling out his phone. 'Then maybe we can make a break for the Seven Angels. I've got some questionable two-day-old doughnuts in my room.'

'Wow, and I thought the date couldn't get any better.'

He smiles before wandering off to make the call.

The street outside is already flowing with water. Across from the shop, people who were out for the night are clambering into taxis. At least some people out there had a normal night, despite the now-severe weather.

If we had taken a different route to the restaurant, Tariq never would have spotted the Cloaker in the first place. And the night would have gone according to plan.

But then someone else could have been killed.

'They're on their way,' Tariq says, returning to me. 'You ready to get wet?'

I nod, and we step outside. The Seven Angels is only a few streets away, but there's a whole lot of rain between here and there.

TWO

HOUSEMATES

TARIQ

He's a little forceful with his tongue, but I don't mind. We've been at it for five minutes now, and it's getting harder to hold back. I don't want to push Liam into anything, but certain parts of my body have other ideas.

The fire roaring in the fireplace beside my bed is making this extra hot; only the rain hammering the windows is keeping me grounded.

'You okay?' Liam asks, pulling away from my lips.

My tongue hasn't been in his mouth for a while now. 'Yeah. Sorry.'

His forehead creases. 'Yeah, I wasn't really into it either.' He rolls off me and onto the bed.

He can take things to heart so quickly sometimes.

Thunder crashes.

'First of all,' I say, rolling onto him, 'you were…' I eye his crotch, 'very into it.'

He blushes and pulls a pillow over his face, but I tug it away.

'Secondly, I'm just annoyed tonight didn't go to plan.' I kiss him softly. 'I just want us to have a perfect date.'

He kisses me back, his lips warm. 'Well, for now, this is perfect.'

I smile. 'You want to stay over tonight?'

'Well, I'm not going home in that.' He gestures toward the window and the storm raging outside.

'Perfect.'

I barely catch the grin spreading across Liam's face before the main light goes out, plunging the room into the warm, flickering glow of the fire.

'What's going on?'

I get up off him.

The streetlights are out, and the only light comes from a passing car.

'Power cut,' I say.

A thumping on my bedroom door makes both of us jump. A flash of white light fills the room for a split second, followed by more distant booms.

The door bangs again. 'Tariq?' A familiar voice calls from the other side.

I open it to find Heather standing there in her long lilac nightie. She quickly scurries in, closing the door behind her.

'Heather, what are you—'

She presses a finger to my lips before I can finish. Liam is definitely amused.

'She'll hear you,' she whispers.

I slowly take her hand away. 'Who's "she"?'

'Maggie. She's afraid of the storm and won't leave me alone,' Heather says.

I drag my fingers down my face. Maggie is Heather's latest ghost friend, a barmaid who died of some disease here at the Seven Angels in the 1700s. Been around about a week. I lose track. Before her, it was Alfred the grave robber and Lydia, the eight-year-old banshee with no concept of an inside voice.

'Hi, Heath—'

'Shhh!' She silences Liam, who's still sitting upright on the bed.

Heather's still adjusting since moving here from the Sarum Wellbeing Centre. She's certainly less... strange, than when Liam and I first met her. But she's still not quite there all the time. Seeing dead people regularly must do that to you.

'Can I stay in here with you boys tonight? Maggie won't look for me here.'

'Of course,' Liam says.

'No,' I say.

We both look at each other.

'Tariq!' Liam nods for me to come over to him. 'Just let her stay,' he says, quietly. 'She's probably scared of the storm and just using Maggie as an excuse.'

'Fine, but you're sleeping in the bed with her. I'll take the chair.'

Liam can deal with Miss Fidget all night long.

'Heather, you can sleep over here,' Liam says, scooting to one side.

She rushes over and climbs in. 'Thank you, my darling.' She gives Liam a hug. 'You're very warm. I do hope you won't be a radiator all night.'

Liam stares at me, and I give him a thumbs up as I pull a blanket from my chest of drawers.

I settle into the armchair, throwing the blanket over me. Liam wraps the duvet around himself, shuffling as far away from Heather as he can without falling out of the bed.

We can't even get through a make-out session without something happening. Maybe the universe is trying to tell us something.

'Can we do anything about that firelight?' Heather asks.

If the universe wants to do some separating, it could at least start with my new housemate.

Thunder, wind, and rain battle outside.

I twist my hand at the fire, and the flames pull toward me. The fireplace empties, and the flames shrink into my hand until the room falls into darkness.

THREE

AN INCONVENIENT RELATIONSHIP

LIAM

Those are definitely the eyes of someone who got no sleep last night. The mirror in the humanities block toilets is brutally honest, highlighting the dark circles that stand out against my pale skin. At least my hair's behaving itself, starting to show hints of lighter blond from the few extra days of sun we've had as spring begins.

I crept out of Tariq's room early this morning, desperate for a proper shower. The one at the Seven Angels doesn't even come close to the one Mum and I have at the flat. When I left, Tariq and Heather were still fast asleep.

It's still early days, but I'm not sure Tariq's adjusting well to living with Heather. It's just the two of them at the Seven Angels, and while Opel and I have our own rooms there, we both prefer staying at home.

I splash some water on my face, pat it dry with paper towels, and step out into the bustling corridor of students.

I miss when Tariq was staying over all the time, but now that I've got full Keeper status and there are no Dark Friars out to kill me, I don't need nightly protection anymore. Besides, I can handle myself these days.

I shoot Tariq a quick message to let him know I managed to drag myself to college this morning and that I'll see him tonight for training.

Even though I'm an official Keeper of the Crossing now, I still need to train regularly alongside Tariq, Opel, and Heather. Well, sometimes Heather. She joins in on her good days. Good days meaning when she's not being hounded by the dead.

As I'm about to enter the refectory hall, a missing poster catches my eye on the student notice board. It's Katie Ford. These were everywhere after she 'went missing' – not just at college, but all over the city. Now, there's just the odd one here and there. Her face always reminds me of what really happened. Everyone else thinks she's just missing, but she's gone, and never coming back.

A lump forms in my throat, but I pull my eyes away and let it pass.

Lily's golden hair catches the light as she tucks it behind her ears. She's mid-bite, a forkful of pasta salad poised between her lips.

'Liam!'

The tables nearby go dead silent. A dozen pairs of eyes snap in our direction.

'Why are we announcing me to the entire hall?'

Lily grins, unbothered by the attention she's drawn. 'Tell us everything!' She yanks me down into the seat beside her with more force than I'd expected.

'Tell you what?'

'She wants to know about your date,' Jack pipes up from across the table, not even bothering to look up from his phone as he scrolls through some chat messages.

'Oh, that.' I unwrap the cling film from the sandwich I packed. 'Didn't happen.'

Lily's shoulders droop dramatically as if the news has physically deflated her. 'What happened?'

'Er… mix up at the restaurant,' I mumble, avoiding her gaze. 'But we spent the night at his.'

I've gotten better at deflecting questions about my Keeper duties. It's easier now that I can truthfully say I'm with Tariq most of the time, even if the details are far from ordinary.

'You spent the night again?'

Jack finally looks up, his face splitting into a grin that's all mischief. 'What base?' He pauses for dramatic effect. 'I mean, you kissed, right?'

I'm already regretting the direction this conversation is heading in. 'Obviously. But—'

'But still no cheek clapping?'

'Jack!' Lily smacks him on the arm.

'No, no cheeks were clapped,' I confirm, my grin widening despite myself. 'I mean, I think last night could've gone in that direction, but we were sort of… interrupted by a power cut.'

Jack's grin turns smug. 'Hey, my first time was in the dark.'

I raise an eyebrow, knowing full well that Jack hasn't exactly crossed that particular finish line yet.

'Jack, Phoebe Green trying to give you a handjob in the fair's House of Horrors doesn't count as your first time.' Lily folds her arms, her expression equal parts amused and exasperated.

Jack's face flushes a deep red. 'How do you know about that?'

'Phoebe told me at her New Year's party. She mentioned you had some trouble…'

'Hey!' Jack slams his hands on the table, inadvertently drawing more attention our way. 'You try maintaining a boner with Count Dracula cackling on loop.'

'…with the tight spaces,' Lily finishes slowly.

A moment of silence hangs between us as Jack processes his outburst.

Jack's had claustrophobia for as long as Lily and I have known him. Back in our first year of secondary, he had a full-on panic attack in a packed science corridor and missed days of school after. Since then, Lily and I always waited for him between classes, to steer clear of crowds. He's been better lately – college is more open, and honestly, I haven't heard him mention it in months.

'Oh…' Jack mumbles, looking down at his hands. 'Well, then pretend the last thirty seconds didn't happen.'

Lily smiles. 'Gladly.' She turns back to me, her eyes sparkling. 'So, basically what you're telling us is that a little thunder and lightning stopped any sexy time?'

'Yeah, well, that, and Heather.'

'Tariq's new housemate? The old lady?' Jack asks.

I frown at him. 'She's like thirty-something.'

Jack shrugs. 'Hey, both my mums are in their forties. And anything over twenty-five is basically ancient in my book.'

Lily rolls her eyes. 'Anyway… so Heather stayed with you two last night?'

'Yeah,' I reply, unable to suppress the sigh that escapes me. 'Turns out she hates storms, so she ended up in Tariq's room.'

'Cock-blocked!' Jack shouts, a little too loudly.

'What was that, Mr Cooper?' Principal Gellar's voice cuts through the air like a knife, sending a jolt of panic through all three of us. She's suddenly beside our table, one eyebrow quirked in stern curiosity.

'Er... nothing.'

'Good. I'm glad to hear it,' she says, her gaze lingering on me for a moment longer than necessary. Those thick eyebrows of hers arch almost comically before she finally moves on, continuing her patrol of the refectory.

I sometimes forget Principal Gellar knows I'm a Keeper. Not that she has ever acknowledged it outside of Guild meetings. It would be stupid of her to do that when ninety-nine per cent of the time I'm with Lily and Jack.

'Man, she's got ears like a bat,' Jack mutters, picking his phone back up.

'You're lucky she didn't hear the whole conversation,' I say. 'Imagine trying to explain "cheek clapping" to Gellar.'

Jack shudders dramatically. 'I'd rather not, thanks.'

I take a bite of my sandwich, letting the taste of egg mayonnaise distract me for a moment.

Tariq really did try to give us a normal date last night, until that stupid demon showed up. He even organised for the restaurant to give us a window seat that had the view over the Market Square. Bet they were pissed they had two no-shows for the best table.

Lily nudges me with her elbow. 'You okay?'

'Yeah.' I force a smile. 'It's just... Tariq and I can't seem to catch a break. Every time we try to have a normal date, something happens.'

Lily's expression softens. 'Maybe it's just bad luck?'

'Or maybe it's a sign,' Jack chimes in. 'You're not meant to be together.'

'Shut up, Jack,' Lily snaps.

'Maybe,' I say, shrugging off the thought. 'Or maybe we're just destined for the most inconvenient relationship ever.'

'Take your mind off it. Jack and I are going exploring after classes later. You want to join?'

Jack offers me an unenthusiastic grin.

'Exploring?'

'Yep! I've told you about the college's local history prize, right?'

She has, about a million times. It's been her obsession for weeks. I nod, bracing myself.

'Well, I've finally chosen a topic.'

Oh God. Please don't let it be Old Sarum. I haven't been back to the Crossing since the whole ordeal with Draven, Layla, and the Dark Friars.

'Grovely Wood!'

Relief! 'What's so special about Grovely?'

'What's so special?'

'You've done it now, mate,' Jack mutters.

'Not only is Grovely one of Wiltshire's largest ancient woodlands, dating back thousands of years, but it's packed with archaeological treasures. Bronze Age barrows, earthworks...'

'Cool, so—'

'And...'

Oh hell, there's more.

'It's been the site of countless historical events. Medieval hunting expeditions, local conflicts. Even during World War II, parts of the woods were used for military training. And don't get me started on the local folklore...'

'No, no, that's fine,' I say, before she can launch into a full lecture. 'Sounds like you've done your research.'

'Yep. Now I just need to get up there and see the area for myself. So, are you game?'

Jack flutters his eyes at me. I have no training until tonight, no Keeper duties on the horizon. Maybe it wouldn't be so bad to hang out with my friends for the afternoon.

'I'm game,' I finally say.

Lily squeals in delight. 'Excellent! We've got a lot of ground to cover, but it'll be worth it.'

Walking. I'm already regretting my decision. The refectory's food counter is suddenly looking very appealing. I'm going to need more than this sad little sandwich to get through the afternoon.

FOUR
GROVELY WOOD

TARIQ

I shove my bike into the Seven Angels courtyard and chain it to the railing by the back door. The front tyre is wrecked. Torn clean open by some broken glass back in Elizabeth Gardens. Should've taken the main roads, but no, I had to shortcut through the storm wreckage. Swerving around a fallen tree didn't help.

The puncture hit right after my last Munch delivery. Usual run to the Pets Corner women. Middle-aged mozzarella junkies who ask for me every week. Sheryl's the worst, always winking like we're flirting.

Not sure if it's me or the extra-hot pizza that keeps them loyal. Not that they know I give it a little boost of heat before I head inside. Some would say its cheating, using my powers. I say it's five-star service.

No shifts, no money. But the tyre can wait until tomorrow. Right now, I need a shower.

Inside, I shrug off my ugly orange Munchrider vest and hang it on the back of the door. My bed's still unmade, creased and messy from last night's guests. I overslept this morning, thanks to the storm, and Heather and Liam's snoring duet.

Liam said he'd call after he was done helping Lily with some college project.

After grabbing a towel, I slip down the hall. I knock on the bathroom door. I've had to get used to doing that with Heather living here. Before, it was just Nathaniel who had the occasional shower, but he's not been around much lately. The Guild's got him searching for the last two Keepers. If they even exist. I told him to let Theo and Lucas handle it, but Nathaniel's too loyal. He'll do whatever the Guild asks.

The shower's hot, washing away the grime of the day.

Back in my room, I pull on dark jeans and a maroon jumper, tucking my pendant stone underneath. I'm still adjusting my hair when there's a knock at the door. 'Yeah?'

'It's me,' Opel calls from the other side. 'You decent?'

I open the door. 'I'll let you be the judge,' I say, holding out my arms.

Opel tucks one side of her black hair behind her ear, studying me for a moment. Her eyes drop to the floor, and she gasps. 'Nude feet!'

I give her a deadpan look. 'You're hilarious.' Leaving the door open for her, I grab a pair of socks and my boots, taking a seat in the armchair to cover up my 'naked' feet. 'What are you doing here? Training?'

'I was,' she says, removing her jacket to reveal her sporty attire underneath. 'But I ran into Nathaniel downstairs. He wants to see us.'

'He's back?'

'Just arrived. Between you and me, he looks majorly frazzled.'

Nathaniel slides his phone across the desk. Google Maps is open, with a pin dropped on the other side of town. Grovely Wood.

'You want us to check it out?' I ask.

'Please,' Nathaniel says, leaning back in his chair and rubbing his temples. 'I'm sure it's nothing, but Peter mentioned seeing quite a few animal remains scattered around up there this morning during his dog walk. As a Guild member, he's suspicious. We should look into it.'

Nathaniel avoids making eye contact, leaning to one side of his chair.

'On the grown-up beverages now, huh?' Opel teases, sliding the phone back toward him, past his oversized Starbucks cup.

'I need the caffeine.' He takes a sip and checks his watch. 'Even if it is 3.30 in the afternoon.'

'I'm guessing no luck in Leeds?' I ask.

'No, just some *Doctor Who* fanatic claiming he can time travel. I should've known he wasn't the real deal when I saw his shed was painted like the TARDIS.' He takes another gulp of coffee. 'The Defensor and Tempus Keepers, if awakened, are still nowhere to be found.'

'You might want to start looking for a Spiritus too,' Opel chimes in.

Nathaniel glances between us. 'Is Heather…'

'Still loca in the casa? Yeah,' says Opel.

'What she means is Heather still hasn't left the building.'

Nathaniel leans back in his chair. 'She needs to get out more. She can't go back to hiding behind four walls. I'll talk to her. We've got to remember, she spent nearly twenty years in that place. This is a big adjustment.' He yawns, removing his glasses and tossing them onto the desk.

He could use some serious sleep. I nudge Opel and move toward the door. 'We'll head over to Grovely Wood and take a look at the scene.'

'Good. Let me know if you find anything. And be careful.'

Grovely Wood lies on the outskirts of Sarumbourne, just beyond the village of Wilton. Opel is driving since I don't have a car, and I haven't driven since I passed my test. I've never really needed to. I walk most places or bike if it's further afield.

We head down a narrow road lined with old cottages on one side. The tarmac ends, giving way to a wooded path. Opel pulls over just before a sign that reads 'Private Road, Residents Only'.

She pulls out her phone. 'The woods are at the top of this farmer's track.'

'Best get walking, then,' I say, stepping out of the car.

There are two paths leading toward the woods, one slightly wider than the other. The wider one must be for vehicles, so we take the narrower path. It's well trodden, and Opel and I have to manoeuvre around thick patches of mud. Two women on horseback approach; they nod as they pass by.

'So, how's lover boy? You done the dirty yet?' Opel asks as we come to less precarious ground.

'I'm not discussing my sex life with you, Opel.'

'That's a no, then.'

'No, we haven't. We can barely manage a date, let alone anything else.'

'Never pegged you for the date type, Tar.' She nudges me with her shoulder.

'Yeah, well, Liam's different. He's—'

'Not as easy?'

'Not as easy as you, you mean?' I give her a side-eye.

She gasps dramatically. 'I'll have you know it was never me who initiated that, it was Thomas.'

Opel and I wouldn't have fooled around that one time if Thomas hadn't dropped those hints. He never admitted anything to me, but Opel said he once told her he was bi-curious. He didn't seem to mind entertaining both of us that night. Awkward as hell. After that, Opel and I knew we were better off as friends.

She and Thomas got closer.

Since he passed, Opel and I haven't gone there again. I wouldn't want to.

'I miss Thomas,' she says, quietly.

'I'm sure Theo does a pretty good job of helping you forget.'

'Sometimes.'

'Are you two... exclusive now?'

She shrugs, but it's not as casual as she wants it to look. 'I guess. As exclusive as you can be with someone who's never really around. It's not the same, though. Theo's... good. Kind. But with Thomas – it was different.'

I don't interrupt. I've learned when to stay quiet around Opel and just let her open up. It's a rarity.

'Thomas and I weren't perfect,' she continues. 'Not even close. Those last few months were rough. You know that. Pushed me away more than once. And I was too stubborn to push back.' She exhales. 'But even with all that... I still miss him. His stupid jokes, the way he used to hum when he was nervous...'

'The way he never let you do anything dangerous without trying to stop you – even though he knew you'd do it anyway.'

23

She gives a weak smile. 'I think part of me thought I'd have more time to figure it out. To forgive him. Or make him forgive me. I don't know.'

We step over a fallen tree, the track lined with tangled hedgerow. Then we round a bend, and Grovely Wood opens up before us.

It's incredible. A long Roman road stretches ahead, vanishing into the trees like it could go on forever. Beeches and ferns flank the path, the foliage thick and endless. I've never seen anything like it in Sarumbourne.

Opel doesn't give it a second glance. Nature has always been lost on her. Instead, she's buried in her phone.

'Going by Nathaniel's pinned location sent to him by Peter, the animal remains should be about a ten-minute walk, somewhere on our left.'

I nod, and we step into the woods, the dappled sunlight filtering through the canopy above.

FIVE

THE BUNKER

My legs ache. We've been trudging through Grovely Wood for nearly two hours now, and Lily shows no sign of slowing down. So far, we've found nothing remarkable, just trees. Impressive trees, sure, but trees all the same. Jack, meanwhile, is climbing a stack of logs despite the large sign that clearly states: 'Do Not Climb These Logs'. Of course, Jack never lets signs dictate his actions; he's intent on filming an update for his followers from the top.

'If you fall and get crushed, that's on you,' I shout up to him.

'Love you too, mate,' he yells back, pulling out his phone as he reaches the peak.

Jack's journalism work has gone digital over the last few months. He still writes for the student news team, but most of his stories are now video segments. His online following has been growing steadily, which has made him more conscious of his appearance. Gone is his thick brown mop of hair, replaced by a more styled, groomed look. He's even started wearing makeup, which Lily helps him apply. A few shitty guys at college gave him grief for it at first, but now Jack's on a mission to normalise makeup for men. Honestly, I'm proud of him for it.

'Over here!' Lily calls.

I leave Jack to his influencer aspirations and find Lily standing in front of the World War II bunker she's been searching for. The small, decaying structure is partially swallowed by nature, crumbling brick walls covered in moss and vines. Trees grow tightly around it, some branches twisting over the top, as if nature is reclaiming it inch by inch.

'You found it. Well done. Can we go now?'

Lily shoots me a withering look and points toward what looks like the entrance. A section of brickwork has been patched up with newer bricks.

'This one's blocked, but I think there's another bunker nearby we can check.'

There is no way I'm spending another two hours traipsing around these woods in search of some other half-ruined bunker. My eyes fall on a gap near the top of the brickwork.

'The wall feels loose,' I say, running my hands over the bricks in an exaggerated inspection. 'Maybe we can still get in.'

'It seemed pretty solid to me.'

'Why don't you grab Jack? I'll keep working on it.'

Lily narrows her eyes. 'Alright.'

Once she's out of sight, I plant my butt firmly on the ground and give the wall a solid push with my legs. The brickwork collapses inward with a low rumble, kicking up a thick cloud of dust. I cough and wave my hand in front of my face, trying to clear the air.

The faint light filtering through the trees barely reaches inside the bunker. I take out my phone and flick on the torch. The tunnel beyond the entrance is long and narrow, its ceiling arched and reinforced with old, ribbed concrete.

Despite the decay outside, the inside looks surprisingly sturdy, with support beams curving overhead in a neat, semi-circular pattern.

'Hey! You did it!' Lily shrieks behind me, making me jump and nearly drop my phone.

She rushes over, snapping photos of the entrance. Jack trails behind her, far less enthused.

'Wow,' Lily breathes, already mentally cataloguing the place for her research. She is practically vibrating with excitement as she stares inside.

'Lily, you're not seriously thinking of going in there, right?' says Jack.

'Of course I am! This is exactly the kind of place I need for my project. We have to explore it.'

I snort. '*We*? You mean *you*.'

'Come on. It'll be quick. I just need to snap a few more pictures, and then we'll be out. Promise.'

Jack has his phone torch on, clearly weighing his options. He sighs and rubs the back of his neck, his resolve cracking.

'Let's just get on with it.' I want to be at home, curled up in bed with a big bowl of cheesy pasta, sending inappropriate messages to Tariq.

Jack looks at me, raising an eyebrow. 'If there's a serial killer in there, I'm blaming you guys.'

'Pretty sure a smart serial killer wouldn't trap himself in a bunker by bricking himself inside.' There might not be a serial killer in there, but Sarumbourne is the home of the Crossing. Anything could be living, or dead, inside. Not that I'm telling Jack that.

'Point taken,' Jack grumbles. 'But if I get murdered, I'm haunting the hell out of both of you.'

Lily claps her hands in excitement. 'Great! Let's go!'

We shuffle through the narrow opening, ducking under the broken wall. The air inside is cold and musty, thick with the scent of damp earth and decayed wood. The floor is covered with dirt, debris, and small stones. Lily leads the way, her phone out and snapping pictures of every inch of the place. Jack and I hold up our phones to light the path ahead, casting long shadows against the bunker's concrete sides.

Jack's keeping close to the wall, his shoulders a little too tense, breathing through his nose like he's trying not to think about how tight the space is.

'You good?' I say.

Jack nods quickly. 'I can't believe this place is still standing.' His voice echoes slightly in the confined space.

Lily ignores him, too absorbed in her photos. 'Soldiers set up encampments here in the woods during the war, safe from prying eyes in the sky,' she murmurs, half to herself. 'These bunkers would have been used to store weaponry and bombs. They don't make structures like this anymore...'

Jack stifles a laugh. 'You mean no one wants a cold, damp hole in the ground? Shocking.'

Lily shoots him a look but doesn't respond, clicking away with her phone. We reach a wider section of the tunnel, and she stops to take a few more photos, crouching down to get better angles.

There's a faint shuffling sound from deeper within the tunnel. Jack and I freeze. I hold up my phone, trying to make out what caused the noise.

'You heard that, right?' Jack whispers, stepping closer to me.

I nod, my heart starting to race. 'Yeah.'

Lily, still focused on her photos, barely notices our sudden change in demeanour.

A scuffling sound echoes through the tunnel, louder this time.

'Lily,' I say quietly. 'Maybe we should head back.'

She waves me off. 'Just a few more shots.'

Jack and I exchange uneasy glances, holding our phones higher, trying to see further into the darkness. The shuffling gets louder, closer now, like something is moving toward us.

'What the hell is that?' Jack whispers.

I take a step forward, squinting into the shadows. And then, out of nowhere, a rat the size of a small cat scurries across the floor in front of us.

Lily screams, loud enough to wake the dead, and bolts toward the entrance. Jack and I don't even hesitate; we take off after her, our feet pounding the damp concrete as we race toward the exit.

'Move, move, move!' Jack shouts, nearly tripping over a loose brick as we sprint back through the tunnel.

We tumble out of the bunker, practically falling over each other as we reach the fresh air outside. The adrenaline is still pumping.

But before I can catch my breath, two dark figures loom out of the trees, and I nearly jump out of my skin.

'Liam!' Tariq says, startled.

Opel is beside him, eyebrows raised. 'What are you doing here?'

SIX

WHISPERS

TARIQ

Liam and his friends are the last people I had expected to find in Grovely Wood, especially crawling out of an old, forgotten bunker.

'We're… uh, researching for a history project,' Lily says between heavy breaths, clearly trying to recover from whatever they just went through inside that bunker.

Opel narrows her eyes at her. 'Sorry, who are you?'

Before I can answer, Liam cuts in. 'Oh, right. You guys haven't actually met. Opel, this is Lily,' he gestures toward his bubbly friend still catching her breath, 'and that's Jack.' Jack, standing slightly behind Lily, gives a half-hearted wave. 'Guys, this is Opel, a friend of Tariq's.'

'Nice to meet you,' Lily says.

Jack barely offers a nod. I've only met Liam's friends a handful of times. Lily's hard to dislike, with all her enthusiasm, but Jack? There's something about him that puts me on edge. The way he is around Liam. Maybe that's it. Their history, jokes, little looks I'm not part of.

'So, what are you guys up to?' Jack asks, breaking the silence.

I lock eyes with Liam. He catches on quick, realising that Opel and I are here on Keeper business.

'Oh!' Liam blurts. 'You two are on your... uh... weekly birdwatching stroll, right?'

Opel shifts uncomfortably next to me. 'Right.'

'Birdwatching?' Lily asks, tilting her head. 'I didn't know you were into that, Tariq.'

'Oh, he's very into birds,' Opel jumps in. 'Birds of prey, mostly. You know, the kind that swoop in for the kill.' She turns her head toward me, glaring slightly as if to emphasise the point.

An awkward silence settles over us. Jack looks between us with raised eyebrows, as if he's trying to figure out the inside joke.

'You don't seem very prepared for birdwatching, though,' Jack comments. 'Where are your binoculars?'

I just stare at Liam pointedly, silently begging him to steer this conversation away from dangerous territory.

'Hey,' Liam begins. 'Maybe we should all head out. It's getting late, and I don't know about you, but I don't fancy being in these woods after dark.'

We've been on the Roman road for five minutes, the silence thick and awkward. No one seems to know what to say. I pick up the pace, hoping Liam will follow and leave Opel with Lily and Jack, despite the disapproving looks she keeps throwing my way.

'Birdwatching? Really?' I ask when Liam finally catches up.

'I panicked. What are you guys actually doing here?'

'A member of the Guild found animal remains up here this morning. Nathaniel asked Opel and me to investigate. You seen anything unusual?'

Liam shakes his head. 'Nope. Nothing.'

'Opel and I heard screaming earlier. What happened?'

'Oh, it was just a rat.'

'All that over a rat?'

He shrugs. 'Hey, it was creepy in there!'

He's looking good today – the maroon hoodie brings out the warmth in his pale skin, and his hair's just messy enough to make me want to run my fingers through it and pull him closer.

'What?'

'Nothing.' I nudge him playfully. 'Just wishing it was just you and me out here.'

I flex my eyebrows suggestively, and he laughs.

Before we can get any closer, Opel barges between us. 'Alright, lover boys, what's the plan? I can't do my job with Mr TikTok and Indiana Jane back there.'

'Opel, those are my friends,' Liam snaps.

'Yeah, I see that. And you know how long it took me to warm up to you. I'm not doing that again.'

Liam looks ready to argue, but I slip between them quickly. 'Okay, how about we—'

A guttural scream pierces the air from behind us.

I spin around to see Lily, her face white as she stares at the ground in horror. Jack is by her side, his hands covering his mouth. The three of us rush over, only to stop dead in our tracks when we see what caused Lily's scream.

The ground is littered with dead animals, birds, rabbits, foxes, even a few deer. Their bodies are shrivelled and dry, as if the life has been sucked out of them. There's no blood, just hollowed-out, empty carcasses.

'What the hell is this?' Jack mutters through his hands.

Liam rushes to Lily's side, holding her steady. She might faint at any moment.

Opel steps between the scattered remains, her focus now drawn to something beyond them.

I follow her line of sight. There are more animal bodies. Hundreds of them. The corpses form a disturbing path that leads deeper into the trees.

'We should call the police,' Jack says.

Opel spins around, ready to object.

'Good idea, Jack,' says Liam, quickly. 'Let's do that. We'll get better signal once we're out of the woods. Let's go.'

Liam tries to guide Lily and Jack away, but Lily isn't moving. Her eyes are fixed on something in the distance, her body rigid.

'Lily?' Liam snaps his fingers in front of her face.

Her gaze slowly lifts to the trees above us. 'Can you hear that?'

I strain to listen. There's nothing but the rustling of leaves in the gentle breeze. Opel shrugs. Liam looks as confused as I am. If even his heightened hearing isn't picking anything up, I have no clue what Lily might be hearing.

'Lily,' I say gently, stepping closer, 'I think maybe you should—'

She shushes me sharply, then steps past Opel, her eyes locked on the strange path of dead creatures. She begins to walk down it.

'Lily, wait!' Liam shouts, starting to go after her, but she doesn't even glance back.

Opel drops her hands to her sides. 'Well, I guess we're following her.'

Without another word, we fall in line behind Lily, heading into the unknown.

We follow Lily deeper into the woods, the stench of death growing stronger as the animal carcasses pile up. Opel sticks close to Lily, eyes darting, nerves on edge. I trail behind, senses sharp. Whatever did this could still be out there.

Liam hangs back with Jack, guiding him through the maze of bodies. Jack stepped in a badger's remains a few metres ago and hasn't shut up about it since.

'Yo, Gretel, wait up!' Opel calls out.

But Lily doesn't stop. She's moving forward like she's in some kind of trance. It's unsettling; only half an hour ago she was fleeing from a rat in a bunker, and now she's marching through a sea of dead creatures like it's nothing.

'Her name's not Gretel,' I mutter.

'We're not exactly following breadcrumbs either,' Opel replies, glancing nervously at the animal remains.

As we walk on, the forest seems to close in around us. The bodies have thinned out, now clustering in a circular pattern around a large open space. At its centre stands a sprawling tree, ancient and twisted, with branches snaking outward in every direction. It's unlike any other tree I've seen before, its gnarled roots gripping the earth as if guarding something. The bark is blackened, burned from within, and a large crack splits the trunk, the hollow dark and ominous.

We all stop, but Lily keeps moving forward, drawn toward the tree like a moth to a flame.

'I don't like this,' Opel says, stepping closer to me while still keeping her gaze fixed on the eerie tree. 'Something's happened here, and I don't think it's anything good.'

'I agree,' I murmur, glancing uneasily at the sky. 'We should head back. We need to inform Nathaniel about this.'

Some distance away, in a small clearing, there's a similar tree, only it's in much better condition than the one in front of us now. They're the same type of tree, but both different from the rest of the forest.

'They're getting louder.' Lily's voice is distant, almost like she's in a dream.

Opel and I exchange glances.

Liam gently grips her shoulder and stares up into the twisted boughs. 'What's getting louder?'

'The whispers.' Her eyes are locked on the tree.

Liam shoots me a nervous look. I strain my ears, but there's nothing. No whispers. No sound at all. It's as if the wood itself is holding its breath.

Lily steps closer to the tree, slowly reaching out toward the blackened trunk.

'Guys,' Jack calls from the other side of the tree. 'There's something over here.'

Opel, Liam, and I quickly make our way around the massive trunk. Burned into the bark of the tree is some sort of mark. A circle with a sharp, floral pattern inside it.

A sudden cry splits the air.

'Lily!' Liam shouts, sprinting back around the tree.

We follow quickly, and my heart stops at the sight of her. Lily is lying on the ground, convulsing violently. Her eyes are wide open, staring into nothingness, and her lips are moving, but no sound comes out.

'Lily! Lily!' Liam cries, dropping to his knees beside her, shaking her shoulders. Jack joins him, also calling her name repeatedly, but she doesn't seem to hear them. She's lost, trapped somewhere far beyond our reach.

'Tariq, we have to do something!'

Lily's convulsions stop. Her body goes completely still, her eyes flutter closed, and for a moment, the woods are completely silent.

'Lily?'

But she doesn't respond. Liam shakes her gently, panic rising in his eyes, but Lily remains still.

SEVEN

CURSED

LIAM

I haven't spent much time in my room at the Seven Angels. In fact, this is only the second time I've set foot in here since I was given my key.

My room at Mum's is warm, and food is provided for me on the regular; also, no offence to Tariq and Heather, this place above the bar is just too noisy for little old me.

The room is similar to Tariq's but smaller, with no fireplace and a tiny window overlooking the courtyard.

The single bed is occupied by Lily, her chest rising and falling. She's alive, but unconscious.

Jack and I are sitting by her side, my leg bobbing as Nathaniel examines her. Tariq and Opel hover by the doorway.

After what happened in the woods, I carried Lily back to Opel's car, her body limp in my arms. We all piled in, Jack barely saying a word, his eyes glued to Lily, terrified. He was confused, furious even, when we brought her here instead of to a hospital. But I assured him Nathaniel could help.

'How long has she been like this?' Nathaniel asks.

'Half an hour, maybe forty minutes,' says Tariq.

'And this happened at Grovely?'

'Yeah,' Opel chimes in. 'Near some massive old tree.'

Nathaniel pulls back Lily's eyelids, his brow creasing as her eyes dart restlessly beneath. He checks her arms and legs carefully. 'Any marks on her?'

I shake my head. 'No, not that I've noticed.'

'Will she be okay?' Jack's voice breaks the silence, trembling with suppressed tears.

Nathaniel turns Lily's hand over, his expression darkening as he studies it. The palm is black, like she's pressed it into thick, oily paint.

'Did Lily touch the tree?' Nathaniel asks.

I nod. 'I think so, yeah.'

He sighs, removing his glasses and rubbing his temples. 'Hm.'

I lean forward. 'What is it?'

'Would you fetch Heather?'

Tariq nods and slips quietly out of the room. The silence that follows is thick with unspoken fear.

'Nathaniel, what's wrong with her?' Opel presses.

But Nathaniel remains silent, either uncertain or unwilling to say. His eyes are distant, lost in thought, and that only makes the dread inside me grow.

'We need to take her to the hospital,' Jack insists, standing up abruptly. 'We can't just sit here! We need real help!'

'I'm afraid they won't be able to help her,' Nathaniel says quietly.

Jack's eyes flare with disbelief. 'What? How do you know that? Who the hell are you?'

'Jack, calm down,' I say, though I'm barely holding it together myself.

Jack rounds on me. 'Liam, who is this guy? She should be in A&E! What's happening?'

Tariq returns, Heather following close behind. Her presence is calming, almost maternal, and yet there's a grave look in her eyes as she hurries to Lily's side.

'Oh, poor girl,' Heather murmurs as she takes Lily's hand in hers. 'What happened?'

'That's what I'm hoping you can tell me,' Nathaniel replies. 'Will you stay with her and young Jack here, while I speak with the others? She may reach out to you.'

Heather nods solemnly, taking a seat beside Lily. She gently strokes Lily's hair, and something about the gesture brings a small amount of comfort to the room. Jack reluctantly takes a step back, watching Heather as though she might somehow make everything right again.

'We need to talk,' Nathaniel says, gesturing toward the door.

Jack moves to follow, but I stop him, pressing a hand to his chest. 'No, Jack. Stay with Lily and Heather. I'll explain everything soon, I promise.'

Jack looks ready to argue, but I grab his shoulders and meet his eyes. 'Please.'

He relents, shrugging me off and settling back beside Lily.

Tariq's face is tight with annoyance. Jack being here is clearly more of a complication than he's willing to deal with right now.

A voice hums.

'Lily?' I rush to her side as her lips move.

'Liam?' Nathaniel calls after me, but I'm already leaning over her.

Her voice is faint, a whisper, barely audible. I lean in closer, straining to hear.

'Wi... wit... tree,' she murmurs.

'What is it, Lily?' Jack asks.

'Witch… tree,' she breathes out.

Dread tightens like a noose around my throat. Nathaniel's face has gone pale, and he gestures sharply toward the door.

'What do you mean *cursed*?' I say as Nathaniel rifles through his bookshelf, pulling volumes aside with an intensity I've never seen from him before.

Tariq casually tosses a small fireball into the fireplace, bathing the room in an orange glow. His calmness seems so out of place.

He's just as on edge as I am.

'Lily has been cursed by a witch,' Nathaniel explains, finally yanking a thick, leather-bound book from the shelf. He flips through the pages with quick, practised hands until he stops at a section titled 'Curses, Hexes and Jinxes'. His finger traces down the page as he speaks. 'I believe the tree she touched was, as she stated herself downstairs, a witch tree. Your friend is clever for recognising it.'

'But we didn't see a witch,' Opel points out.

'You wouldn't,' Nathaniel says. 'Witches rarely linger near their graves once they've broken free. I presume the witch's earthly prison was shattered, and she laid a curse on the tree, waiting for an unsuspecting victim to come too close. Centuries ago, witches were often buried under trees specifically chosen to contain their lingering power.'

'So how did this witch get out?' Tariq asks.

'The tree,' I mutter, the memory of its charred trunk flashing through my mind. 'It was split down the middle, like it had been burned.'

'The storm,' Opel says, realisation dawning in her eyes. 'That massive storm last night. Lightning must have struck the tree.'

Lily had heard whispers in the woods, something drawing her closer to the tree. Was that the witch, manipulating her? Leading her into a trap?

'I still don't get it,' I say. 'How do you know Lily's been cursed?'

Nathaniel turns the book toward me, showing a detailed sketch. The image is eerie, disturbingly familiar.

'That's what we saw on the tree!' Tariq says, eyes wide.

Nathaniel nods. 'It's a witch's mark. The witch left her imprint on the tree, and now it has infected Lily. Her erratic eye movements are another clear sign – she's caught in the witch's power.'

My breath catches. 'But will she be okay?'

Nathaniel studies the book. He turns the pages with deliberate care, the sound of paper scraping against paper almost deafening in the quiet room.

'Nathaniel?' I press, my voice barely steady.

His eyes are full of worry. 'We need to find the witch, and quickly.'

'Why?' Tariq asks, though I can already see the dread in his eyes. We all know where this is heading.

'The curse ties Lily to the witch,' Nathaniel says heavily. 'To break it, the witch must be killed.'

Opel throws her hands up. 'Kill a witch? Seriously? How do we even find her? It's not like she's going to be wandering through town buying cauldrons at Lakeland!'

Nathaniel closes the book with a heavy thud. 'We'll need to learn more about this particular witch. Why she was buried here in Sarumbourne, and what kind of power she wielded before her death. I'll notify the Guild to begin a search—'

'What if we can't find her?' I say. 'What happens to Lily?'

Nathaniel hesitates, looking between the three of us.

'If we cannot stop the witch, then she will die.'

The room tilts. My knees threaten to give out. Die? That can't be right. This was supposed to be a simple day. Safe.

How did everything go so wrong?

Tears sting the back of my eyes, but I push them down.

Tariq steps closer, placing a comforting arm around me, but his presence does little to stop the rising panic inside me.

Before anyone can say another word, Jack bursts into the room, breathless and frantic. 'This place has too many bloody rooms!'

'Jack, what's wrong?' I ask.

Jack's eyes are wide. 'Something's wrong with Heather!'

As we rush into the room, Heather is doubled over in the chair beside Lily. Her hands are gripping her head, her face contorted in pain. Nathaniel is at her side immediately, kneeling beside her.

'Heather? What's happened?' Nathaniel's voice is calm.

I barely hear his words before Tariq is pushing Jack and me toward the door.

'Take him out of here,' Tariq orders, his eyes intense as he gestures to Jack.

Before I can argue, the door to my room slams shut behind us, and suddenly Jack and I are alone in the hallway.

Jack looks confused. 'What the hell is going on, Liam?'

I press my hands to my temples, trying to calm the rapid thudding of my heart. 'What happened in there?'

Jack's hands are trembling slightly. 'I... I don't know. One minute she was holding Lily's hand, and then she started acting like she was in serious pain. I thought she was having a migraine or something at first – my mum gets them sometimes – but then... she started yelling.'

'Yelling what?'

Jack takes a deep breath, like he's trying to make sense of it all. 'Something about white robes. And arches. Statues. And... a witch. None of it made any sense, Liam. It was like she was out of her mind.'

Everything about this day has spiralled out of control. Hell knows what Jack is thinking right now.

'You said you'd explain what's going on, Liam. What are we doing here? Who are these people? Really?'

'I know, I know. I will explain, Jack, I promise. But not right now. Please, just trust me a little longer, okay?'

Jack looks at me, his face hardening with frustration.

The door opens, and Nathaniel steps out. His face is calm but stern, and his eyes find mine immediately. 'Liam, we need you.'

I squeeze Jack's shoulder reassuringly before heading back into the room.

EIGHT

THE CLOISTERS

TARIQ

The sky deepens from dusky blue to indigo, the first stars flickering through. Liam, Opel, and I cross the empty grounds of Sarumbourne Cathedral, the evening chill brushing our skin. The sprawling lawn feels peaceful, but there's an edge to it, shadows pooling beneath the swaying trees.

Ahead, the path leads to the Cathedral. Its towering spire cuts into the dark sky, while golden light spills across the Gothic facade. Shadows gather in the arches and windows, tracing the curves of the ancient stone.

'Hey, kid, slow down,' Opel calls after Liam, who's pulled ahead of us, his steps quickening as we draw nearer to the Cathedral.

'He's worried about his friend.'

Opel shakes her head. 'If he goes barging in there, we'll lose any element of surprise.'

'We don't even know if Heather is right about this,' I mutter. 'She said herself she's never had a premonition before.'

Back at the Seven Angels, Nathaniel explained that the Spiritus Keeper can occasionally catch glimpses of both the future and the past. But Heather had never displayed that ability until today, and we're all on uncertain ground

44

now. It's even more unusual that she's developed a new ability this late into her Keeperhood.

'Yeah, well, at least it's distracted her from talking to dead people for five minutes,' Opel adds.

Liam has finally come to a stop. We catch up to him just as he stands in front of the Cathedral's huge arched doors, staring intently at the entrance. It's clear what's drawn his attention. There's a pair of security guards patrolling the grounds near the far corner of the building.

'Since when did the Cathedral get extra security?' he says quietly.

'Since that hammer attack on the Magna Carta's casing earlier last year,' says Opel. 'I see them roaming all the time when I head home.'

I sometimes forget Opel's family home is here in the Close. An inheritance on her father's side.

'We need to be careful,' I whisper. 'If they see us sneaking around, we'll be in trouble.'

Opel huffs, pulling her jacket closer against the wind. 'Any suggestions on how to break in?'

Liam's eyes are sharp, focused. 'Let's head around to the other side. The cloisters entrance has a smaller door; I might be able to break the lock.'

We move quietly, ducking into the shadows as we skirt around the Cathedral.

The snap of the lock hitting the floor echoes through the still air, followed by the soft creak of the door as Liam pushes it open. We slip inside the Cathedral's cloisters. There's a security camera mounted high on the wall, its glassy dome rotating toward us.

Shit. 'Opel!'

She's faster than my panic, raising her hand before the camera can adjust. The lens jerks sideways with a sharp crack, the wires snapping free. It hangs uselessly, the little red light blinking out. No footage. No evidence.

Liam shuts the door behind us, the sound reverberating. The arched walkways stretch into the distance, moonlight spilling through the slender, Gothic columns, casting long, silver shadows.

'Where exactly are we going?' Opel whispers.

'No idea.' I scan the shadows. 'But let's start looking. Be on your guard.'

As we move deeper into the cloisters, the open quadrangle comes into view, soaked in pale moonlight. The grass and neatly planted shrubs glisten. I've spent afternoons here, reading and relaxing, but at night, it's different – ancient and menacing.

We round a corner into another long corridor lined with statues. They stand like watchmen, tall and stoic, their faces swallowed by shadow. Bearded men in robes clutch swords to their chests, their hollow eyes fixed on us.

Opel catches sight of another camera and disables it just as deftly as the first.

'Heather saw statues in her vision,' she says, glancing nervously at the stone figures. 'And archways. What else?'

'Priest,' Liam adds.

'No, I don't think she said anything about a pri—' Opel's voice falters as Liam stops in his tracks. We almost collide with him. There's a figure lying on the floor a few metres ahead.

My heart leaps into my throat. It's a man, his body half-obscured by the shadows but unmistakably dressed in black and white robes. His beard catches the faint light, silver strands glinting in the dark. His arms are splayed out, his robes fanning across the stone.

'Is he...?' Liam whispers.

When we finally reach the priest's body, a wave of nausea hits me. His eyes are missing. Deep, hollow sockets ooze blood, staining his cheeks in thin, meandering rivers. His mouth hangs open in a silent scream, his face twisted in the last moments of unutterable terror.

'Holy shit.' Opel covers her mouth.

I crouch down, reaching hesitantly toward the priest's hand. His skin is still warm to the touch. 'This just happened,' I say, my throat dry. 'Whatever did this... it's still around.'

We exchange glances, dread settling. We're not alone here. Something is watching us.

'We should go,' I say.

But as we turn back to retrace our steps, a figure steps into our path. It stands unmoving, cloaked in shadow. Details are hidden, as if the darkness itself has taken shape.

The figure raises an arm toward us, and I instinctively ignite a fireball in my hand, the flames casting flickering light on the ancient stone walls.

'Keepers,' the figure hisses. The voice is feminine, cold, and wicked.

'Tar...' Opel starts to warn, her eyes fixed on the figure, but my attention is suddenly pulled elsewhere.

'Please tell me you guys hear that,' Liam says.

Whispers, sinister and indistinct, curl around us, growing louder and more frantic. They seem to be coming from all directions, as though the walls themselves are speaking.

'Guys.'

I follow Liam's gaze. The stone statues of robed men are no longer rooted to their pedestals. They're stepping down, breaking free from the stone with a slow, grinding sound. Their faces, once calm and serene, now appear twisted and fierce. Their swords, once ornamental, are now raised and ready for battle.

'Well, this can't be good,' Opel says.

The statues advance on us, their movements eerily human.

I hurl my fireball at the nearest statue, hoping to slow it down. The flames hit it square in the chest, but the stone only blackens, leaving the statue otherwise unscathed.

Opel steps forward. A blast of telekinetic energy slams into two statues, sending them crashing into each other. They crumble to the ground in a cloud of dust and debris.

Liam charges at another statue, catching its sword mid-swing and twisting it from its stone grip. In one swift motion, he drives the blade back into the statue's chest. The stone figure splits apart and crashes to the ground in two shattered halves.

'Where's the witch?' Opel asks, scanning the shadows beyond the statues.

The figure is gone.

Two more statues close in on Liam, from either side. Without thinking, I sprint toward him, crashing into his side just as the statues' swords come down. The blades smash together in the air.

I pull him to his feet.

The swordless statues twitch and start to rise again, but they're no match for Opel's power. They are flung against the walls, shattering into rubble. She dusts her hands off as she steps forward. 'Well, that was oddly satisfying.'

'Any more of them?' I ask.

'I think that's it,' Liam says, his breath heavy.

'Shame,' Opel quips, smirking. 'I was just getting warmed up.'

'They weren't particularly challenging,' I say, my gaze sweeping the corridor. 'The witch probably just used them to slow us down.'

Liam's face tightens with anger. 'That shadow... Was it the witch?'

'Had to be,' I say.

'Then we need to go after her,' Liam says, turning away.

I grab his arm. 'Wait, Liam. We don't even know what we're up against.'

'And we have no idea where Sabrina has gone,' Opel adds, glancing nervously around.

Liam's fists clench and unclench.

'I know you're worried,' I say, my voice softening. 'But we can't help Lily unless we're smart about this. We need to know more.'

His eyes meet mine, searching for reassurance. Slowly, he nods. I pull him into a quick, firm hug, feeling the heat of his body still thrumming with adrenaline.

'Who goes there?' A beam of torchlight sweeps across the stone walls, coming closer.

'Time to go,' Opel says.

We bolt for the exit, dodging the scattered debris of the broken statues as we race back the way we came. Behind us, the sound of footsteps and shouts grows fainter.

NINE

THE HANDSEL SISTERS

LIAM

Jack is asleep on the edge of the bed when I enter the room, his head resting gently on Lily's arm. Nathaniel agreed Jack could stay, on the condition that he didn't wander off on his own around the Seven Angels. Jack looks drained, a world away from the animated friend I've known all these years.

Lily's hand has darkened. The inky shadow has crept further, stretching up her arm. Carefully, I lift the sleeve of her shirt. The darkness has spread, slithering up around her shoulder like poison.

I sit down opposite Jack, easing into the chair to avoid waking him. Lily's face is peaceful yet ghostly, and it's hard to reconcile the severity of what's happening with how serene she looks. I shouldn't have let her go to those woods. But even if I had tried, she would've found a way. Lily's always been headstrong, always the one at the front of the line. Back in school, she'd be the first one on the bus for school trips, having packed everything we needed, my stuff included, because she knew I'd forget.

Gently taking her good hand in mine, I tuck a strand of her golden hair behind her ear.

'I'm sorry, Lily.' Tears sting the corners of my eyes.

Jack stirs at the sound of my voice, his eyes fluttering open. He rubs them groggily and looks at me with a tired smile.

'You're back,' he says, stifling a yawn. 'Did you find anything to help Lily?'

I shake my head.

We'd told Jack we were out looking for a solution for Lily's condition, trying to give him enough information without being too specific. But how could I tell him the truth? That we're hunting a witch to break the curse she's laid on Lily? It sounds ridiculous, even to me.

'You should head home, Jack,' I say, my voice gentle but firm. 'Get some proper sleep.'

Jack shifts in his seat, narrowing his eyes at me. 'I could say the same to you.'

'I can't.'

'Why not? What aren't you telling me, Liam?'

He's at the end of his patience.

'I want to know. Now.'

'You'll know everything tomorrow, I promise. Just… give me tonight. Please.'

Jack leans back in the chair, his jaw set in frustration. I haven't seen him this irritated since I spilled my drink all over his keyboard during one of his epic *World of Warcraft* battles. He's not happy, and I don't blame him. I hate keeping him in the dark. The rule of keeping our identities a secret is beginning to grate.

'I'm not leaving Lily,' he says firmly.

Lily doesn't stir, still locked in whatever nightmare this curse has thrown her into.

'Jack, she's stable. We're watching her, I swear. But there's literally nothing more you can do right now.'

He's quiet, staring at her with such intensity, like he's urging her to wake up through sheer force of will. He wants to stay, but he also knows that sitting here won't change anything.

'This isn't normal, Liam. None of this is.'

'Look, Cassie's probably terrified no one's come home.' I grab Lily's bag and offer it to him. 'Her parents are halfway around the world on that cruise. Lily wouldn't want her alone.'

He wants to stay, but something flickers behind his eyes at the mention of Lily's dog.

He grabs the bag, but not gently. 'I'll go, but I'm not going far. And if anything changes, anything, you tell me. Immediately.'

'I promise.'

He leans over, presses a kiss to Lily's forehead, then straightens, eyes still on me.

The door shuts behind him with a thud that feels heavier than it should. And just like that, it's quiet again, just Lily and me.

We gather in the library on the top floor of the Seven Angels. I haven't been in here since Nathaniel gave me a tour of the building, right after I became a Keeper.

Opel and Tariq are already on one of the sofas when I appear. Opel has her feet propped up on the coffee table, looking as laid-back as ever.

Tariq spots me first, flashing me that warm smile that always lifts my spirits, even in moments like this. It's a welcome distraction.

'Liam.' Nathaniel emerges from the corner with a teacup in hand, naturally. 'I trust Lily is being watched over?'

I nod. 'Heather's with her.'

'And Jack?' Tariq asks.

'I sent him to check on Lily's dog. I don't know if he'll be back tonight.'

'Best he stays clear of things here, I think,' Nathaniel says.

'I need to tell him something,' I say. 'He can't be kept in the dark forever.'

Tariq crosses his arms. 'You know we can't—'

'I know. We're not supposed to reveal we're Keepers. But that rule was partly meant to protect the people we care about.' I turn to Nathaniel, holding his gaze. 'Well, one of my best friends is downstairs, cursed by a witch and barely hanging on. How protected is she now?'

A heavy silence settles over the room. Nathaniel opens his mouth to speak.

'The kid's got a point,' Opel interrupts, to everyone's surprise. 'I say he tells Jack. At least then Jack might understand how dangerous things are and keep his distance.'

Tariq turns to her. 'Are you serious? The boy has no business knowing about this. He won't get it.'

'He's my friend, Tariq. He'll understand if I can just talk to him.'

'Enough,' Nathaniel says firmly. 'This is a unique situation. I'll speak to the Guild about what can be done concerning your friends.'

I grind my teeth in frustration. The Guild. What will they do? Will they allow Jack to know the truth, or will they intervene to keep him quiet? They're supposed to be the good guys, but Heather is a prime example of what they'll do if things become problematic.

Nathaniel clears his throat. 'We have more pressing matters to discuss.'

I sink into the sofa opposite Tariq, avoiding his gaze.

'Did you find something out about the witch?' Opel asks, leaning forward.

Nathaniel places his teacup on the table. 'Witches. Two, to be precise.'

'Two?' Tariq echoes.

Nathaniel nods. 'The Handsel sisters were originally from Denmark. They arrived on our shores in the early 1700s, drawn to the Crossing. As witches, they believed proximity to the Crossing would enhance their powers.'

'And what happened to them?' I ask.

'In 1737, there was a smallpox outbreak in Sarumbourne. It killed over one hundred and fifty residents, and the two Handsel sisters were accused of witchcraft. They were executed without a formal trial.'

Opel leans in further. 'Executed how?'

'They were bludgeoned to death in front of crowds in the Market Square. Their bodies were dragged to Grovely Wood, where they were buried far apart from one another.'

'Apart?' Tariq frowns. 'Why?'

'To prevent them from conspiring after death,' Nathaniel continues. 'A beech tree was planted over each grave, meant to keep their magic buried with them.'

'Until last night when the storm cracked open the evil piñata?' Opel says, cutting to the chase.

'Exactly,' Nathaniel replies. 'But only one of the sisters was released. The other is still trapped beneath her tree.'

'Until this witch brings her sister back,' I say.

Nathaniel nods. 'The priest you found... magic specialists at the Guild believe his missing eyes are likely part of a resurrection spell.'

'Resurrection?'

'She wants to bring her sister back,' Tariq says.

Opel sits up. 'Why doesn't she just split her sister's tree and set her free?'

'The storm was the catalyst for her return, the power from the strike must have been enough to dismantle her earthly cage.' Nathaniel paces around us, hands in pockets. 'She won't have enough power to do the same. She will have to resort to a spell, which is a longer process to put together.'

'What does that mean?' I ask.

'Spells require ingredients, such as the eyes of this priest, for example.'

'What else is she looking for?' Opel says.

'I'm working on it,' Nathaniel continues. 'With help from the Guild, we should have an answer by morning. I've arranged a meeting first thing. You'll all be there.'

'What happens if the witch's spell works?' Tariq says.

Nathaniel's expression darkens. 'Then we'll have two powerful witches on our hands.'

TEN

ASSIGNMENTS

TARIQ

The last time I was in the jury room at the Guildhall, I was making out with Lucas.

It's been a few years, but the memories hit as I take in the deep red walls and the oil paintings of past Guild members glaring down from their gilded frames. Morning sunlight floods through the arched windows, too bright for this hour. I squint against it.

Lucas sits at the far end of the long, dark wooden table. He blows me a kiss as I find my own chair.

Liam nudges me gently. 'You okay?'

'Yeah, just… it's early.'

Across the room, Opel giggles at something Theo whispers. His hand's in her hair, their heads close as they gaze out the tall windows. They look happy and connected. Must be one of their good days.

'Why have we been summoned so early?' Lucas's voice cuts through the moment, and he stretches lazily, ruffling his shaggy white hair. 'I'm not usually awake at this ungodly hour.'

Theo snorts. 'Yes, you are. Only you're just usually coming home.'

Lucas glares at his older brother. 'You wish you had my stamina.' He smirks again at me. 'You remember my stamina, don't you, Tariq?'

Heat is creeping up my face. But I'm not giving Lucas the satisfaction. He's doing this to stir things up, and I'm not biting.

Liam watches me closely, expecting me to offer a comeback. He probably wonders what Lucas means, but now's not the time to explain my past mistakes.

Lucas raises an eyebrow, still waiting for a reaction. Before I have to say anything, Charles and Nathaniel enter the room.

'Apologies for the early hour,' Charles says as he takes a seat at the head of the table. 'Nathaniel and I needed time to strategise before we move forward.'

He gestures for everyone to take their seats. Liam slides in next to me, with Nathaniel sitting on his other side. Theo and Opel sit together as well, Opel still holding Theo's hand.

'Move forward with what, exactly?' Lucas huffs, leaning back in his chair with his arms crossed like a petulant child. 'Can someone actually explain why we're here?'

'Patience, Lucas,' Charles says, holding up a wrinkled hand to silence him.

Lucas groans dramatically but falls quiet, albeit with a pout.

Charles starts talking, rehashing everything Nathaniel told us last night about the Handsel witches. Nathaniel jumps in, covering the eyeless priest at the Cathedral and updating them on Lily.

He says her name, and it hits Liam. There's a strain behind his eyes.

'…and it would appear that the physical side of the curse is spreading,' Nathaniel finishes.

'Curses are nasty things. How long do we think the girl has?' Charles asks.

Liam is staring intently at Nathaniel now, his eyes misty. I reach under the table and give his leg a light squeeze.

Nathaniel hesitates, then answers. 'I can't be sure. A few days, perhaps. What I do know is that while Lily gets weaker, the witch is growing stronger. They're linked by the curse. If we can destroy the witch, we'll break the curse on Miss Boynes.'

'Then why are the Keepers sitting here?' Lucas interrupts again. 'Shouldn't you all be out hunting down this Wicked Witch of the West?'

Nathaniel ignores the jab and gestures toward Charles, who takes over. 'That's why you and Theo have been summoned,' Charles explains. 'Nathaniel?'

Nathaniel clears his throat. 'We believe the witch is gathering ingredients for a spell, a resurrection spell for her sister. She needs three key components.'

'How do you know she hasn't already collected them?' Theo asks, much more calmly than Lucas ever could.

'Because one of those components is in this room,' Nathaniel says.

We all exchange confused looks, glancing around as if we're trying to figure out who or what it might be.

Lucas snorts. 'I hope it's not the silverware.' He nods toward the antique cabinet behind us. 'Grandfather is rather attached to those.'

Charles shoots him a sharp look, like he might smack him across the head.

'Not the silverware. It's something much more precious to you. Or Theo.'

Lucas's smirk fades.

'Us?' Theo pulls his hand away from Opel. 'What do you mean?'

'The witch already has a pair of eyes,' Nathaniel explains. 'Now she needs an ear and a tongue.'

'From both of us?' Theo asks, sceptical.

'No,' Charles says. 'Just one of you. But we don't know which.'

'Why not?' Lucas snaps.

Charles sighs deeply. 'Because our ancestor was one of the men responsible for bludgeoning the witches to death. The resurrection spell means the youngest descendants pay the price. That's one of you two.'

'But the entire town lynched them,' Lucas says, sounding defensive. 'Why are we the ones being punished?'

'Because, according to the eyewitness accounts, it was your ancestor, along with two others, who dealt the final blows,' Nathaniel says. 'That's why the witch is targeting your family.'

Lucas shakes his head, disbelief clouding his face. 'They should have burned them at the stake,' he mutters. 'We wouldn't be in this mess if they had.'

Typical Lucas, thinking he knows best after hearing about the situation for all of ten minutes.

'What's the plan?' Liam speaks up for the first time since we sat down. 'Are we using these two as bait or something?'

'Bait?' Opel echoes. 'I say let her have Lucas, he'd be far better off without a tongue.' She grins.

Theo bursts into laughter, and the rest of us struggle to suppress our own. Even Nathaniel's lips twitch in amusement.

'You're funny, Keeper,' Lucas sneers, leaning back in his chair. 'I knew my brother was putting up with you for more than just your—'

Before he can finish, Lucas's collar tightens sharply around his throat. His hands fly to his neck, panic in his eyes as he gasps for breath.

'Want to finish that sentence?' Opel says.

Now it's my turn to smirk.

'Miss Everleigh,' Charles intervenes, though his glare is firmly on Lucas. 'Please release my grandson. I'm sure he meant no disrespect.'

Lucas nods frantically. Opel relents, and Lucas sucks in air, rubbing his throat with a scowl.

Theo pulls Opel close, his protective side flaring as he shoots daggers with his eyes.

'Right, back to Liam's question,' Nathaniel says, taking control of the conversation again. 'We're not sure where the witch will strike next, so we're assigning each of you a Keeper for protection. Theo, Opel will stay with you. Liam, you'll be with Lucas.'

'What? No way,' I blurt out before I can stop myself.

Everyone stares at me, except Lucas, who seems pleased. 'Don't worry, Tar,' he says with a sneer. 'I'll happily have Liam by my side.' He winks in Liam's direction.

I glare at him, my blood boiling. The last thing I want is Liam playing bodyguard with my, for lack of a better word, ex. It's not even about Lucas being my ex; I just don't trust him. Especially not with Liam, my... well, whatever we are right now.

'Tariq,' Nathaniel continues, 'you'll be keeping an eye on Sergeant Sarah Waters of the Sarumbourne Police team. She's the youngest known descendant of the Waters family involved in the witch killings.'

I nod, reluctantly.

'Well, that's settled,' Charles says, clapping his hands together. 'I trust the Keepers to do their duty and keep my grandsons safe. And the sergeant as well.'

'Wait,' Liam interjects, catching everyone by surprise. Charles, who was already standing, pauses mid-step. 'What about Jack?'

Nathaniel shifts uncomfortably, clearly torn between his duty to the Guild and his sympathy for Liam.

I hope the Guild will make the right decision and keep Jack in the dark. The rules are clear; Jack has no business getting involved. Not to mention, I find him irritating. This isn't a personal grudge, just... practicality.

'Yes, Nathaniel has explained the situation with Mr Cooper,' Charles says after a brief cough. 'The unfortunate situation with your friends is to be discussed at our next Guild meeting.'

'Situation?' Liam says.

He glances at me, as if weighing his options. I shake my head slightly, trying to communicate that it's not worth it.

'You all know your assignments,' Nathaniel says. 'Stay safe until we know more.'

Charles gives a final nod and leaves the room, with Opel and Theo trailing behind him.

Lucas lingers, stepping up to Liam and resting a hand on his shoulder.

'Looks like you're stuck with me for a while, Auctus,' he says with a crooked smile.

Lucas is the last person I want near Liam. But this isn't my call. I have to trust Nathaniel's judgement, even if I don't trust Lucas.

Besides, I've got my own mission now: find the sergeant, and make sure she doesn't lose any body parts.

ELEVEN

FAMILY TRAITS

LIAM

I move away from the foul stench of the Market Square's public toilets, where Lucas is currently taking care of his 'emergency', after whining that he needed to take a piss. He could have easily gone at the Guildhall before we left just five minutes ago, but no, that would have been too simple.

The Square is unusually busy, and it's not even market day. People buzz around like bees under a clear blue sky, their chatter blending into the sounds of the city. I lean against a lamppost, letting the cool metal press into my back. Above me, baskets of vibrant flowers sway in the gentle breeze, the only pleasant part of this situation.

A family stops in front of me, browsing the menu posted outside of Leonardo's. This is where Tariq and I were supposed to go on a date. Not that I'm bitter or anything, but a slice of pizza would really hit the spot right about now. Instead, here I am, babysitting Lucas.

My phone buzzes in my pocket, and I pull it out to see a text from Jack.

I'm back at the Seven Angels with Lily and that strange lady who keeps talking to people who aren't even here. Where are you?

Typical Jack, ignoring my instructions. I told him, this morning, to head to college without me, that I'd handle keeping an eye on Lily, or, more accurately, have Heather do it while I met with the Guild. But clearly, he didn't listen.

He went home last night after checking on Cassie, and I'm glad for that. He needed the rest, but it looks like he's taken matters into his own hands again. Now, I'm stuck in a dilemma: either I don't tell Jack anything and risk losing him as a friend, or I tell him everything and go against the secrecy of the Keepers. I have no idea what the Guild will decide to do about this, or how long it may take.

I'll assess Jack's mood when I get back. For now, I ignore the message.

'Right, Auctus,' Lucas calls as he saunters out of the toilets with an annoyingly cheerful expression. 'I'm empty. Let's fill me up again.' He flashes a grin as he strolls past me.

'Lucas, we're going to the Seven Angels,' I call after him, trying to rein him in.

He spins around, walking backward through the crowd. 'That can wait. I've got a better idea.'

Of course he does. He would make this difficult. Unfortunately, I'm tethered to him now. Not that I'm doing this solely for his protection. If the witch comes for him, it'll be my chance to stop her, and save Lily in the process.

'Come on!' Lucas shouts over the throng of people now separating us. 'I want to get at least three pints in me before Elphaba shows up.'

Lucas wipes his mouth with the back of his sleeve, before slamming his empty pint glass down on the table.

We're sitting in a booth at Wetherspoons. It's far from my scene, filled with day-drinkers who are at least double my age and twice as rowdy. There's a particularly loud group near the bar, but at least Lucas had the sense to choose a booth tucked away from the chaos.

'I could get you a shot of rum to spice up that Coke, if you like?' Lucas says, eyeing my drink as if it personally offended him.

'I'm good. My mum says lunchtime drinking is a low point of society.'

Lucas mockingly clutches his chest, pretending to be insulted, before shaking it off with a laugh. It's strange being this close to him in the daylight; he's actually kind of attractive. His white hair is wild, hanging over his face. He has these cute dimples, and his eyes…

'You'll be far more interesting with an actual drink in your hand, and far less concerned with staring at my face.'

I blush. Caught.

'Sorry. It's just… your eyes. Are they…'

'Violet?' A sly smile creeps across his face. 'Yep. It's a Martindale family trait. Some of us inherit low-level, crappy magic; others get the most luscious eyes you've ever seen.'

He leans forward, giving me a better look. Then he holds up his hands, showing off his nails, perfectly manicured and tinted the same striking shade as his eyes.

'So, Theo got the magic, huh?'

My question shifts something in him. Lucas leans back, his mood visibly dimming.

'Barely. And what he has got is nothing special. All our grandfather uses him for is to create the Keeper pendants. You saw it yourself when you got yours.'

'Back when I was a "Debbler", you mean?'

Lucas blinks, looking genuinely surprised. 'Did I call you that?'

'A few times,' I confirm, trying to keep my voice even.

He makes an awkward face, scratching the back of his neck. 'Wow. I was probably...' He holds up his empty pint glass and mimics taking a swig. 'Accept my apologies. The Guild doesn't use that term anymore. I should know better.'

His apology catches me off guard: it's sincere. But he's only one pint in, and the day's still young.

I check my phone and see another message from Jack, this one just a string of question marks.

'Can we go to the Seven Angels now?' I ask.

Lucas stands up, stretching lazily. 'Absolutely not, we're finding you a proper drink first.'

I groan, slumping back in the booth as he strolls toward the bar. This witch better show up soon.

TWELVE

WITCH GOT YOUR TONGUE

TARIQ

Liam's sent a photo. An empty beer glass with a caption: *Lucas 1, Liam 0. Wish me luck.*

I curse under my breath. Why aren't they at the Seven Angels? I told them to stay put, especially with the witch out there.

Lucas must have dragged Liam to one of his haunts, which is one of the many reasons things never would've worked between us.

Lucas could be charming when he wanted, and his disdain for the Guild was refreshing. But the party boy act got old fast. Drugs, drinking, hanging around Bloodtakers, He crossed too many lines. But Charles allowed him back into the Guild.

Now he's got Liam stuck in his orbit.

I'm about to fire off a reply when I catch sight of Sergeant Sarah Waters emerging from the back of Sarumbourne Police Station. I recognise her face from the weblink Nathaniel sent me. I shove my phone in my pocket and duck behind a parked car.

She's younger than I expected for a sergeant, pretty too. She waves to a colleague before crossing the car park toward the sports field.

According to our Guild contact inside the police, she's just finished her shift and should be heading home, which is only a five-minute walk from here.

I wait until she's a safe distance ahead before I slip out from behind the car and start tailing her.

Sarah turns down one of the quieter, nicer streets just off from the field. The neighbourhood feels almost too peaceful. I follow her at a safe distance, watching as she passes by an old church that's been converted into a community hall. As she rounds a bend, she disappears from sight. I quicken my pace to keep up.

By the time I reach the corner, she's slipping between two hedges, heading down a short path toward her front door. I approach slowly, watching as she enters her house and shuts the door. The street is quiet, no sign of anything out of the ordinary. No sign of the witch.

There's a narrow alleyway to the side of the house, leading around to the back.

'I wouldn't go snooping around there, love,' an elderly lady calls, from the other side of the road.

'Sorry?' I probably look like some kind of stalker.

'She's part of the police. A sergeant.' The woman points with her walking stick.

I force a smile and the lady shuffles down the street and out of sight.

I make my way toward the alleyway. But before I can reach the end, there's a scream from inside. The sound cuts through the air, followed by a crash of breaking plates.

I rush back to the front, and pound on the door.

'Sarah!' I shout, but there's no response except another muffled scream from inside. More shattering.

I'm about to slam my shoulder into the door when something catches my eye. The vines that crawl up the wall beside the door begin to move. They writhe and twist unnaturally fast, growing thicker, and spreading across the front door. In seconds, they've completely blocked the entrance, twisting over the frame and sealing it shut.

The witch is here.

I grab the vines, trying to tear them from the door, but they resist. They twist and shift in my hands, suddenly sprouting sharp thorns. One pierces my palm, sending a bolt of pain shooting up my arm. I hiss, pulling back quickly. Blood wells from the tiny punctures.

I race to the nearest window and press my face against the glass. The angle is awkward, but I manage to catch a glimpse of the kitchen inside.

The sergeant is sprawled out on the floor, her body twitching as if she's in agony. A dark, cloaked figure looms over her.

I sprint around the side of the house. More of the same twisted vines have tangled over the back door.

Focusing on the heat building within me, I step back, fire sparking. I press my hands to the vines, willing the flames to surge forward. The vines crackle as they catch fire, curling and withering under the heat. Smoke rises into the air, but I don't let up until every inch of the foliage has turned to ash.

With the vines gone, I shove my shoulder against the door. It gives way with a loud crack, the wood splintering beneath the force. I stumble inside, immediately searching for Sarah.

She's still on the kitchen floor, shaking. Blood covers her face, and her eyes are wide with panic. She's clutching her face, fingers digging into her cheeks as she writhes in pain.

The witch is nowhere to be seen. But the front door is now ajar, swaying slightly on its hinges.

'Sarah, can you hear me? You're going to be okay, just hang on.'

She whimpers, her eyes flickering open as she tries to focus on me. Her lips are swollen and bruised. Blood pools beneath her head. She can't speak.

I pull out my phone and dial triple nine.

'I need an ambulance, right now.' I quickly rattle off the address and hang up.

Sarah's breathing is laboured, but she's still conscious. I keep my hand on her shoulder, trying to offer some small measure of reassurance.

The witch was here, waiting for her.

Sarah might be alive, but the witch has her second spell ingredient.

THIRTEEN

THE CHAPEL

LIAM

'Good boy!'

Lucas applauds as I finish off the last of my cider, his grin widening with every drop I swallow. We somehow made it through three more pubs before I caved and let him buy me a drink. He's been delighted ever since. Lucas knows the barman here, which is the only reason I'm not being thrown out for underage drinking. To my surprise, Lucas is only nineteen, and he's holding up pretty well considering this is his fifth pint.

'Okay, that was pretty good,' I admit, feeling the tingle of sweet apple in my mouth.

'Told you.' He takes another swig of his own drink.

'Now, can we go?'

'Look, your friend Milly—'

'Lily,' I correct him.

'…Lily. She isn't going anywhere. You can't do anything to help her until you Keepers have vanquished the witch. And the only way you'll find her is sticking with me.'

He's right, in his own annoying way. There's nothing I can do for Lily at the moment, and Lucas is my one link to the witch and possibly breaking the curse. I've had no more messages from Jack, and there's been radio silence from Tariq too.

'You checking to see if your boy has messaged?'

I slip my phone back into my pocket.

'Tariq's always been pretty elusive. I wouldn't worry,' Lucas continues, like he knows something I don't.

I've wondered about Tariq and Lucas's history for a while. Ever since Tariq and I ran into Lucas in Elizabeth Gardens a few months ago. That was the first time I met Lucas. There's always been something between them. I caught it again earlier at the Guild, the way Tariq's face tightened when Lucas was near. Not to mention Lucas's forward comments.

'What's the story with you guys?'

Lucas shrugs. 'We used to fool around, and now we don't. That's basically it.'

His bluntness hits me like a slap. It was a different time in Tariq's life, but knowing that Lucas knew him like that, in ways I haven't yet, it stings. The casual way Lucas throws it out there makes it worse, like it's nothing to him.

'Don't look so glum, I bet you guys have… oh, wait. You haven't yet, have you?' His mouth falls open.

'We're working up to it.' My cheeks heat up. 'We're trying to actually date without something getting in the way. Besides, Tariq's happy to wait.'

'Hm.'

'What?'

'Nothing, it's just… I never pegged Tariq as the waiting type. Unless… wait. You have done it before, right?'

It's like he's trying to expose every crack, every insecurity I have about Tariq and me, and it's working.

'Okay, we're done here.' I stand up, but he catches my arm, holding me in place.

'Hey, no judgement, Auctus,' Lucas says.

'Why do you call me that?'

'Because that's what you are.'

'Maybe if you want to be the next head of the Guild, you should start acting like it. Like calling Keepers by their actual names.'

Lucas raises his eyebrows, looking both shocked and impressed at my sudden outburst.

'Who says I want to be the next Guild leader?'

'You're telling me you don't?'

Lucas doesn't answer right away. He just takes another sip of his beer, staring off into space.

'A lot of the Guild would rather see Theo take over. He's their golden boy.'

'Well, he's not the one who suggested letting a Keeper die just to replace her with a fresh one,' I remind him, unable to keep the bitterness out of my voice. It still bothers me, the way Lucas once coldly dismissed Heather's suffering when she was locked away by the Guild.

'So, I'm a little opinionated.'

'Do you stand by what you said?'

'What does it matter? The Spiritus—'

I glare at him.

'I mean... Heather. She's back in the fold now, confident and fighting fit, am I right?'

He knows full well she's not.

'She's still adjusting.'

There's something infuriatingly captivating about Lucas, the way he dances on the line between charming and irritating, pushing buttons just to see how far he can go. Maybe it's the cider talking, but I almost find it alluring.

The sun sinks lower, casting long shadows as Lucas and I finally leave the pub. I steer him toward the Seven Angels. But, of course, Lucas has other ideas, leading us further away from the bustling city centre and deeper into the quieter part of town.

'Lucas, where are we going now?'

'You'll see.' He raises his eyebrows mischievously before skipping ahead.

We cross the street, narrowly avoiding a bus that honks angrily in our direction. Lucas doesn't even flinch, just laughs it off and rounds another corner.

He's got this way of moving that feels completely carefree, like nothing in the world can touch him.

'If you used some of that super-speed of yours, you'd keep up with me!'

'I don't think it's wise after that second cider you made me have.'

'Don't the Guild have a "don't drink and power up" policy?'

I laugh, the cider warm in my stomach. 'You tell me!'

We turn another corner, and my laughter dies in my throat as a familiar figure walks toward us. Mum, carrying a bag of shopping.

'Liam?'

'Mum! Hi!' I try to sound less tipsy than I am.

Lucas slows beside me, suddenly quiet.

'What are you doing in town?' Mum asks. 'I thought you had History Insiders with Lily after college on a Friday?'

'Er… right. I do. It got cancelled. Lily is… sick.'

Mum looks at me, her eyes narrowing. Her gaze shifts to Lucas.

'Oh, Mum, this is Lucas. Lucas, this is my mum, Marie.'

Lucas holds out his hand, slightly unsteady, but still polite enough. Mum takes it, though she does so with a hint of reservation.

'Nice to meet you. Where's Tariq?'

'Oh, er…' The cider is definitely slowing me down now. 'He's working.'

Her nose crinkles slightly, and then she waves a hand in front of my face. 'Have you been drinking?'

'What?' I laugh, trying to play it off, but she can smell the cider on my breath.

Lucas steps in smoothly, putting an arm around my shoulders. 'We've just been to the cinema,' he says with a perfectly straight face. 'Liam tried their new apple ice-blast slushy. Big mistake.'

'Oh.' Somehow Mum looks even more concerned. 'Well, those things are dreadful all the same.'

'Agreed,' Lucas says, faking a laugh that sounds a little too real.

Mum looks between the two of us, her expression softening. 'I best get this shopping back home. I don't suppose I'll see you for dinner tonight, love?'

'No can do, sorry. I'll make my own when I get in.'

'Okay.' She reaches to gently slap my cheek. Then she turns to Lucas with a polite smile. 'Look after him.'

'I will,' Lucas promises with a wave. 'Nice to meet you, Marie.'

I wait until Mum's completely out of sight before letting out a long breath I didn't realise I'd been holding.

'Well, she seems lovely,' Lucas says, still draped casually over me.

'She is.' There is a pang of guilt inside me, knowing she's going home alone. 'And thanks, for the apple ice-blast save.'

'You're welcome. Now, let's go.'

'Lucas, can we just—'

'Last place, I promise. You owe me now.'

I'm not going to win this. 'Fine. But this is really the last stop.'

It's getting dark as the Chapel comes into view directly ahead of us, its grand, historic facade illuminated by vibrant pink and purple lights. Only in Sarumbourne would you find a nightclub inside an old religious building.

Lily's always gushing about its classical architecture, the tall arches and elegant columns, quite a contrast to whatever's happening inside.

Outside, a small group gathers, eager to start their night early, spilling into the street under the soft glow of the streetlights.

I stop dead in my tracks. 'Absolutely not.'

Lucas turns back, flashing a grin. 'The Chapel is the best place in town. You gotta do it.'

'I want to get back to my friends. Besides, my ID literally says I'm seventeen. There's no way I'm getting past those bouncers.'

'You don't need to get past them.' Lucas winks. 'I'll go in the front, and you can sneak around the back. There's a window. I used it all the time before I turned eighteen. I'll meet you there.'

'You're joking, right?'

'You owe me. Remember? I saved your arse earlier with your mum.'

'I don't care, Lucas. I'm not sneaking into a nightclub.'

'Well, that's where I'm heading.' He begins to back away across the road. 'Your call.'

'Lucas!' But he's already halfway across the street.

'What if the Wicked Witch is inside?' He pretends to bite his nails in terror.

'Fuck sake. One drink. Then we go.'

Lucas draws an X across his chest with his finger as he grins and joins the queue.

Heading toward a side gate, I slip around to the back of the building. There's a series of windows – most of them are out of reach. One is slightly lower than the rest, but it's still going to be a squeeze to fit through, even if I can get up there.

I check my phone. A missed call from Jack. He's probably wondering where I've been all day. I want to check in, to ask how Lily's doing, but it'll just lead to a string of questions I'm not ready to answer.

'Up here!' Lucas shouts from the open window.

He's already dangling halfway out.

'It's too high.'

'Oh come on, give yourself a little super-boost.'

With a sigh, I step back, then run forward and leap up. Lucas grabs my hands, pulling me up until I'm halfway through the window. But his grip slips, and I collapse on top of him. We both crash into the door of a toilet cubicle, laughing.

'You alright?'

'Yeah,' I say. His dark, purple eyes meet mine, and I find myself lingering there for a second longer than I should. I pull away, brushing myself off.

We're pressed against each other in the small cubicle.

'You're very hot.'

'What?' I blush.

'I can feel your Keeper heat radiating off of you. Relax.'

Has he experienced this with Tariq before?

'Come on.' He opens the door and steps out. 'Let's have some fun.'

We make our way into the main part of the club. The place is vast and open, with a mezzanine balcony wrapping around the perimeter, like in an old-style theatre. The walls are lined with curved wooden railings, and the lights flash across the room in bursts of neon colours. The bar, sleek and modern, glows invitingly. It's quiet right now. I imagine many are still pre-drinking and changing their outfit multiple times until they settle on something night-out worthy.

Lucas is already at the bar by the time I catch up.

'Welcome to the Chapel.'

He pulls out his phone and holds it up in front of us.

'What are you doing?'

'Don't you want to remember your first time in here?'

I adjust my messy fringe before he snaps a few photos of us. He hands me another pint of cider, and we clink glasses.

'Cheers, Liam.'

He actually used my name for once.

The brief warmth vanishes as the air around me suddenly shifts. The room feels colder, a chill creeping in. A strange, uncomfortable tingle runs down my spine.

We're being watched.

FOURTEEN

KETCHUP DISASTER

TARIQ

'Tariq? What the hell happened to you?'

Opel rushes over as I enter the training room at the Seven Angels. My hands and clothes are soaked in blood, which explains why so many people stared at me on the way here.

'Is that your blood?' Theo asks, following closely behind Opel.

I shake my head, still catching my breath. 'The witch. She got the sergeant. Took her tongue.'

Opel tucks her dark hair behind her ears. 'So that means…'

'Either me or Lucas are next.'

'Where is Lucas?' Opel asks.

'I told them to come here.'

Theo snorts. 'Did you really think my brother would listen to you?'

He has a point. Lucas rarely listens to anyone. Who knows what kind of trouble he's dragged Liam into.

Frustration boils inside me, and I throw up my arms in exasperation.

'Jack's with Lily,' Opel says. 'Maybe he's heard from Liam?'

Good call. I nod, striding out of the training room. I nearly run into Nathaniel as he's entering.

'Tariq? What—?'

I brush past him, leaving Opel and Theo to explain.

The door to Liam's room clicks shut behind me. Jack is slumped in the armchair, elbows braced on his knees, eyes fixed on the floor. Not even a flicker of acknowledgement. Lily lies beside him, her chest barely rising. The mark on her neck has deepened, curling up toward her jaw like ink in water.

'How is she?'

Jack is still. 'Do any of you even care?'

I bite down on my temper. His best friend's dying. I get it. Is he the only one allowed to care? We don't have time for this.

'We're doing everything we can...'

'Really? Because no one's told me anything since this started.'

'It's for your own good.'

'Right. What is it? Drugs? Are you all part of some underground ring?'

'Yeah... it's a real high-level operation.'

Jack doesn't smile.

'Do you know where Liam is?'

'I was hoping you could tell me that,' I say.

He stares at me like I've grown a second head. 'You think I know? I've been trying to call him all evening. He's ghosted me since this whole thing started.'

The way he says it, as if he has some claim over Liam, grates on me.

'So, you haven't heard from him?'

Jack grabs his phone and tosses it onto the end of the bed. 'See for yourself. No reply, no read receipts. Nothing.'

His gaze drops, scanning me for the first time. Blood-stained sleeves. Dirty hands. His eyes narrow.

'Ketchup disaster,' I say flatly.

He doesn't buy it.

The door creaks open behind me, and Opel pokes her head in.

'Tariq, you need to see this.'

I follow her into the corridor. She thrusts her phone into my face, the bass-heavy thrum of music blaring from the screen.

'Opel, what the hell are you showing me?'

'Look at the video.'

It's an Instagram live. The camera pans over a crowded nightclub, a mess of bodies swaying to the music. I squint at the blurred figures under the strobe lights.

'It's the Chapel. So what?'

Opel zooms in, and then it becomes clear. The crowd is parting, and a dark, barely visible mass is moving through them.

'The witch,' I murmur.

Opel nods grimly.

'Guys!' Theo rushes toward us, holding out his own phone and shoving the screen in my face.

It's a photo. Lucas, beaming, standing in a nightclub.

And next to him… Liam.

'Let's go.'

I bolt down the hallway, Opel and Theo calling after me. I nearly slam into Nathaniel for the second time as he steps out of the training room.

'Tariq, what on earth—?'

'Can't stop. Liam's in trouble!' I shout back, taking the stairs two at a time.

FIFTEEN

HEXING ON THE DANCEFLOOR

LIAM

I slam my empty glass on the bar, wiping my mouth on my sleeve. Lucas grins, mimicking me. The bar feels more crowded now. Someone pushes in behind me, forcing me closer to him.

'Okay, drink's done. Now we go.'

'What?' Lucas leans in, his face inches from mine.

The music's roaring now. Full blast. I can barely hear myself think, let alone what Lucas is saying. But there's something else too. My powers don't include a spider sense, but something is tingling.

'We should go!' I say, louder.

'Nuh-uh, we're dancing.'

He grabs my arm and pulls me into the crowd.

Lady Gaga's 'Abracadabra' pulses through the speakers as Lucas drags me onto the dancefloor. He's already lost in the music, all elbows and enthusiasm. I'm just trying not to get hit in the face.

Something shifts.

A prickle along my neck. My breath fogs in front of me. It shouldn't. Not in here.

The guy next to us is rubbing his bare arms. A girl clutches at her sequined top, suddenly aware of how little it covers. Her boyfriend shrugs off his hoodie and wraps it around her shoulders.

My skin feels tight. The sweat I'd barely noticed a moment ago turns clammy, cold.

Not everyone feels it. Some dancers keep moving, caught in the beat. But a wave of discomfort is spreading.

I pull out my phone, but before I can unlock it, Lucas snatches it, laughing, and slips it back into my pocket with a playful wag of his finger. He runs his hands through his hair, his back brushing against me. For a second, there's warmth. Weirdly soothing.

No. I need to focus. Tariq. Think about Tariq. Lucas is just being… Lucas.

The beat drops. Jack made Lily and me do a TikTok to this song. I tanked it, but we laughed for ages.

My friends. I should be with them.

Lucas moves deeper into the crowd.

But something's changed. The air behind him ripples. People near the source of it start backing away. But most still don't notice. They keep dancing, hypnotised by the lights and bass.

The witch.

She moves like liquid shadow through the dancers, strobe lights making her shape flicker. There, then gone, then closer.

'Lucas!' I push forward.

He doesn't hear me.

Through a tangle of limbs and shoulders, it's like moving through glue. Some dancers watch me pass, but they don't move. The music's got them. Or something else has.

Each breath feels sharper, colder. Ice in my lungs.

'Lucas!' It's swallowed by the beat.

He's still dancing. Still oblivious.

The witch is nearly on him. Her pale, claw-like hand shoots out from the shadows. Without thinking, I lunge forward, tackling him to the ground. The crowd parts, some gasp, others laugh.

'I didn't peg you for the rough-and-tumble type, but I like it,' Lucas says.

The witch is gone. But she's still here. Still close.

I haul him to his feet. 'We need to go!' I shout over the music, gripping his arm.

Lucas jerks his arm away. 'What the hell are you—'

The temperature plummets again. A gust of wind rips through the club, sending drinks and napkins flying. The lights flicker and dim. Screams rise as people scramble toward the exits. The music continues in the chaos.

'Look!' I point toward the ceiling. A swirling dark mass, like a storm cloud, forms above. But it's not a storm.

Frost begins creeping over the walls and floor. Glass shatters as ice coats the bar. It's coming straight for us.

The dark mass above dissipates, and the witch emerges. Suspended in the air.

Lucas's face drains of colour. 'What the f—'

'Run!' I pull him toward the back exit. This time, he doesn't resist.

We bolt through the panicked crowd, dodging overturned chairs and people scrambling for safety. Something breaks behind us, but I don't look back. I just run, dragging Lucas until we burst through the doors into the night air.

'I knew it.' Lucas gasps, leaning against the wall. 'I knew the witch would come for me, not Theo.'

'Yeah, well, congratulations. Now we just need to stay alive.' I fumble for my phone with trembling hands.

Tariq. I need Tariq.

The phone rings once. Twice. My pulse pounds in my ears. Come on, come on…

Finally, Tariq picks up. 'Liam?'

'She's here.' My voice is shaking. 'The witch. She's after Lucas.'

'I'm coming. Almost there.' The line goes dead.

But I didn't even tell him where we are.

Lucas is still breathing heavily. 'Let me guess. Knight in shining armour?'

The exit door behind us bursts open. A body flies out and hits the alley wall with a sickening thud.

Lucas gasps. 'Shit.'

It's the barman who served us, frozen solid, his face twisted in terror.

Another sharp noise, and Lucas is yanked off his feet, by some unseen force, and dragged back into the club.

I chase after him, his screams echoing as we re-enter the icy hell.

Inside, the nightclub has transformed into a frozen wasteland. The music is distorted, the strobe lights casting green and red beams. Ice cracks underfoot as I stumble forward, slipping, catching myself.

'Get off me!' Lucas cries.

The witch is pinning Lucas to the floor. She presses his face into the ice.

I charge forward, crashing into her. We both slide across the frozen floor, smashing into furniture as we go.

I scramble to get up, but she's there. Her eyes lock onto mine. Pale, dead.

'Keeper.' Her clawed fingers close around my throat, cold and unyielding. My strength is draining, my body going numb. My vision blurs as frost creeps over my skin.

'Keepers betray. Keepers die.' Her face is hidden by a hooded robe.

Just as the darkness closes in, someone calls out. My name. It's not Lucas, it's…

The witch screeches as flames explode behind her, lighting up the frozen room in hues of orange and yellow. She slithers away, retreating into the shadows.

Tariq stands over me, a ball of fire glowing in his hand.

'I've got you.' He kneels beside me, his hands warm as he presses them to my neck. The chill begins to fade, replaced by the comforting heat of his touch.

Tariq's warm hands steady me as he pulls me to my feet. My legs feel weak beneath me, but his heat keeps me grounded.

'You were supposed to be at the Seven Angels!'

I'm still catching my breath. Does he really want to do this now?

Lucas is being helped up by Opel and Theo.

'How did you find us?' I ask.

'Your little selfie with Lucas is all over Instagram.'

'Tariq, I wasn't—'

'Guys,' Opel says. 'Sabrina's back.'

Before any of us can react, the witch drops from the ceiling, like a shadow torn loose. Her cloak snaps around her, throwing jagged shapes across the ice-glazed walls.

'The Martindale is mine.'

She thrusts her hands outward. Shards of ice explode across the room, shredding tables and shattering glass. I throw up an arm as a chair leg flies past my face, splinters nicking my skin.

The cold slices straight to the bone. But there's no time to feel it.

Tariq steps up, flames roaring from his palms, the heat blasting back the worst of the chill. Opel moves with him, face carved into fierce focus. A broken chair lifts from the floor and hurtles toward the witch, smashing into her shoulder. She hardly flinches.

Power thrums under my skin, bright and sharp.

I grit my teeth and charge.

Ice spikes punch up from the floor, missing by inches. I weave through them, my boots slipping, lungs burning with cold air.

'Stay together!' Tariq shouts, but the wind tears his voice away.

I don't stop.

I launch forward, fist swinging. The impact jars up my arm as I slam into the witch's side. She staggers, skidding across the frozen floor.

I'm barely upright when she whirls back, a gnarled hand cutting the air toward me. A grip like iron clamps around my throat.

But the pressure vanishes quickly as Opel blasts another barrage of debris.

Tariq appears at my side, flame spinning. He drives the witch back, the fire wrapping around us like a living shield. The heat sears the icy wind, giving us a second's breathing room.

Lucas stumbles away from the fight.

His gaze locks with Theo's, just for a moment.

Then Lucas bolts.

'Lucas!' Theo shouts, but his brother is already gone.

Theo's shaking with barely restrained fury.

And the witch sees it.

She smiles. If you could call that twisted thing a smile.

She unleashes a violent burst of energy.

I'm knocked off my feet, skidding along the frozen floor. Opel crashes into a nearby pillar. Tariq stumbles backward, his flames dimming.

We're all down.

Before I can get my bearings, the witch moves swiftly toward Theo. He doesn't have time to react. Her hand shoots out like a viper, and before any of us can stop her, she slashes at his head.

Theo screams as the witch rips his ear clean off. Blood splatters onto the ice, staining it red as Theo crumples to the ground, clutching the side of his head.

'Th-Theo!' Opel cries, trying to force herself up.

The witch looms over Theo, victorious. Seconds later, she's gone, with her last remaining spell ingredient in tow.

SIXTEEN

FADING

LIAM

J ack is already on his feet as I step into my room at the Seven Angels. He marches toward me.

'Jack, let me explain—'

But he brushes past me, slamming the door behind him.

I sink into the armchair; it's still warm from where Jack had been sitting. Across from me, Heather sits in her own chair, holding Lily's hand. Her presence is a calming contrast to Jack's abrupt exit.

'He's a bit dramatic, that one,' Heather says.

I force a small smile. 'He has every reason to be.' I haven't explained anything to him. I'm keeping him in the dark.

'How is she?' The curse has worsened, the dark markings spreading across one side of her face like a creeping shadow.

Heather starts to respond but hesitates, her eyes flicking to the empty space beside her.

'Now's really not the time,' she mutters under her breath. 'No, I'm… okay, fine.'

She stands abruptly, letting go of Lily's hand. 'Spirits. Worse than a needy dog!'

I smile faintly.

'She'll be okay, Liam,' Heather says, before she heads out the door to talk to whoever is bothering her.

I don't see how Lily will be okay. We have no idea where the witch is or how to stop her. She could have completed the spell to bring her sister back by now. Meanwhile, Lily's life is slipping away.

I rest my chin on Lily's arm, feeling the sting of tears welling up.

'Lily… can you hear me in there?'

Her eyelids flutter, as if she's dreaming.

'Lily, I'm so sorry. I never should've let you go near that tree. This is all my fault.'

A floorboard creaks outside the room. Maybe it's Tariq or Nathaniel, about to burst in with news about the witch's whereabouts.

But there's nothing.

Lily's chest rises and falls.

'Maybe I should've told you,' I say quietly. 'About being a Keeper. About what's really out there. If you'd known… maybe you wouldn't be lying here now.'

I wish we were back at college, back when her biggest concern was whether she'd win that bloody history prize.

My fingers graze my pocket.

'Do you remember this?' I hold up a small, smooth crystal to the weak light. The edges catch a dull gleam. 'You gave it to me once when I needed it. Said it would promote healing.'

I'd kept it, even though I never really believed in all that. I didn't get it, still don't. But she does. And that is enough.

I swallow, setting the crystal down gently on the table beside her.

'I'm giving it back. Maybe… maybe it'll help.'

She doesn't move. Doesn't stir. Just lies there, caught in whatever nightmare the witch has her in.

I lean down and press my lips to her forehead. Her skin is cool.

'I need you to come back, Lily.'

The door creaks open, and I wipe my eyes. Heather takes her seat beside Lily again and slips her hand back into hers.

'Thank you, for staying with her.'

Heather gives me a small, tired smile. 'I'm just glad I can help. In some way.'

I push open the heavy wooden door to Nathaniel's office. The familiar scent of old books and candle wax greets me. Nathaniel and Tariq are standing over a large, leather-bound book spread out on the desk, deep in discussion.

'Liam.' Tariq glances up, his expression grave.

'We need to find the witch.' I ignore him. 'We need to stop her before it's too late.'

Nathaniel sighs, running a hand through his beard. 'We know where the spell will take place. But… Liam, you must understand. We don't know how the witch can be stopped yet.'

I step closer to the desk, my heart pounding. 'How about we beat the crap out of her? We don't have time to wait, Nathaniel. Lily's life is on the line.'

'I understand that. But if you go in unprepared, you'll be walking straight into fire. The witch's magic is old, powerful. And if she has her sister now, then who knows what we're up against.'

'Lily doesn't have time,' I say through gritted teeth. 'Every second we wait, she... we can't just sit here.'

Tariq rests a hand on my shoulder.

The door behind me bursts open, and Heather rushes in, looking frazzled. She's swatting at the air as if her invisible ghost companions are following her.

'I think I've got it. I know how to stop the witch.'

Nathaniel raises an eyebrow. 'You know...'

'Water.' She cuts him off, breathless. 'Water drawn from the earth where a witch has been buried is their Achilles' heel.'

'How do you know that?'

'I didn't know. Lily did.'

I straighten up, my heart leaping. 'Is she awake?'

Heather's expression turns sombre. 'No... she's still unconscious.'

'Oh.' I frown.

'When a witch dies,' Heather continues, 'their spirit leaves, but not cleanly. Their power... it lingers. It seeps into the earth.'

'Nathaniel,' Tariq begins. 'You told us that the witch trees become infected above and below the ground.'

'Well, yes.' Nathaniel adjusts his stance. 'It corrupts everything around it.'

'The ground water carries that corruption too,' Heather says.

'It becomes toxic to them,' Nathaniel says.

'Exactly,' Heather agrees. 'It's like they're own decay carries a poison to them.'

'Okay, first of all, ew.' I scrunch up my nose. 'Second of all, how did Lily tell you this?'

'I communicated with her... spiritually.' Heather hesitates. 'Your friend is one knowledgeable nugget, Liam, but—'

'But what?'

'She's fading… if we don't stop the witch…'

'Then we go now,' I say.

Tariq is at my side. 'I'm with you.'

Nathaniel hesitates. 'Liam, if we're wrong about this…'

'I don't care if we're wrong,' I snap. 'We have to try.'

Before anyone can say more, there's a noise outside the office door. A faint scuffling sound, like someone or something moving quickly past.

Nathaniel crosses the room in a few long strides and pulls the door open, peering into the hallway. He shakes his head, frowning.

'I'll call Opel.' Tariq takes out his phone, already dialling.

She's with Theo at the hospital, along with Lucas.

'Tar?'

He's put her on speaker.

'We're heading to Grovely. We think we know how to stop the witch.'

'I'm coming with you.'

'You should stay with Theo, he needs you.'

'Boy's conked out on morphine, he won't miss me. Besides, Lucas can stay with him.'

Lucas is protesting in the background.

Opel's voice crackles through the speaker, sharp and determined. 'I'm coming to help kill that bitch.'

Tariq opens his mouth to argue.

'I'll drive and pick you guys up on the way. Be ready.'

The call cuts out.

Tariq sighs. 'We're doing this.'

I nod. There's no turning back now. We're going after the witch. And this time, we'll finish it. For Lily's life.

SEVENTEEN

BEAUTIFUL WICKEDNESS

TARIQ

Grovely Wood is a different beast at night. The towering trees cast twisted shadows, their branches swaying with a restless rustle. Moonlight filters through the canopy, barely breaking the patchwork of darkness below. The air is thick with the earthy scent of damp soil and decaying leaves. Every step we take is muffled, like the forest is swallowing the sound.

Liam's pace is quicker than Opel's and mine. He's desperate to stop the witch and save Lily, but he can't rush this. If she spots us before we spot her, we're dead.

'So, have we talked about the plan if Sabrina brings back her sister and they start *Hocus Pocus*-ing all over town?' Opel says.

Somewhere in the distance, an owl breaks the stillness with its call.

'Sorry, Theo made me watch the sequel recently.'

'I'm just glad Theo's going to be okay.' My eyes are still on Liam, who's a few paces ahead.

'Should've been Lucas. In fact, the witch could've taken all his appendages. That would've been fun.'

'I personally would prefer him without a tongue.'

'The guy's a knob. At the hospital, all he did was rant about how Theo's always in the limelight, always getting the attention. Like Theo let the witch cut off his ear for the attention. Honestly, he's a twat.'

The selfie Liam and Lucas took at the Chapel flashes in my mind. 'I'm just glad Liam doesn't have to babysit him anymore.'

'Right? That was the other thing. Lucas couldn't shut up about Liam. "Liam this, Liam that." It's like, find another fixation.'

Lucas is doing what he always does. He uses people, then tosses them aside.

Up ahead, Liam's stopped.

We catch up with him. There's a faint violet glow shimmering beyond the trees.

Liam moves forward, but I grab his arm. 'Wait. We don't know what that is.'

He shrugs me off. 'It's the witch. I'm going!'

Before he can get too far, he's yanked back, as if an invisible rope has tied him down.

'Hey!' Liam protests. 'We agreed no using powers on each other!'

Opel relaxes her fingers, and Liam topples to his knees. 'That was before you were about to do something stupid.'

'She's right, Liam. We have to be smart about this. I want to save Lily too, but we don't know what's waiting out there. Nathaniel wasn't sure how long this resurrection spell would take.'

'I'm sorry. I just... I can't lose her.'

I grip his chin, lifting his gaze to mine. 'We've got this.'

He nods, taking my hand and managing a half-smile.

'Can you boys get a room later?'

A twig snaps nearby. We look behind us, but there's nothing.

'Follow me,' I say. 'Slowly and stay low.'

The violet light is blinding, and now that we're closer, the source is evident. The other witch tree is on fire. But instead of glowing with oranges and reds, it's ablaze with purples and flickers of white. The crackling fire sends shards of the tree to the ground, its energy growing wilder.

'I don't see the witch.' Opel crouches between Liam and me, squinting past the bushes to get a better view.

'She has to be close.'

As if on cue, a hooded figure steps out from the other side of the burning tree. She moves slowly, circling the flames and tossing what looks like a powdery substance into the fire.

'What is she—' Liam is silenced when the witch pulls a pair of gooey-looking eyes from her satchel, holding them up as if offering them to the flames. Then, without hesitation, she throws them into the fire.

The inferno surges, casting wild shadows across the clearing. Its violet glow pulses like a heartbeat, unnatural and furious. Whispers slither through the air, low, hissing, too many voices to understand.

Opel steadies herself beside me. 'She's started the spell.'

'I need to get to her witch tree, just beyond here.' I keep my voice low. 'I can draw the water up from there.'

'We need a distraction,' Liam says, and then he's gone, a blur disappearing into the flickering light.

Opel stands. 'Damn, super-speed.'

'Go. Help Liam – I've got the water.'

She nods once and darts off into the trees.

I crouch low, heart pounding, and weave through the undergrowth. Dry branches scrape my arms as I push through, careful not to snap anything that might give me away. The heat thickens as I near the first tree. The flames crackle loud, and the glow paints the underbrush in shades of deep red and bruised purple.

'Keeper!' The witch's voice slices through the air – harsh, echoing, close.

Liam's in the clearing, facing her down, Opel just behind him.

There's no time. I push on.

The scorched remains of the second witch tree loom ahead, blackened bark still reeking of smoke from the lightning strike. I skirt around it, avoiding any sort of touch. I don't want to end up like Lily.

I drop to my knees on the far side of the tree, press my hands to the ground, and shut my eyes. The soil is cool, and rough against my palms.

The heat inside me races through my arms, through the roots, into the soil below. The earth resists at first. Then it loosens, softens.

Shouts echo faintly from the clearing – Liam, Opel, the witch. Clashes, bursts of sound.

They're buying me time.

Sweat drips down my temples, stinging my eyes. I drag a sleeve across my face and push deeper.

The ground answers. Water bubbles up, dark and thick, until a shallow pool forms beneath my hands.

I rise slowly and lift my arm. The water follows, rippling upward into a hovering sphere. The liquid quivers as it grows.

A snap – somewhere behind me. A twig?

I freeze.

The flames from the other tree aren't bright enough to show what's moving through the trees.

Heart hammering, I edge toward the clearing, keeping the water steady in the air above my hands.

And stop.

No Liam. No Opel. Just smoke, fire, and silence. The clearing is empty.

Only the flames remain, crackling, growing louder with each passing second.

'Tariq!' Liam's voice cuts through the silence.

He's bound to a tree, thick vines snaking around his body. Opel is restrained the same way, her cries muffled by foliage.

'Behind you!' he shouts.

I spin, and there she is. The witch steps forward, her hollow eyes locking onto mine.

I hurl the ball of death water at her.

She mutters an incantation in a language I don't understand, and the water halts mid-air.

I push hard, willing the sphere to find its target. But she has it on pause, and for a moment, studies it, before whipping her hand around it.

The water evaporates into steam, rising into the air above us.

'Your effort was not without merit, Keeper. But luck was never on your side.'

Something coils around my legs and pulls me off balance. I'm dragged backward, my back slamming into the rough bark of a tree. Vines snake around me, binding my hands behind my back. The bark scratches painfully against my skin as I struggle.

The witch approaches, lowering her hood. Blond hair spills out, long and matted. Half her face still rots with decay. Maybe she was beautiful once, but now she's something twisted, unnatural.

Liam struggles against the vines. One of them snaps as he tries to break free. But another appears, binding him tighter.

'You must be the Auctus Keeper.' Her voice is more human now.

'Leave him alone!'

She scans me with disdain.

'You appear more selfless than the Elementa I once knew.'

Something ripples under her mangled cheek. It's like she's slowly restoring herself. As if with every moment that Lily weakens, she's restored, growing stronger.

'It won't save you, though.' She walks back toward the burning tree. 'If only Evangeline had listened to me. You Keepers are much the same as ever.' Her hands rise as if communing with the flames. 'Troublesome you were, troublesome you remain. Ever interfering, ever in the way.'

She returns to her sister's grave. The witch tree is still burning bright. Whispers swirl around us again.

'Stop!'

She doesn't even glance back. She reaches into her satchel, pulls out Theo's severed ear, and tosses it into the fire.

The flames explode, shooting high into the sky before retreating inward. The violet light fades, replaced by normal orange flames.

'My sister shall soon crawl from this tomb.'

'Then what?' I fidget in my bindings. 'The world has changed. You don't belong in this time.'

'You are right. Sarumbourne is different. Familiar places are not the same.' She smiles coldly. 'Time was wrested from us. Now, the hour is ours. Once we claim our power, we shall have our vengeance upon this city and its people.'

Opel wriggles her mouth free from the vine. 'What the hell are you seeking vengeance for? You were the one who diseased the city in the first place!'

The witch draws a breath, moving closer, examining Opel from head to toe.

'Is this what the history books have told you?'

Opel turns her head to the side, screwing up her face. 'It's 2025, you might want to work on your dental hygiene.'

The witch strikes her across the face before commanding the vines to tighten their grip on her.

Liam struggles to speak through the vines, and the witch waves her hand, loosening the vines around his mouth.

'Please,' Liam pleads. 'Do whatever you want, just remove the curse from my friend. She doesn't deserve this.'

The witch cocks her head, intrigued. 'Friend?'

'The blond girl who was here with us the other night,' he continues. 'Her name is Lily.'

The witch raises a hand to silence him. 'I know the girl of whom you speak. She's got brains, and a strength inside for which I yearn. That's why I chose her.'

'Spare her,' Tariq says.

'I cannot grant your request even if I wanted to.' The witch stares me down. 'She is bound to me now. Her life force sustains mine. The renewal is nearly complete.'

Liam's face crumples in despair as the vines wrap back around his mouth.

Lily must be close to the end.

Something moves in the shadows behind the witch. It's fast – too fast for her to notice.

A voice rings out. 'Sustain this!'

The witch spins just in time to see the glint of a flask as its contents are hurled toward her. The liquid splashes across her chest, and the moment it touches her skin, she screams, a raw, agonised wail that cuts through the stillness of the forest. The scent of burning flesh fills the air, thick and nauseating, as steam rises in ghostly tendrils from her body.

Her skin blisters and peels in an instant, dark veins splitting open as the liquid eats through muscle and sinew like acid. She claws at herself, her nails raking down her own arms in a desperate attempt to rid herself of the searing agony, but it is useless. Her fingers curl inward, the flesh melting away until only blackened bone remains.

She stumbles backward, her legs giving out beneath her as they, too, begin to wither. The bubbling, oozing ruin of her body collapses onto the forest floor, her robes pooling around what little is left of her. A guttural rasp escapes her lips, half a curse, half a plea, but it dies in her throat as her skull finally gives way, cracking and crumbling into dust.

Silence falls. A soft breeze stirs the trees, carrying away the last wisps of steam. All that remains is the lingering scent of decay and a heap of tattered fabric, dark and empty, as if no one had ever stood there at all.

'Whoa, that was gross!' Jack steps out from the shadows, holding an empty flask in his hand.

EIGHTEEN

ATTACHMENTS

LIAM

The vines wrapped around me dry and shrivel, cracking like brittle wood before snapping apart. I stumble, collapsing onto my hands and knees, coughing dirt as I try to breathe in the cool night air.

The witch tree no longer burns. The last echoes of the witch's whispers fade, leaving an unsettling silence around us.

Hands grip my arms, hauling me to my feet. It's Jack, brushing dirt off my shoulders with an oddly calm expression.

'Mate, that was insane.'

'Jack! What are you... I mean, how did you...'

I throw my arms around him. He hugs me back, and just like that, we're okay. No explanations necessary.

He pulls back. 'This sort of reminds me of that time in school when you got stuck in the science block's cupboard. Remember? I had to break down the door with Mr Pierce's chair.'

'Yeah, he was pissed.'

'I think the only reason I didn't get detention for destruction of property is because Mr Pierce neglected the health and safety rule of not leaving his students alone in the lab.' He slaps my back. 'You were always getting yourself into trouble, mate.'

'And you always show up to bail me out.'

The moment lingers. Warm, easy. Familiar.

'How did you find us?' Tariq's voice cuts through, sharp against the softness.

Opel and Tariq stand nearby, now also vine-free, and equally stunned by Jack's sudden appearance. Both of them look a little worse for wear. Scratched, bruised, but alive. Opel prods the witch's raggedy remains with her foot.

'I followed you guys.' Jack gestures in the direction of the path we took. 'I overheard you talking with that Nathaniel guy and figured I'd tag along. I wanted to help. For Lily.'

'So that was you outside Nathaniel's office?' I knew I heard something.

He nods. 'Yeah. The journalist in me couldn't help it. Not that this will be going anywhere near the student news team.'

Opel's eyes narrow. 'You've been following us through the woods this whole time?'

'Pretty much.'

'Are you stupid or something?' Tariq folds his arms tightly across his chest.

'Tariq.' I adopt the same pose. 'Jack just saved our lives.'

Tariq scowls, but Jack's already countering. 'Yeah, if I hadn't been here, that witch would've turned you into a frog. Or probably something more aggressive for you, like a crocodile.'

Opel stifles a laugh. 'I think we should be grateful Liam's nerdy little friend decided to show up.'

'It's Jack, but thanks.'

Tariq looks between Jack and me, unreadable. Something flickers across his face before he sighs and drops his arms.

'Let's just hope killing her broke her spell. Otherwise, we've got her sister to deal with.'

My phone buzzes in my pocket. I pull it out to see a message from Heather.

'Lily's awake!' My voice comes out louder than I mean it to.

'What?' Jack practically lunges over my shoulder to read the screen himself.

'Nathaniel's assessing her.' I read the message. 'But it sounds like she'll be okay.'

'That's brilliant, Liam.' Tariq puts his arm around me, almost knocking Jack out of the way in the process. 'Why don't you and Jack start heading back to the car? Opel and I can hang around here, make sure Witch 2.0 is staying put.'

Jack and I make our way through the woods, guided by our phone torches along the narrow path to Opel's car. The night air is thick with the lingering smell of smoke and damp earth.

Jack's been talking nonstop since we left the clearing, explaining how he never actually left after bailing on me at Lily's bedside at the Seven Angels. Instead, he started poking around, trying to piece together what was really going on. He stumbled into the Varga Room where we train, then found the library on the top floor, and couldn't resist flipping through one of the books left out on the coffee table.

Then he overheard our plan outside Nathaniel's office and caught a taxi to Grovely Wood to follow us.

'When I saw what Tariq was doing with the water, I thought it was incredible, like he was Aquaman, or that one from *The Last Airbender*... anyway, then the witch caught him, and... well, I had this bottle in my bag, so I filled it with water from the puddle he'd made. Snuck up on the witch while she was busy with you guys, and Dorothy Gale-d her ass!'

I'm impressed. 'You actually thought to do that?'

'Hey, I may not pay attention in class, but Lily's life was on the line.'

'Well, you did good. Even if I'm not thrilled you put yourself in danger.'

'Why? Because I don't have special powers?'

I stop, watching as he walks ahead. 'How much exactly did you read back in the library?'

'Not much. Honestly, most of it went over my head, but I got the basics.'

'So, you know Opel, Tariq, and I are...'

'Keepers? Oh yeah. And I'm sorry, mate. The way Lily and I acted last year. That wasn't fair. We shouldn't have been so dismissive.'

'Jack, you don't have to apologise—'

'No, I mean it. We thought you'd just had a real bad nightmare.'

'You did go full sceptic on me.'

'I know. But once I started reading, things clicked. All the weird stuff these last few months. The vending machine incident. You know that lad you took out with the ball? He ended up in A&E with a cracked rib. Not to mention all your freaky Spider-Man reflex moments.'

'Thanks for reminding me of my greatest hits.'

'What I'm trying to say is… I should've trusted you. I'm sorry.'

We fall into silence, and a mix of emotions floods in. Part of me feels he should be sorry; what happened to me was huge, and my friends weren't there when I needed them. But I know that if our roles were reversed, I'd probably have doubted him too. Besides, Nathaniel and the Guild made it perfectly clear I had to keep my Keeper identity hidden.

'Now you know, Jack, it changes everything. This is… it's dangerous.'

'Yeah, yeah. I've heard all the superhero best friend speeches.' He playfully punches me on the shoulder before carrying on up the track.

Now that Jack knows, surely this means the Guild will have to intervene somehow? Nathaniel won't be happy, although I hope us being alive might be a small saving grace.

Right now, though, all I want is to get back to Lily.

Nathaniel and Heather part quickly as Jack and I rush into the room back at the Seven Angels. Lily is sitting up in bed, and she barely has time to grin before we're on her.

'You're okay!' Jack squeezes me and Lily in a three-way bear hug that has us all gasping to breathe.

'I'm okay.' Her voice is muffled from the pressure of Jack's embrace.

I pull away, leaving Jack clinging to her like some tree-hugging sloth. Lily looks like she's been through it, kind of like she would after a night sampling Jack's made-up cocktails. Her skin has returned to its usual pinkish tone. Her hair is flat, her eyes are tired, but she's Lily.

'Jack, this is sweet.' She tries to wriggle free. 'But seriously, please get off me. You smell like a bonfire and... I don't even know what else.'

'Oh, right, sorry.' Jack finally lets go, staying seated on the edge of her bed. 'Long night. Burning trees, dead witch... wait. Do you know about—'

'She knows,' Heather says.

'You know?' I take a seat in the chair beside her.

'I know all of it.' She's looking at me with a mix of tired relief and understanding.

'Hold on, both of you know?' Nathaniel says, hands sinking into his pockets, his face a mask of frustration.

Jack and Lily nod in unison.

'Know what?' Opel says, entering with Tariq just behind her.

'That you're the Keepers,' Lily says.

'...of the Crossing,' Jack finishes.

The room falls silent.

I explained to Tariq and Opel in the car that Jack knows about us. They were quiet about it, and I understand why. This has to be the first time that their identities have been exposed like this.

Heather must've told Lily, or maybe Lily pieced it together herself, knowing her. Then she probably questioned Heather until she cracked.

Judging by the thunderous look on Nathaniel's face, I'm going to say he's not thrilled about the current situation.

'My office. All of you. Now.' Nathaniel walks out.

Opel and Heather follow.

I squeeze Lily's hand. She squeezes back.

Jack shifts to leave.

'Not you.' Tariq points. 'This is Keeper business.'

I step between them before Jack can respond. 'Stay with Lily. I'll be back down in a bit.'

Jack nods, resuming his place beside the bed.

We've been in Nathaniel's office for five minutes, and the silence is unbearable.

Opel is perched on the windowsill, her fingers absently tracing the edges of her pendant as she stares out at the dark courtyard below. Is she actually looking at anything or just avoiding the awkwardness?

Tariq sits beside me in one of the armchairs, his foot tapping a restless rhythm against the floor. It's like he's vibrating with the need to move, to act, to be anywhere but here. Across from us, Nathaniel is leaning back in his chair, hands pressed together in a contemplative pose, his gaze fixed somewhere beyond us. Heather appears to be whispering to someone that the rest of us can't see. Her lips move, her eyes dart to the empty air beside her.

Did I mess up by letting Jack and Lily into this world? I didn't mean for them to know, it just… happened.

'So…' Heather's voice cuts through the silence like a clap of thunder, and I nearly jump out of my seat. 'Maggie was just wondering if—'

Nathaniel shoots her a look of 'this is really not the time'.

'Maybe later, Maggie,' Heather whispers to the air.

Nathaniel leans forward, his chair creaking. 'Before we get to the obvious, I assume the witch is vanquished?'

'Yeah, she's dead,' Tariq replies.

'And what of the spell? And her sister?'

Tariq glances at Opel. 'We hung around for a while, but there was no activity.'

Nathaniel narrows his eyes. 'Are you sure?'

'There was nothing,' says Opel. 'Killing the witch must've broken the spell, just like it did with the curse on Lily.'

'Spells and curses are different beasts.' Nathaniel leans back in his chair. 'But if there was no evidence of resurrection, then it does indeed sound like the remaining witch of Grovely Wood is still bound to the earth.'

His shoulders relax slightly. I hope this bit of good news might soften the blow of what's coming next.

'Will Lily be okay now?'

Nathaniel removes his glasses. 'The curse has left her.'

'That girl's a tough cookie, Liam.' Heather offers me a warm smile.

'She may have some lingering effects,' Nathaniel continues. 'Sharing a lifeforce with the witch, even briefly, could leave traces. I suggest keeping a close eye on her in the coming days.'

Lily is alive. That's all that matters.

'Not to ruin the happy ending...' Opel slides off the windowsill. 'But we now have two regulars who know we're Keepers.'

'They won't tell anyone anything.'

'This isn't just dangerous for them, Liam, it's dangerous for us,' Tariq says. 'They could be a distraction.'

The irritation under my skin threatens to boil over. Surely Tariq, of all people, should understand. Jack and Lily aren't liabilities.

Nathaniel raises a hand. 'I think I should speak to Liam alone.'

Opel throws up her arms. 'This affects all of us.'

'But it will affect Liam the most.' Nathaniel opens the door for them. 'Opel, you have Theo to attend to. I imagine he's not getting much rest, with Charles and Lucas at his bedside.'

Opel falters, as if realising she'd forgotten about her boyfriend. She recovers quickly, striding out of the room.

'I can stay…' Tariq offers, though I'm not sure who to.

'No.' I want him to know I'm annoyed. He knows how much Lily and Jack mean to me, yet he talks about them like they're dirt under his boots.

He blinks, his face briefly clouding with… hurt, maybe? Then he leaves without another word. Heather bops me lightly on the head as she passes, the door clicking shut behind her.

Nathaniel doesn't look at me immediately. Instead, he rummages through his desk drawer.

'Nathaniel, I'm sorry about—'

He pulls out an old, worn photograph and places it on the desk between us. It's a picture of two boys, maybe my age. I recognise Nathaniel instantly, his curly black hair and bright blue eyes are unmistakable. No beard though. He's got his arm around another boy, smaller and freckled, both of them laughing at whoever took the photo.

'Who is that?'

'His name was David. He was my best friend. Funny, adventurous… we were both huge *Star Wars* fans. He died when we were seventeen.'

'What happened?'

Nathaniel's gaze lingers on the photo. 'I made the mistake of telling him everything. He became obsessed with it. He wanted to be part of it, to do what I was doing. Being a Keeper. One night, after a screening of *The Phantom Menace*, we ran into trouble. A shapeshifter.' His voice cracks slightly. 'I told David to go home, but he followed me. When the creature turned on him, I tried to use my powers to protect him. But I panicked, something went wrong, and he... he stumbled. Hit his head and... he died instantly.'

My throat tightens. What can you even say to that? A thousand words fight their way to the surface, but none of them feel right. *I'm sorry* is too small, too empty for something like this. Telling him it wasn't his fault feels like a lie... because he doesn't believe that, and maybe I wouldn't either if I were in his place.

'The Guild covered it up, of course,' Nathaniel continues. 'They told his family he'd had an accident.'

'Did you get into trouble?'

He shakes his head, his eyes glossier than before. 'They gave me a lecture and sent me on my way. I've lived with it ever since.'

Nathaniel places the photo back in his drawer with a deliberate care that feels heavy, final. He leans back in his chair, his gaze fixed somewhere above my head.

'I know you didn't mean for your friends to find out about you, Liam. This is a unique situation. But I hope you can understand that however much they know, they must stay away from it.'

The words hit me hard. 'But how?'

'I'm not saying you should break your friendships. But Opel, Tariq, even Heather, they don't have the same ties as you do. It's easier for them.'

I shake my head. It's not easier for them; it's just different. 'They've cut themselves off from having those kinds of relationships. I can't do that. My friends are like my family. I need them.'

Nathaniel tilts his head, studying me carefully. 'And that need, Liam, is what makes you a Keeper like no other. But it's also what makes you vulnerable. This world, our world, it doesn't have the room for attachments like theirs. Trust me when I tell you that holding on to them will make everything harder. For you, and for them.'

My fists clench in my lap, but I force myself to breathe through the anger, the fear. 'So, what do I do? Push them away? Pretend they mean nothing to me? I won't do that. I can't.'

Nathaniel exhales slowly. 'The Guild are still due to talk about this, and I don't know what the outcome will be. But, ultimately, you will be responsible for them, Liam. Their safety, and their silence, will be on you. Do you understand that?'

The gravity of his words sinks in. 'I understand.'

'Good. Then start by making *them* understand. This isn't a game; it's life and death. And if they get too close...' He trails off, but the meaning is clear.

I look to the drawer where the photo is now hidden away, thinking of David and the life Nathaniel lost in one terrible moment. Is this what it means to be a Keeper? To carry the weight of two worlds and always feel like you're failing one of them?

'I won't let anything happen to them.' I'm not sure who I'm trying to convince, Nathaniel or myself.

PART 2

NINETEEN

THE CAVEAT

TARIQ

Call Me by Your Name rests in my hands, the edges of the cover soft and curling. I've tried picking up something else tonight, but nothing stuck.

I flip a page without really reading it. The words blur. Aciman always writes like he's letting you in on something personal, like every line's peeled straight from his own chest.

Liam's prize-giving was tonight. We were supposed to go together, but we've barely talked since everything with the witch and his friends. I said sorry... for snapping, for being weird when they found out about us, but it didn't seem to land. Maybe he's still angry. Or maybe he's just done trying.

Opel says he's been seeing Lucas. They 'had coffee', apparently.

Lucas is getting more of Liam than I am lately, and yeah, that gets under my skin.

I close the book and press it to my chest, staring up at the cracked ceiling.

There's a knock at the door.

'Not now, Heather.'

'It's me.'

The door creaks open, and Opel walks in wearing workout gear. Her ponytail swings behind her like she's ready to conquer the world – or at least a punching bag in the training room.

'Wow, you're a state.'

She gives me a once-over like I'm just a heap of dirty clothes.

'What?'

'I'm pretty sure I've seen you in those trackies all week. Your stubble's looking... undefined, and your hair...'

'Okay, you can stop now.'

She snatches the book from me and I sit up in protest.

'Haven't you read this, like, a hundred times?'

'It's a good book.' I shrug.

'Is it? Or do you just see yourself and Liam in Oliver and Elio?' She flips to the back to skim the blurb.

'There's no similarities, Opel. I just like the story.'

'There's an age gap.'

'Yeah, of seven years. Liam and I have three. Three.' I grab the book back and place it on my bedside table. 'Can we not?'

'So that's why you're moping.'

'I'm not moping.'

She plops onto the bed, shoving my feet aside. 'I told you to talk to him if you want to work things out. And by talk, I mean actually talk, Tar, not send him some half-arsed message.'

She's right, the WhatsApp apology wasn't my finest moment.

'He won't talk to me. He comes here to train when he knows I'm at work. He's avoiding me.'

'You were pretty harsh about his friends.'

'So were you!'

'Yeah, but I'm not the one he's been falling for like a lovesick puppy these past six months.' She leans back, crossing her arms. 'Look, Liam's friends knowing isn't ideal…'

I snort. No, it's a bloody disaster.

'But,' Opel continues, undeterred, 'it's done. Like Nathaniel said, Liam's the one who'll carry that burden every day. Cut the kid some slack.'

I blink at her. 'Who are you, and what have you done with Opel Everleigh?'

She ignores me, whipping out her phone. A moment later, mine buzzes. I pull it out and see she's forwarded an email. It's a booking confirmation: a one-night spa break at the Blackhill Manor, a swanky hotel in the New Forest, on the outskirts of Sarumbourne.

'What the hell?'

'I got it for Theo's birthday, but he's not keen on spas while he's still recovering from the whole no-ear thing. Couldn't get a refund, so… you go. Take Liam.'

'Opel, this is… I can't.'

'Yes, you can. You need some quality time. Make this your chance. No distractions, and hopefully, no Crossing drama.'

She's got a point. It might be the reset we need. 'Okay. I'll ask him.'

She grins. 'Great. There's just one caveat.'

The little excitement I'd mustered starts to deflate. 'What is it?'

'You're taking Heather too.'

'You've got to be kidding.'

'Nathaniel has organised it.'

'Nathaniel?'

'She needs to get out of this place as much as you do – more so, in fact.'

I flop back onto the bed, groaning. A romantic getaway with a chaperone. Perfect.

TWENTY

LATE-NIGHT MESSAGES

LIAM

'Congratulations, Lily Boynes, on your very impressive history prize.' I raise my pint of Coke.

Our glasses clink. Coke spills down my thumb and I wipe it on my jeans without thinking. Jack takes a huge gulp of his drink like he's in a beer advert, then coughs when an ice cube hits the back of his throat.

'Thank you, boys.'

We brought her to the Cosy Club to celebrate. It's her favourite place. Old bricks, weird wallpaper, big armchairs that look stolen from a museum. The place feels like it's been around forever, which is kind of Lily's thing. Plus, because it's partly a restaurant, they actually serve us under-eighteens.

'I mean, just look at it!' Lily pulls a small, silver-plated paperweight from her bag, and places it reverently on the table. The light catches on its surface, making the engraved letters glint. 'It's so pretty!'

'Can I hold it?' Jack reaches out.

'Not with those hands! Go wash them first.'

Jack laughs, but Lily levels him with a look that says she's dead serious. With an exaggerated sigh, he drags himself upstairs to the toilets.

'You never told me what you submitted.' I lean in to examine the engraving.

'Well… I sort of changed my project last-minute, after… you know.' She waves her hand vaguely, her smile faltering.

I nod quickly, trying to ease her discomfort. Lily hasn't talked much about what happened with the witch or the curse she endured. It's unlike her, as she's always been the 'let's talk about everything' type, but I've respected her silence. Nathaniel's warning about sharing too much has been ringing in my ears, too, so I haven't pried.

'I ended up focusing on the Handsel sisters… before they were witches I mean,' she continues. 'They were settlers from Denmark. They came over on boats in big groups. It's such an overlooked part of local history, and the judges apparently hadn't heard much about it before. I guess my "personal connection" gave it a unique edge. Not that I mentioned that in my report!'

'Good call.'

Lily relaxes into her chair, swirling the ice in her glass. 'So, as grateful as I am for the celebratory drinks, shouldn't you be practising or… whatever it is you Keepers do?' She glances around to make sure no one's listening.

'I've been training all week. Besides, I wanted a normal night for a change.'

'Normal?' Jack cuts in as he reclaims his seat, lunging for the trophy again. 'What's normal these days?'

'Are you avoiding Tariq?' Lily's eyes are on Jack and her trophy but her question is aimed squarely at me.

Lily tried to have this conversation with me the other day at college, but I had to rush off to catering class. The truth is, I *am* avoiding him. Because we'll go around in circles. I'll mention Lily and Jack. Tariq will get pissed that I'm still hanging out with them, even though they know about my identity. You'd think Lily almost dying and Jack saving our lives would be enough to earn his trust. But no. He doesn't see them the way I do, and I don't want to have that fight.

I shrug. 'I just wanted to spend time with you guys.'

'Liam O'Connor. I know how you feel about him. Put aside whatever petty drama is going on and fix it.'

Easy for her to say. She's not the one caught in the middle.

'Yeah, mate. At this rate, I'm gonna be getting some before you do.'

Lily glares at him. 'Oh, really? And from who, exactly?'

'Phoebe. She asked me to the May Masquerade.'

Lily's eyebrows shoot up in surprise. 'She didn't tell me!'

'Congrats.' I punch his arm. 'When you guys finally hook up, let me know. I'll stand in the corner and cackle like Dracula on that ghost train.'

Lily spits out her drink, laughing so hard she has to clutch her stomach.

Jack glares. 'Funny guy. Did your superpowers come with super-fast jokes too?'

'Did I forget to mention that?'

Lily shakes her head, still chuckling. 'Can we finish our drinks? Some of us have to be up at stupid o'clock tomorrow.'

My phone buzzes. Tariq's name is lit up on my screen. I slide the phone into my pocket without answering.

'Student council slave duty.' Jack takes a big glug of his drink.

Lily groans. 'We've got five new students starting next term. Principal Gellar wants us there bright and early to welcome them.'

Jack grins. 'Sucker!'

Lily glares at him but then lets out a perfect Count Dracula impression that has me choking on my Coke.

It's almost eleven at night when I finally get inside the flat. I'm knackered. Classes, the prize-giving, drinks with Lily and Jack. It's been a day. My legs feel like lead as I drop my bag by the door and head straight for the kitchen.

'Hello, love.'

Mum's curled up with a cup of tea, wearing her bright Winnie-the-Pooh pyjamas.

'Mum. Sorry, I didn't think you'd still be awake.'

'Late shift tomorrow. I can have a lie-in. How was the awards?'

'Good.' I grab a glass and fill it with water. 'Lily won the local history prize.'

'Oh, good for her. Nothing for you?'

'That would actually involve me entering something. Which I didn't.'

She nods but gives me that look. The one that says maybe I should have entered something. I take a sip of water, avoiding eye contact.

'It's fine, Mum. Not everyone's destined to win a paperweight with "academic excellence" etched into it.'

She raises an eyebrow. 'It wouldn't kill you to try, though.'

I shrug. 'Maybe next year. Or maybe I'll invent my own award. "Best Avoidance of Academic Pressure".'

That gets a tiny smile out of her.

'Just don't leave it too late to figure out what you're good at, Liam.'

Demon fighting. Saving the world from unimaginable evil.

'I'm really tired.' I head toward my room.

'That boy stopped by for you today.' Her words catch me like a lasso. 'The skinny, white-haired one. Met him briefly in town with you.'

'Lucas.' What was he doing showing up at my home?

'That's the one. He did tell me, but you know me... brain like a sieve.'

'I'll message him.'

'I don't see Tariq much these days. Everything okay between you two?'

She knows it isn't. 'All good, Mum. He's just... busy.'

She nods, slower this time. Like she doesn't buy it, but she won't push.

'Goodnight, Liam.'

'Night, Mum.'

I close my bedroom door behind me, setting the glass on my desk before stripping off my clothes and collapsing into bed. Mum's door clicks shut down the hall, and guilt tugs at me for brushing her off. But I'm too tired to talk. It's not like there haven't been nights when I waited up for her to get home, only for her to rush straight to bed after a late hospital shift.

Pulling my phone out, I check Tariq's message:

Free tomorrow night?

That's it? No explanation, no details. Just typical cryptic Tariq. Am I free? Yes. Do I want to be? That's another question entirely.

I ignore it and open my chat with Lucas instead. My thumbs hover.

Lucas is complicated. Last week, he asked to meet, and I agreed on three conditions: no sneaking me into clubs, no alcohol, and no telling Tariq. Things between Tariq and me are already tense. I didn't need Lucas rocking the boat.

I send him a message. *You called?*

We ended up having coffee after one of my training sessions. He made a joke about me being all hot and sweaty, and then we eventually moved on to talking about his family. As much as he despises his brother at times, he feels bad for what happened to him at the Chapel, and running out on us. He also thinks his grandfather is too old to be the head of the Guild, not in his right mind for the role. He wants to change things if he ever takes over.

The conversation seemed almost genuine. But then, right at the end, he hugged me and said, 'Thanks for the date.' I still don't know if he was joking, and we haven't spoken since.

My phone buzzes.

I was in the neighbourhood thought I'd check on my favourite Keeper.

I roll my eyes and reply:

Your favourite Keeper is fine.

Almost immediately, Tariq messages:

You awake?

Damn it. He can probably see I'm online. *Yeah*, I reply.

Lucas fires back:

I hear you and Tariq aren't talking?

How does he even know that? Probably Opel. She tells Theo everything, and Theo's gossip chain likely runs straight to Lucas. Great.

Before I can answer, another message from Tariq:

Look outside your front window.

My heart skips. I throw back the covers, painfully aware I'm only in boxers, but too tired to care. Mum's already got her bedtime audiobook playing anyway.

Light spills through the parted living room curtains. Beneath the streetlamp, Tariq waits, irritatingly handsome as always.

What are you doing here? I message.

He puts a finger to his lips and points toward the front door.

The air in the communal hallway is cool. I'm shivering by the time I reach the door.

'You're practically naked.' Tariq's eyes flick down, his lips twitching into a grin.

'I was going to bed. What are you doing here, Tariq? Is it a Keeper thing? Did Nathaniel—'

'No. It's not that. You just… didn't reply to my message.'

'The one asking if I was free?'

He nods. 'Yeah. Opel gave me this One Night Retreat spa voucher. Blackhill Manor. I thought… maybe we could go. Talk.'

Talk. At a spa. That's… not what I expected at all.

'You should've led with "spa".'

A flicker of relief crosses his face. 'So, you'll come?'

A night alone. No demons. No drama. Just… us. It sounds suspiciously like hope.

'Yeah. Sure.'

His grin spreads. 'Great. I'll pick you up at six. Opel's lending me her car.'

I blink. 'You don't drive.'

'I do. Technically. I just haven't in, uh… three years.'

'So, there's a chance we die en route.'

He shrugs. 'Worth it. Just pack an overnight bag. And swim shorts. Not that I'm complaining, but maybe something less… translucent than those boxers.'

My white CKs are on full view. My ears go hot, and I close the door on his laughter.

———

Back in bed, my mind whirls. Ten minutes ago, I was dreading how to talk to Tariq. Now, I'm going to a spa with him. How did that happen?

My phone buzzes. A swim shorts emoji from Tariq, followed by water splashes.

Lucas has messaged again. Just a string of question marks.

All's fine between Tariq and me, I reply, adding, *He's taking me to a spa tomorrow.*

Hopefully, that'll shut down any rumours. Not that Tariq and I are actually 'fine'. But maybe, by tomorrow night, we'll figure out where we stand.

TWENTY-ONE

THE NEWBIES

LIAM

The projector hums at the back of the classroom, casting *Bedknobs and Broomsticks* onto the screen. I sink lower in my seat, watching Angela Lansbury waltz around the room with a broomstick. A witch. Of course. Just when I've spent the last month trying to shove everything about witches and curses to the back of my mind, Mr Hurley hits me with this. At least she's a good witch. Not the kind that leaves you with nightmares or removes various body parts from you for some spell.

Jack isn't even pretending to pay attention. He's hunched over his phone, Phoebe's name lighting up the screen with every new message. His thumbs move so fast it's like it's not even attached to him, his face pulled into this intense focus that, honestly, I wish he'd aim at the film for five seconds so Mr Hurley doesn't lose his shit. Too late. The film is paused. Angela Lansbury's mid-jump, broomstick hanging in the air.

I nudge Jack. But he just nudges me back.

'Jack.' Mr Hurley's voice slices through the quiet, and Jack flinches, nearly dropping his phone.

Mr Hurley folds his arms, creasing his blazer. 'Maybe you'd like to explain how this scene uses mise en scène to establish tone.'

Jack's eyes dart to me. I shrug, smirking. He's on his own.

'Well… er…' Jack coughs as the entire class turns to look at him.

Mr Hurley tilts his head, peering over the rims of his glasses.

'The broomsticks… er… dance?'

A snort escapes me before I can stop it. Jack kicks me under the table, hard enough to sting. A ripple of laughter spreads through the room.

'Perhaps you should spend more time on the big screen here,' Mr Hurley says, gesturing to the projector, 'and less time on that smaller screen of yours, yes?'

'Yes, Mr Hurley. You got it.' Jack lifts his phone in mock surrender before shoving it, very obviously, into his bag.

The projector whirs back to life, and Angela resumes her dance.

'You really said, "The broomsticks dance"?'

'Don't be a twat, Liam.'

The refectory buzzes with the chaotic energy of lunch hour: trays clattering, chairs scraping, and the constant murmur of overlapping conversations. Jack and I are halfway to the food queue when we hear our names being shouted from across the hall.

'Oh no.' Jack groans. 'Can we just turn around?'

'It's Lily.' She's at one of the larger tables, surrounded by a group I don't recognise.

'Yeah, with the newbies. She's on induction duty.'

'Right, crap.'

'Glad you're finally on my level.'

Lily waves us over, both arms flailing like she's directing traffic. Jack looks longingly at the exit.

'Come on.' I nudge him forward.

When we reach the table, Lily pulls me into a quick hug. There are five unfamiliar faces around her, all watching us like we're part of some unannounced inspection.

Two boys sit at one end of the table: one clutches his bag like it's a life jacket, his eyes darting nervously; the other wears a thick chain necklace and looks as if he'd rather be anywhere else.

The three girls are more varied. One, with fiery red hair and a wide, friendly smile, waves at us immediately. Another is buried in a college prospectus, barely looking up.

The third girl is already standing and extending a hand toward us. 'Hello. I am Eva.'

I can't place her accent.

She's strikingly pretty. Almost unnervingly so. Her thick blond hair gleams under the fluorescent lights, and there's a confidence in her handshake that feels out of place among the usual nervous energy of us first-years.

Jack blinks, mouth slightly open. 'Ah… uh…'

'Eva, this is Jack,' Lily says, saving him.

'Liam.' I give a small wave to the others at the table.

'It's nice to make your acquaintance.'

She's well spoken, and very polite. There's something familiar about her.

'Eva still needs to register at the admin office,' Lily says, glancing at me. 'Liam, could you—'

'I'll take her!' Jack interrupts, far too eager.

Eva smiles, looping her arm through Jack's and leading him toward the door.

Lily rolls her eyes, turning to the red-haired girl. 'Velora, catering's next on your timetable, right?'

Velora nods, her grin as bright as her hair.

'Perfect. Liam has catering too.' Lily looks at me pointedly. 'Would you mind showing her the way? I've got to take these guys to the library, and as you know, that's now a trek since they've moved everything to that mobile room on the other side of the grounds.'

'Sure.' I attempt to sound more enthusiastic than I am.

'Lifesaver. I'll come find you after class.'

'Let's take this station.' I slide my bag under the counter. Velora does the same and hops onto one of the high stools beside me.

We're early, which means we've snagged the best workstation. It's tucked in the back of the catering room, far from Miss Nott's usual orbit, and right by the window. The sunlight streams in, bathing the counter in a soft glow, and it's a welcome buffer from Miss Nott's booming voice. She's a decent teacher, but subtlety? Not her strong suit. My ears are usually ringing by the end of class when I sit too close.

'Will it be a practical today?' Velora asks, pulling out a notebook.

'Uh... What day is it? Oh! Friday. Yeah, it's probably some kind of salad. Waldorf, I think?'

Velora smirks and tucks the notebook back into her bag, then glances at her phone, quickly tapping out a reply to a message.

'So, Velora—'

'Call me Vel,' she says with a grin. 'I hate Velora. It makes me sound like a room spray or something.'

I laugh. 'Noted. Vel it is. So, how long have you been in Sarumbourne?'

'Few weeks. Transferred from Edinburgh.'

'Wow. Why here?'

Vel adjusts her glasses, hesitating for a moment. 'Oh, we've got family here. It's just me and my mum. She used to live here ages ago when she had me, but then Scotland seemed more appealing. Until…' Her eyes drop back to her phone. Her smile fades.

The classroom door swings open.

Miss Nott strides in, followed by a horde of students scrambling for the remaining workstations.

'It's just me and my mum, too.'

Vel glances up and offers me a small smile.

'Settle down, everyone!' Miss Nott shouts.

Vel winces, covering her ears.

'Sorry, should've warned you. Miss Nott's basically a human megaphone.'

'We're going to jump straight into making Waldorf salads. Equipment's under your workstation, ingredients are in the pantry. Off you go!'

Vel blinks at me. 'That's it?'

'Yeah, pretty much. She's more about *instructing* than actually, y'know, teaching.'

Vel's knife skills put mine to shame. Watching her slice through an apple is like seeing a professional chef at work: clean, precise, and freakishly fast.

She tosses the slices into the bowl of celery I've just finished chopping.

'Wow, you're amazing at that.'

'Thanks.' Vel grins. 'I cook a lot for my mum. I've watched way too many YouTube videos on slicing and dicing. Probably the only catering skill I'm actually good at, though.'

'Don't sell yourself short. Anyway, I'm pretty sure you can't be worse than me.' I scan the room, then lean in conspiratorially. 'Wanna know a secret?'

Vel tilts her head. 'What?'

'I only took this class for the free food.'

Vel bursts out laughing. 'Preach!'

We both laugh, and for a moment, it's easy. Normal. I'm regular Liam. Not Keeper Liam.

'Alright, time for the grapes.' I reach into a bowl and grab a handful. I lay them out on the chopping board and grab a small knife. Carefully, I halve them.

'You're not bad yourself.'

'Thanks... ouch!'

Shit. Balls. Fuck.

Pain shoots through my finger. I drop the knife and stagger back, clutching my hand. The sting is sharp, and blood is pooling beneath my grip.

'Oh God, are you okay?' Vel is by my side in seconds, pressing paper towels into my hand.

'Yeah, yeah, I'm fine.' Though the growing red stain says otherwise.

Vel rushes to Miss Nott, who hands her the first aid kit. Miss Nott looks like she's about to come over, but Vel waves her off with a quick nod, as if to say, *I've got this.*

She's back in a flash, opening the kit and pulling out what she needs.

'You YouTubed first aid too?'

Vel giggles. 'Something like that.'

I don't look. She unwraps my hand. For someone who's battled demons and been stabbed in the gut, you'd think I'd be fine with a little blood.

Vel cleans the cut with practised ease, then applies a bandage. When she's done, she lingers for just a second too long, her hand wrapped around mine. There's a warm, tingling sensation, sort of like pins and needles.

'Sorry.' She steps back and gives me an awkward smile. 'All patched up.'

'Thanks.' I flex my hand. The pain's already gone, and I can move it without wincing. The bandage is neat and precise; even Mum would be impressed.

Vel grabs the next bowl, holding it out to me. 'Walnuts?'

I've been craving sunshine and fresh air all afternoon. After starting the day squinting at a screen in film studies, then forcing myself to be sociable with Vel in catering, I've just sat through another two hours of darkness and cinema talk. My eyes feel fried.

Jack, of course, spent most of it banging on about Eva. Apparently, they 'get on like a house on fire', and he's already catching feelings; even though he's known her for all of ten minutes.

Now he's thinking of ditching Phoebe and asking Eva to the May Masquerade instead. So not like Jack. It's a dick move, but I'm not getting involved. He can sink that ship solo.

I step out onto the college veranda. Lily's sitting cross-legged on the grass, typing furiously on her laptop. The sunlight catches the edges of Craythorn Forest behind her, the trees lush and green against the bright sky.

'No more newbie duty today?' I toss down my bag and unzip my hoodie. It's surprisingly warm for mid-spring.

She shakes her head, still focused on her screen. 'Just finishing this history essay.'

'What essay?' I sit, cross-legged, on my hoodie.

Lily gives me a sharp look.

'I'm kidding.' I nudge her arm. 'I finished mine at the start of the week.'

'What? You?' Her mouth drops open in mock shock. 'How?'

'Don't act so surprised.'

'But you never hand in your history coursework on time.' She closes her laptop like this requires her full attention.

'Tariq's taking me to a spa for the night.' I hope this will distract her from wanting to check my coursework for all of its errors.

Lily makes a sound that could shatter glass and pulls me into a tight squeeze.

'Liam! This is it!'

'This is what?' I croak, trying to breathe.

'The night!' She releases me, wiggling her eyebrows suggestively.

My face heats. 'Wait, what? No. Definitely not *that*.'

'Are you sure? A spa? You'll be all hot and naked. Plus, I'm betting you're sharing a room.'

'First of all, I don't think this is a nude spa. Secondly, I think he just wants to talk. We haven't spoken properly in weeks.'

'Okay, so you'll talk and then have sex.'

'Change the subject!' My cheeks are on fire. 'You're making me nervous.'

Her grin is unapologetic, but then her gaze shifts past me, and her smile vanishes. She shields her eyes from the sun.

Jack's sitting with Eva, under a tree. She's giggling at something Jack just said.

'What the hell?'

'Yeah,' I say. 'Jack said he was meeting Eva after class.'

'He's supposed to be taking Phoebe to the dance next week. What's he doing?'

'You know Jack,' I shrug. 'He gets obsessed with a girl for a while, then moves on.'

'Yeah, I know. I've been that girl, remember?'

'Don't worry. By next week, he'll probably be back on the Phoebe train.'

Jack offers Eva a sip from his can of Coke Zero.

'He'd better be. What does he even see in her?'

'Phoebe?'

'Eva! She's a bit… odd.'

I raise an eyebrow. 'Suits Jack, then.'

'No, but seriously,' Lily says. 'There's something off, but I can't put my finger on it.'

I frown, replaying my brief interactions with Eva. 'Yeah… there was something familiar about her.'

We both fall silent, lost in thought, until a football whizzes past, nearly hitting Lily's bag. A group of boys run by, one almost tripping over himself.

'They have an entire field, but they have to play here. They're going to injure someone.'

'Speaking of injuries…' I hold up my bandaged hand.

'What did you do to your finger?'

'Let's just say it's karma for making a salad. Vel patched me up.'

'Vel?'

'Yeah. She's surprisingly good at first aid. Like she's got a side hustle as a nurse or something.'

Lily hesitates. 'Don't say anything, because I shouldn't even know this, but she's a carer. For her mum.'

'Oh.' I blink, the pieces falling into place.

Lily nods solemnly. 'I don't know what condition her mum has, but Vel's basically looking after her full-time. It must be tough. College is hard enough without other responsibilities.'

'Tell me about it.'

A shout cuts through the air, drawing our attention. One of the football boys has kicked the ball at Jack, nearly knocking him sideways. They're laughing in response. One of the boys curses loudly, throwing an insult my mum wouldn't approve of. Jack throws the ball back to them, but Eva's face is hardening. The boys jog off, still chuckling, already bored of the moment. Eva brushes herself off and offers Jack a hand.

'That was uncalled for.' Lily shoves her laptop into her bag.

'Yeah, bit awkward. You walking home?'

She nods and we pack up our things.

As we head off, Jack lingers with Eva. But she's still watching the footballers on the field.

TWENTY-TWO

BLACKHILL MANOR

TARIQ

Opel's car jolts forward as I pull up outside Liam's building. The engine shudders, then stalls completely. I must've let the clutch out too soon. Again. All the lights on the dashboard blink accusingly before the whole thing goes dead. I take a deep breath, gripping the steering wheel tighter than necessary. I hate cars.

A sharp gasp from the back seat makes me jump.

Heather is pressed against the window, her hand flat on the glass. Her eyes dart over the building's facade.

'What's up?' Though I already have a pretty good idea.

'How old is Liam's house?'

'It's a flat. And I don't know. Old, I guess?'

Her gaze stays fixed on the building, her face tight with concentration. 'There are dead ones in there.'

'Don't tell Liam that. And if you ever meet his mum, definitely don't tell her either.'

She turns to me, one eyebrow arched.

'Also, no ghost stuff tonight.'

Heather holds my stare. 'You sound like Agetha.'

'Who the hell is Agetha?'

'An old bat at the Wellbeing Centre. Used to say I was making it all up.'

Sometimes I forget Heather spent years in that place, because that's what the Guild decided was best for her. It must have had an effect on her that I can't even imagine.

The passenger door swings open, and Liam climbs in, his rucksack slung over one shoulder. The fresh, citrusy scent of his shampoo hits me instantly, clean and bright. His damp hair curls slightly at the ends.

We're going to a spa. Why does he look so effortlessly put together?

Still, it's cute. He's cute.

'You guys okay? You look like you've seen a ghost.'

'No!' Heather blurts, a little too loudly. 'No ghosts. There are no ghosts. None. Zero.'

I shoot Heather a pointed look, and she flashes an awkward smile before retreating into silence.

'Wait… Heather, you're actually out in the real world.'

'Nathaniel's idea,' I say.

'I don't know how I feel about it yet.' Heather waves me off.

'She has her own room,' I whisper.

That earns me one of Liam's soft smiles.

A finger on his right hand has a bandage around it. 'What happened?'

He holds it up. 'Oh, I sliced it open in catering today. It's all good.'

'They trust you lot with knives in that place?'

I turn the key in the ignition again, praying this time will be different. The car sputters to life, but as I try to find the biting point, it jerks forward and stalls. Again.

'For fuck's sake.' I smack the steering wheel.

'That's the sixth time he's done that since we left.'

'You're counting?'

Liam covers his mouth to stifle a laugh.

'It's Opel's old banger of a car.'

'Is it, though?' Liam teases.

I grit my teeth and try again, this time managing to coax the car into motion. We pull away, and I flip down the visor to block the glare of the setting sun. Its orange glow spills across the windscreen, painting everything in warm hues.

Liam waves to his mum, who is watching from one of the upper windows.

It's dark as we approach Blackhill Manor, tyres crunching over gravel between rows of trees. The drive winds deep into the New Forest.

A massive cedar looms to the left, branches clawing at the sky like it's guarding the place. The headlights catch the red-brick hotel as it comes into view. Sharp rooftops, crooked chimneys, windows flashing pale in the dark.

'Whoa.' Liam leans forward to get a better look. 'The photos online do *not* do this place justice.'

The entrance glows ahead, its golden light spilling through the arched doorway like a beacon. Warm. Inviting.

'Finally,' Heather groans. 'What a journey that was.'

I glare at her in the rearview mirror, and she doesn't miss it.

'Oh, but lovely,' she adds with a syrupy smile. 'I especially enjoyed going over the cattle grids at forty miles per hour.'

Liam snorts.

I pull into a space between two spotless BMWs, kill the engine, and get out. The air's thick with damp and the smell of wet grass. Liam helps Heather drag out her second suitcase, because apparently one isn't enough for a single night. I grab my bag and slam the boot shut.

Inside, the reception is all charm and polish. Wooden beams, soft lighting, lavender in the air. The kind of place that wants to feel like home, but probably costs more than rent.

At the desk, the woman behind it looks up and gives the kind of smile that's been rehearsed a thousand times.

'Hello. Welcome to Blackhill Manor. Are you here for dining or staying?'

'Staying. We've got the one-night spa thing.' I unlock my phone and slide it toward her.

'Wonderful.' The woman taps at her computer. After a moment, she pulls out two keycards. 'The single room is 114, on the first floor.'

I take the card and pass it to Heather, who's busy giving the place her own version of a hotel inspection.

'It's very… busy here.' Her face is twisted into a frown.

The receptionist looks around at the empty room.

'Busy with… paintings,' Liam says quickly.

The receptionist chuckles politely. 'Yes, we have a large collection of artwork on display. John Blackhill, the property's original owner in the 1600s, was a collector.'

'He'll be around here somewhere,' Heather mutters under her breath.

'Sorry, what was that?' The receptionist studies Heather.

'Where's the other room?' I interject.

'Ah, room 211. That's on the second floor.' She hands Liam the second keycard. 'Our spa is open until 11pm.

And if you'd like to dine with us tonight, let me know, and I'll book you a table.'

We head toward the stairs, Heather trailing behind, still scanning every inch of the space like she's expecting something – or someone – to jump out at her. Maybe bringing her to a centuries-old hotel in the middle of a forest wasn't Nathaniel and Opel's brightest idea. A place like this is probably crawling with spirits.

On the first floor, we stop outside room 114.

'This is you.' I unlock the door and it beeps.

Heather casts a suspicious glance up and down the corridor before finally stepping inside.

The room beyond looks as harmless as any other hotel room. Still, Heather studies it like she's searching for hidden traps.

'We're just upstairs,' I say.

'Will you be okay?' Liam asks.

Heather nods absently and steps inside. 'Spent almost seventeen years on my own in a room. This is nothing.'

Liam shrugs at me. 'See you down at the spa?' he asks her.

'Oh, absolutely not. Spas are dreadful things. No. I'll be just fine in here.'

That's a relief. It means some alone time with Liam. Maybe we'll actually get a chance to talk, just the two of us.

'Hello, lovely to meet you,' Heather says suddenly, her voice carrying from somewhere deeper in the room.

Liam and I freeze. I quickly pull the door closed before we hear any more.

'Think she'll be alright?' Liam asks.

'In an old building full of spirits? She'll be right at home.' I nudge him. 'Come on, let's find our room.'

TWENTY-THREE

BUBBLE TROUBLE

LIAM

I forgot how ridiculously hot Tariq looks shirtless. His chest is toned in ways I didn't even think were possible, muscles carved like a sculpture come to life. Even the harsh fluorescent lights of this changing room don't dull him. They just make him look unfairly, ridiculously good.

He unzips his jeans, and I spin around so fast I nearly drop my trainers. Focus, Liam. I shove my shoes and socks into one of the higher lockers, pretending I haven't spent the past thirty seconds gawking at him like an idiot.

'You're safe. I came prepared.'

I risk a glance. He's already wearing his swim shorts. They're tight, black, and tied neatly at the front with a white cord. Of course, they fit him perfectly. He grins, stuffing his clothes into his bag and casually pushing it into his locker like we're not having completely different experiences here.

He adjusts his pendant so it falls perfectly between his pecs.

'You're taking your time.'

Yeah, because I've been staring at you like some kind of drooling mess. What is wrong with me?

Facing my own locker, I tug off my T-shirt.

The mirror near me reflects everything I wish it didn't. My chest is pale, like the rest of me, and speckled with the beginnings of chest hair. Not enough to commit to the whole rugged look, but just enough to look awkward. It's the worst kind of middle ground. Could my body just pick a lane already? Either let me be smooth or give me a proper hairy chest to be proud of.

Still, there's a little definition in my arms from all the training I've been doing since I became a Keeper. Even Jack noticed last week, calling them 'guns'. I'd never aimed for that kind of thing, but... I'm not mad about it.

'You look good.'

I jump, realising he's standing closer now. He's tying the belt of one of the fluffy white robes we were handed at the spa entrance, but his eyes linger on me for just a second too long.

'Thanks.'

I move to unbutton my trousers, but then it hits me: I didn't put my swim shorts on under my clothes like Tariq did. They're still in my bag. My face burns.

'Err...' The noise escapes before I can stop it.

Tariq looks up in the mirror, raising an eyebrow. 'You alright?'

'Yeah. I just... left my swim shorts upstairs.' Maybe I can throw my clothes back on, pretend to go grab them, and change in the room, where I can panic in peace.

But, of course, Tariq is already rummaging through my bag. 'No, you didn't.' He holds them up triumphantly. 'They're right here.'

'Oh. Uh… thanks.'

I take the shorts, my fingers fumbling as I grab them. My trousers loosen and fall to my knees, leaving me standing there in nothing but my boxers. Tariq doesn't even blink. He just turns back to the mirror, fiddling with his hair like this is all perfectly normal.

Sure, he's technically seen me nude before, when I was a wounded mess, and he helped me into the shower. Eyes shut the whole time. Practically saintly.

But this? This feels different. I'm about to get naked. Properly. In front of Tariq. Stay calm, Liam.

I shove my trousers into the locker, glance over my shoulder, and confirm Tariq is still preoccupied. Thank Gaga. I hook my thumbs into the waistband of my boxers and yank them down, the cold air of the changing room hitting me all at once. I grab my swim shorts, pulling them on in a rush.

And, of course, I nearly trip over myself in the process.

'Careful there.' Tariq steadies me with one hand as he passes by. He doesn't linger, though, just heads toward the toilets. 'Just taking a pee before we head in.' He disappears through the door.

Relief floods me as I adjust the waistband of my shorts. Crisis averted.

The door creaks open again, and Tariq's head pops back around the corner. 'By the way, you've got the cutest bubble butt I've ever seen.'

Before I can respond, he's gone.

My entire body goes warm, and I spin toward the mirror, checking my reflection. Yep, my face is definitely red.

Stepping into the spa feels like entering another world. The air is warm and thick with the faint scent of essential oils. Soft light glows from sconces on the walls, reflecting off the calm surface of the water.

Ahead, the pool shimmers. A pillar rises from its centre, gentle streams cascading into the water. Steps curve into the shallow end, where Tariq is already disrobed and stepping in.

'You should take that off.' He nods toward my hand.

My finger is still bandaged. 'Right.'

It'll just come off in the pool anyway. Hopefully, it's healed a little, and the water might even help.

Unwrapping the bandage, I peel it back gently. Then stop, cold.

The cut is gone. No scab, no mark, not even a faint line where it should be.

It looks… normal.

'Everything okay?'

'Yeah. It's just… my finger. It was cut open earlier. Pretty badly. This new girl I met had to patch it up.'

'And now it's fine?'

I hold it up to show him. 'Like it never happened.'

He frowns slightly. 'Weird.'

'Do Auctus Keepers… heal fast or something?'

Tariq shakes his head. 'Not as far as I know.'

That's unsettling.

Removing my robe, I follow him into the pool, the warmth of the water climbing over my feet, legs, and up my body until I'm fully submerged. 'This is pretty nice.'

Tariq looks around, his eyes wide with awe. 'It's incredible.'

I don't think he's ever been to a spa before. Mum and I went to one a couple of years ago, but it wasn't half as fancy as this.

Tropical plants line the walls, and a huge skylight reveals a starry night above us.

'And we've got the place to ourselves,' Tariq adds, a mischievous grin spreading across his face.

He wants to kiss me. I want him to. The moment couldn't be more perfect. But we came here for a reason, and we can't just gloss over it.

'We should talk.'

Tariq tilts his head, playful. 'Should we?'

'Tariq, this is why you invited me here. Remember?'

'Can't we do the talking bit after?'

I push him back, maybe harder than I meant to. He loses his footing and disappears under the water.

He resurfaces, shaking water from his hair. 'Point taken.'

'I can go first, if you—'

'No.' He swims to the side and rests against the pool's edge. 'Let me. I know why you've been avoiding me.'

'You do?'

He sinks lower into the water. 'I haven't been fair to you or your friends. I know I can be… difficult sometimes. But it's only because I worry about you.'

'I'm not helpless anymore, Tariq. I've been monster-hunting with you for months now—'

'It's not about that. Your strength and speed have come such a long way. I know you can handle yourself. I just…'

He trails off, and the familiar frustration simmers up in me. This is what happens. He goes quiet, and the conversation dies. But not this time.

'Just what?'

His fingers ripple through the water. Finally, he sighs. 'I don't want to see you hurt. You've got good friends, Liam. And your mum. If something happens to them, it'll crush you. And I can't see you go through that.'

I hesitate. This isn't just about me, it's about him. Tariq lost his parents in a car accident as a kid. Then Thomas, his friend and fellow Keeper. He's lost nearly everyone he's ever been close to.

I swim closer, the water rippling softly between us.

'Tariq, I get it. Really, I do. Losing people... it's part of life. You can't protect me from that.' I meet his gaze. 'Okay?'

He stares at me for a moment before nodding. 'Okay.'

There's a pause. He paddles around me, then stops in the middle of the pool. He twists his finger slightly and a little whirlpool spins in my direction. It disperses as it hits my chest.

'I actually have something to ask you.'

'Go for it.' I lean back in the water, looking up through the glass roof at the night sky.

'Did you really have a coffee date with Lucas?'

I collapse into the water, almost going under. I splash to stay upright.

Of course, he knows.

'Yes.' I spit out water. 'But it wasn't a date.'

Tariq arches a brow.

'He kept asking, so I said yes. It was just coffee. He wanted to thank me for protecting him from the witch. And he's going through a lot, with his brother and the Guild. I think he just needed someone to talk to.'

'I don't trust him.'

'Like you don't trust Jack, or Lily?'

That gets a reaction. Tariq freezes, eyes narrowing.

'I don't not trust them. I just… don't like how easy everything is with them. They always know what to say to you. Always know what you're thinking.'

'They've been my best friends for years.'

'I know. That's the part I struggle with.'

He looks away, ashamed maybe, but it's the closest thing to an admission I've ever heard from him.

'You could've just said you were jealous.'

'I'm not proud of it.'

'I didn't ask you to be proud. Just honest.'

He finally looks at me. 'I'm working on it. Okay?'

I swim to the other side of the pool and pull myself out, water streaming off me.

'Where you going?' Tariq follows, his feet splashing behind.

The jacuzzi is small and round, surrounded by pillars. I slide in, the hot water melting away the last of my tension.

Tariq steps in after me, beads of water trailing down his muscular body. 'I've never been in one of these before. They're supposed to bubble, right?'

A small sign is stuck to one of the pillars: 'Jets out of order. We apologise for any inconvenience.'

'Rubbish.'

Tariq nudges me, grinning. 'Allow me.' He closes his eyes, and within seconds, the water beneath us rumbles. Bubbles erupt, growing larger and larger until foam spills over the sides.

'Tariq!'

'Whoops.' His eyes snap open. He smooths his hand over the water, calming it to a gentle simmer.

'Show-off.' I wipe water from my face.

Tariq pulls me toward him, his emerald eyes sparkling. 'What?'

'Just thinking.' He moves closer.

'About what?'

His hand trails softly down my back, pausing when he reaches the waistband of my swim shorts.

'Something else that's bubble-like.'

'You weren't meant to be looking.'

'Sorry.' He's so close now that our noses are almost touching. 'I couldn't help myself.'

Our lips meet, softly.

As our kiss deepens, everything melts away. My body sinks into his like it's second nature, and I let myself savour the feeling of his touch.

I push forward, and he moves with me until he's seated, pulling me onto his lap. His tongue rolls against mine, slow and deliberate, his hands tightening on my hips as if he's afraid I'll pull away. I'm not going anywhere.

The bubbles around us begin to fade, but I barely notice. His concentration must be slipping – he's usually better at keeping his powers in check.

I push him back slightly, just enough to adjust, and we fall into the deeper part of the jacuzzi. The water splashes over the edges as we shift, nearly submerging us both. I'm pretty sure I've swallowed half the tub since we started making out, but I don't care.

This feels too good to stop.

His fingers brush against my waistband again, this time slipping beneath the fabric of my shorts. My breath catches, and I should probably say something to slow things down, but his touch is so intoxicating that all I can do is let myself sink further into the moment.

He pauses, pulling back just slightly, his forehead resting against mine. His eyes search mine, checking for something, uncertainty, hesitation, but he doesn't find it.

He kisses me again, slower this time, like he's savouring every second. His touch feels different, more careful, more deliberate, as if he knows how much this moment matters.

I'm about to lose myself completely.

'There you boys are!'

We spring apart, water splashing over the sides. Heather stands above us in something I'm pretty sure Opel has lent her; it's very dressy for her. Either way, she's entirely out of place here in the spa.

'Heather!' I splutter. 'What are you—'

'Most of the dead here aren't chatty, thank goodness. So, I thought we could have dinner while I'm not being bombarded. I booked a table under Tariq's name.'

'My name?' Tariq groans.

'Yes, dear. I don't work. How else do you expect me to pay? Out you get,' Heather commands. 'I'm starving.'

I exchange a look with Tariq. He's struggling to calm down, below the surface, just as I am. 'Can you give us a minute? We'll meet you in reception.'

'Don't be long.' Heather turns, pausing as if she's bumped into something invisible. 'Not tonight.' She moves around whoever it is before leaving.

Tariq and I laugh.

'Can we count this as a date?'

'Definitely.' I climb out of the jacuzzi. 'And I really could eat, to be fair.'

'Me too.' He moves to follow, but quickly sinks back into the water. 'Actually, I'll meet you outside.'

'Are you still…?'

'Yep. Like the Cathedral's spire.'

I laugh, slipping on my robe. 'Don't be too long. Dinner's on you, apparently.'

I leave Tariq blow-drying his hair in the changing room and step into the spa lounge, the faint scent of eucalyptus still clinging to my skin. Pulling my phone from my bag, I see I have two missed calls. Three messages. All from the same person. Lucas.

Hey. I need to see you.

Answer your phone, Liam!

I'm coming to you!

That last message was sent thirty minutes ago.

I never told Lucas where I was going with Tariq – only that it was a spa. He wouldn't know where to find me… unless, of course, he spoke to his brother. Or Opel.

Damn it.

Why would he come all the way out here, at night?

I quickly call his number, my heart thudding. It rings once. Twice. Then cuts to voicemail.

No answer.

The walls of the spa feel like they're closing in. Tariq's going to flip when he finds out Lucas is on his way. And me? I have absolutely no explanation to give him.

Shoving my phone into my pocket, I head straight for reception.

TWENTY-FOUR

THE BLOODTAKERS

TARIQ

The blow-dryer hum fades as I switch it off and toss it onto the counter. My hair's still damp, but I don't care.

Talking to Liam didn't implode the night like I'd half expected. He didn't storm out, didn't recoil when I told him the truth. He just listened.

He's right: I am jealous of Jack. Of how easy everything seems when he is with him and Lily.

Maybe honesty could have broken us. But it didn't. If anything, it made things clearer. Lighter.

There's still a lot I haven't told him, especially about Lucas. That past is complicated, and ugly in places, and I'm not ready to lay it all bare. But I will. I want to. Just not yet.

Tonight wasn't perfect, but it was real, and right now, that's more than enough.

I just wish we'd had more time to finish what we started in that jacuzzi.

My phone buzzes with a voicemail. I press play while walking to reception. Opel's voice filters through, laced with her usual exasperation.

'Hey, Tar. We just had Lucas here, ranting and raving about some Bloodtaker he's been involved with. Theo and he got into it. Big argument. Drama, drama. Usual Lucas crap. Just a heads-up: he's talking about finding someone who'll help him. He might be on his way to you. Just tell him to do one. Anyway, hope you and Liam had a chance to talk. Oh, and check on Heather – realising now that sending her to a seventeenth-century hotel in the middle of the New Forest might not have been my brightest idea.'

The voicemail ends, and before I can process it, I step into the reception and stop dead. Liam and Heather are standing by the entrance. And there, slumped in a chair between them, is Lucas.

'Leave!'

Lucas flinches, shrinking back into the chair. His white hair is grimy, his clothes are torn, and he's paler than normal.

'Tariq, wait.' Liam steps between us.

'No. Opel left me a message. He's in trouble again, aren't you?'

Lucas fidgets, looking anywhere but at me.

'Yes,' Liam says. 'But I think we might be too.'

'What?'

Heather moves closer. 'Perhaps we should take this conversation somewhere quieter. The dead – and the living – are watching.' She nods toward the reception desk and a man in a suit. The manager.

There's a sign for the lounge and I motion toward it.

The warmth of the roaring fire does little to ease the chill crawling up my spine as we step inside. The room is empty, no other guests in sight. Lucas collapses into an armchair, Heather standing stiffly beside him.

Liam catches my arm before I can move closer. 'Look, I know how this looks.'

'Like he's making up some drama to ruin our night together?'

'Really, Tariq? You think he'd taxi all the way out here just to—'

'Yes. I told you. I don't trust him.'

'I know that. But I asked you to trust me. And I believe him. He says he's in trouble—'

'With a Bloodtaker. Again.' I cross my arms. 'You think this is the first time?'

'I don't know much about Bloodtakers. Only that's what you call vampires because, to quote you, "the name has become uncool since *Twilight*". But Lucas mentioned just now about owing a clan his blood. That's more than one Bloodtaker, right?'

I shove past Liam, grabbing Lucas's arm and yanking up his sleeve. Two puncture marks gleam red against his pale skin. 'Back to your old tricks?'

Lucas jerks away. 'Piss off.'

'Are those bite marks?' Liam asks.

Heather clears her throat. 'He's their supplier.'

Liam blinks. 'Supplier?'

'He lets Bloodtakers feed off him. For a fee,' she says.

'They don't kill?'

'Why would they? The Bloodtakers get hot blood whenever they want it. They don't have to hunt. And humans get paid.' I glare at Lucas. 'Some get addicted to the bite.'

'But if they've already bitten him, what's the problem?'

I don't look away from Lucas. 'This wasn't a bite from a clan member, was it?'

Lucas's mouth twists in frustration, but he says nothing.

'Lucas made a pact with a clan,' Heather says. 'Only they're allowed to feed from him. If a lone Bloodtaker, or an outcast, feeds, then it's a violation.'

'What happens if the pact is broken?' Liam asks.

Heather's expression hardens. 'Death.'

Liam stiffens, his eyes locked on Lucas. 'Why didn't you go to your grandfather? He could've gotten Nathaniel involved. We could have been on this sooner.'

Lucas's gaze drops.

I kneel to look into his eyes. 'Because you can't admit your mistakes, can you?' I straighten up. 'He's already been kicked out of the Guild once. Can't let Granddaddy Charles see you've failed again.'

His head snaps up, his eyes burning. 'Do you really want to talk about mistakes?'

Heather hushes us. 'The ghosts are restless. Bloodtakers are approaching.'

Panic flashes over Lucas's face.

'What do we do?' Liam asks.

I move to the window, peering out at the darkened grounds. The wind rustles the trees, shadows flickering in the moonlight.

'Heather, go to the manager. Tell them there's someone on the grounds with a gun and to tell all the guests to stay in their rooms. Meet us upstairs when you're done.'

Heather hesitates but nods, heading for the reception.

'Liam, call Nathaniel. Then Opel. Tell them what's happening.'

Liam pulls out his phone and steps aside.

I grab Lucas by the arm, hauling him to his feet. 'You're coming with me.'

He stumbles after me as I head for the stairs. Whatever storm is coming, we'll face it head-on. But if Lucas has put Liam in danger, I'll make sure he regrets it.

TWENTY-FIVE

REPEAT OFFENDER

LIAM

I take the stairs two at a time as panicked voices echo up from the lobby below. The hotel is in chaos. Guests are rushing to their rooms, slamming doors, while others are dragging suitcases and barking at receptionists. Whatever Heather told the staff, they must have believed her.

Opel and Nathaniel are on their way. Neither of them sounded thrilled about us getting involved with Lucas, but they couldn't argue when I told them what was coming. There's a hotel full of guests all at risk from a clan of Bloodtakers. They promised to get here as fast as possible.

How did tonight escalate so quickly? Less than an hour ago, Tariq and I were tangled together in a jacuzzi and totally relaxed, and now we're barricading ourselves in a hotel, waiting for a siege of bloodthirsty monsters.

This is going to be a long night.

When I reach our room, the door is ajar. My pulse quickens as I push it open, finding the lights off. Moonlight spills through the window, highlighting Tariq's figure. He's standing there, rigid, his arms crossed and his jaw clenched, bathed in silver light.

In the bathroom, a faint glow from the mirror light casts Lucas's naked reflection against the tiled wall. He's just slipping one of Tariq's T-shirts over his pale, wiry frame when our eyes meet. He half smiles, like he's trying to be charming, or at least less of an inconvenience, but I don't return it. His discarded clothes are crumpled on the floor, dark with stains I don't want to examine too closely.

I move to Tariq at the window. 'Anything?'

'Not yet.' His eyes are fixed on the shadows. 'Bloodtakers are shifty. They'll lurk in the dark until their leader gives the signal.'

'Opel and Nathaniel are on their way.' I rest a hand on his back, trying to ground him, or maybe myself. 'I haven't seen you this tense since Draven.'

He shakes his head. 'One or two Bloodtakers we can handle. A whole clan? Almost impossible.'

'They're only here for Lucas, though, right? If we can talk to them—'

'You can't reason with Bloodtakers, Liam. They might look human, but they're predators. Fast, strong, unpredictable, and deadliest at night.'

'Okay, so how do we stop them? Holy water? Crosses? A little stake to the heart?'

Tariq scoffs, finally glancing at me. 'Do you happen to have any of those on you?'

Of course not. Where is Buffy when you need her?

'The best weapon we've got is me.'

'Oh, sure, just put yourself on a pedestal.'

Flames bloom in his palm, bright and alive, illuminating the hard set of his jaw. 'Fire is lethal to a Bloodtaker.'

Before I can ask more, Lucas steps out of the bathroom, clutching his old clothes. The flame in Tariq's hand dies instantly, plunging the room into dim light again. Tariq's entire demeanour shifts, his shoulders tensing and his gaze hardening as if Lucas's mere presence grates on him. He crosses the room, snatching the bundle of clothes from Lucas without a word.

'What are you doing?'

'Getting rid of these.' He holds up the tattered fabric. 'Bloodtakers can track his scent a mile away.' He pauses in the doorway, turning back to me. 'Lock the door behind me. Don't open it for anyone except me or Heather.'

'Tariq…'

He disappears into the hallway.

Lucas locks the door behind him with an exaggerated click. 'Bit dramatic, isn't he?'

He takes a seat on the bed. Tariq's T-shirt hangs awkwardly on him, too loose on the shoulders and chest. But it's an improvement. Less like someone on the brink of collapse, but not by much.

'Can you blame him? You've lured a pack of Bloodtakers to us.'

Lucas groans, slumping onto the edge of the bed and rubbing at his shoulder. 'You're Keepers. It's your job to hunt monsters. I've done you a favour bringing them to you instead.'

'Bringing them to a hotel full of innocent people is what you call a favour?'

He tilts his head back and kneads his shoulder.

'Why do you do it?'

He doesn't look at me. 'Do what?'

'All of it. The drinking, the partying, the… blood donations. Don't tell me you made a pact with a clan of

Bloodtakers for money. Your family's one of the wealthiest in Sarumbourne.'

Lucas raises an eyebrow. 'Who told you that?'

'Your family live in the Cathedral Close. The Martindales own the Seven Angels.'

He smirks faintly. 'My, my, Tariq has been quite the chatterbox.'

'Don't change the subject. Why?'

'Why?' He finally meets my gaze, purple eyes blazing. 'So you can run back to your perfect boyfriend and tell him there's a reason I'm in this mess? That I'm just a broken little human who's had some bad luck, and maybe he should pity me?' He leans forward. 'Do you think that'll make him trust me?'

'Lucas...'

'Let me ask you something. Do you trust him?'

'Yes.' The answer comes easily.

'Then he's told you everything? About his past?'

I hesitate. Tariq hasn't told me anything. Not really. Most of what I know, I've pieced together from Lucas's cryptic comments, or sometimes his not-too-subtle ones. And honestly, I haven't wanted to press.

Lucas watches my silence and leans back, a self-satisfied glint in his eye. 'Thought so.'

'I know he lost his parents young. I know he was in the foster system until Nathaniel found him.'

Lucas gets up and wanders to the window, staring out into the dark. 'Did he ever tell you how his parents died?'

'He said it was a car accident.'

'True enough. A drunk driver pulled out on them one night while they were driving home. Tariq was in the back seat.'

Tariq was in the car? He never told me that.

'The car was forced off the road and into a ditch. His parents died instantly. Tariq took an injury to his lower back. I'm sure you've seen the scar.'

I nod, remembering the first time I noticed it, in his bedroom, long before I'd had the courage to ask about it.

'The driver's name was Leon Strainer. He only did five years. My father was killed two weeks after he was released. Hit-and-run. Drunk driver.' His voice falters, and he swipes at his face. 'It was Strainer. I know it was. But my grandfather and Theo thought I was just imagining things. The police said there wasn't enough evidence to charge him.'

'Lucas…'

'I was supposed to meet Dad that night. I was the one who saw him in the road.'

A single tear tracks down his cheek, and he brushes it away roughly.

'The last thing he said to me was "rollers" and "van". After his funeral I did some googling. That was the name of Strainer's company, Rollers Painting. He drove a white van. I told the police everything, but it didn't matter. They let him walk.'

My throat feels tight. 'So, the same man who killed Tariq's parents… killed your father?'

Lucas nods. 'When Tariq became a Keeper, Charles had Nathaniel introduce us. He thought we could help each other through our grief. And we did. But we also pieced together the truth, and we made a decision. Strainer had to pay.'

My heart sinks. I don't like where this is going. Is Lucas about to tell me he and Tariq took revenge? I didn't know

Tariq was that kind of person. I don't know if I want to hear any more. 'Lucas, are you saying…'

A sudden pounding on the door cuts me off, making both of us jump.

I rush to the door. 'Who is it?'

'It's Heather! Let me in!'

I unlock the door, and Heather bursts in, slamming it shut behind her. 'The Bloodtakers are here.'

TWENTY-SIX

NO VACANCY AFTER SUNSET

TARIQ

E mergency lights cast a dull glow across the lobby, shadows bleeding into every corner. The fire in the lounge is out, but smoke still clings to the air. The front door swings open and shut in the breeze, letting in a cold draught that creeps down my spine.

It's too quiet.

The guests have either bolted or locked themselves in as instructed.

My stomach twists. There's a body on the floor. The receptionist. She has the same navy blazer, same ponytail that had bounced while she checked us in.

Her hand's ice-cold. The warmth she'd had earlier is gone.

I move her hair gently and reveal two neat punctures at her neck.

Bloodtakers.

Heat stirs at my palms, sharp and hungry. I push it down and scan the shadows, moving into the restaurant.

The place is a wreck, with overturned chairs and tables, smashed plates, and half-eaten meals littering the floor. Whatever happened here, it was fast.

It's been a while since I've dealt with Bloodtakers. They're usually content to stay in their own shadowy corners of the world, keeping out of sight and out of trouble.

Porcelain crunches under my boots as I move through the mess. Every nerve's awake.

Decades ago, the Bloodtaker clans in Sarumbourne struck a deal with the Guild: no human kills. They're allowed to feed, but only from willing donors, those reckless enough to sell their blood for cash, like Lucas.

In return, the Guild pretends not to notice them, and the Keepers leave them alone. It's not ideal, but it works. Most of the time.

Still, accidents happen. There are the clanless ones. The rogues who don't follow the rules. They're the ones we hunt when they cross the line.

But we're not technically in Sarumbourne. This hotel is neutral ground, a place outside the Guild's hold. Out here, the Bloodtakers don't have to play by anyone's rules.

They can kill here.

But so can Keepers.

A flicker of movement catches my eye. My breath hitches as I step around an overturned dessert cart, following the blur of shadows.

A low, guttural hiss slices through the silence.

I whirl, but something slams into me before I can react. The impact sends me crashing through a row of chairs, their wooden legs snapping as I skid to a stop.

She's on me in an instant, her long black hair whipping around her face. Her eyes are unmistakable: pure black, with that eerie yellow pinprick at the centre. It's the mark of all Bloodtakers, and right now, those eyes are locked on my neck.

Her jaw and fangs extend with a sickening click, and as she lunges closer, I gather my legs beneath me and kick with all my strength. She's flung backward, hissing in fury as she regains her footing.

I scramble to my feet, fire sparking to life in my hand. The flames crackle and twist, a brilliant, living warning. I thrust it forward.

'Take another step, and you'll burn.'

She freezes, her lips curling back in a snarl.

'Where is Errett?' Her clan leader is the one I need.

Another Bloodtaker rushes me from the side. This one doesn't even make it halfway. My fire connects, and he goes up like kindling, his screams cutting off as he disintegrates into ash.

But the female doesn't waste her chance. A chair hurtles through the air, crashing into my shoulder. Pain explodes down my arm as I stumble, landing hard on a table.

Before I can recover, she's on me again. Her weight pins me down as she snaps at my neck, her cold breath brushing my skin.

I twist and thrash, but she's stronger, her fangs inching closer. My pulse pounds in my ears. This is it, this is how I go.

'Get the fuck off him!'

Liam!

The Bloodtaker is yanked off me so fast I barely register the movement. One moment she's on me, the next she's flying across the room, crashing into the remains of an overturned table.

Liam grabs my arm, pulling me to my feet. His soft, brown eyes are wide with concern, but there's a smirk on his lips.

'I'm the only one who gets to bite you.'

Despite everything, I grin.

It's short-lived. The Bloodtaker is already recovering, her black-and-yellow eyes blazing with rage. She charges, but I shove Liam aside and hurl a fireball at her.

The flames engulf her mid-leap. She screeches, clawing at the air as her body turns into ash.

The silence returns. Liam dusts ash off his hoodie, his smirk fading as he glances around the wreckage.

'How many more do you think there are?'

I tighten my fist, feeling the residual heat still lingering in my palm. 'Enough. What are you doing down here?'

He crosses his arms. 'You mean, other than saving your life?'

That came out harsher than I'd intended. 'Sorry. And... thank you.' I kiss his forehead. 'But I need you to stay back up in the room.'

'Heather's with Lucas. I told them to barricade themselves in.'

I want to argue and send him back to safety, away from this. But we've been around this bend before.

'Anyway, it looks like you could use a hand.'

'Come on. We need to find their leader.'

We leave the restaurant, moving down a dim corridor toward the first set of rooms on the ground floor. Most of the doors have already been kicked in, but thankfully, the rooms inside are empty. No bodies. Not yet, anyway.

Liam wanders into one room, the furniture inside reduced to splinters. The mattress is overturned, and there's shattered glass everywhere.

'Can you hear anything?'

Liam tilts his head, closing his eyes as he listens. I wait, holding my breath. If there's anyone who can catch the faintest sound of movement, it's him.

After a few moments, he shakes his head. 'Nothing.'

'Let's check the next floor.'

We step back into the corridor, making our way toward the staircase. Every shadow feels alive, every flicker of light a potential threat.

'Why don't you trust Lucas?'

That stops me mid-step. 'Is that a serious question?'

Judging by his expression, it is.

'Alright. Let's look at this objectively, shall we? Back at your first Guild meeting, he suggested we kill Heather to wake a new Keeper. He called you a Debbler, remember that? He dragged you into a nightclub despite you being underage. He gets bitten by Bloodtakers. He has no regard for a hotel full of innocent people.'

'Okay, you made your point.' Liam holds up his hands. 'He *did* apologise for the Debbler thing.'

'Oh, how nice of him.'

Liam's gaze sharpens. 'So, this has nothing to do with Leon Strainer?'

The name hits me like a punch to the chest. My mouth opens, but no words come out. How does he know about Leon? He can't know. Not unless... Lucas.

Of course.

'We've got Bloodtakers to catch.'

'Tariq...' Liam's voice is softer now.

'Tariq Ashar.' A new voice cuts through the air, one that sends a chill down my spine.

It's louder, and all too familiar.

We both freeze, our eyes snapping to the lobby below.

Standing over the body of the receptionist is Errett, the Bloodtaker clan leader.

His vampiric eyes gleam with malice, his sharp grin stretching unnaturally wide. 'Any vacancies for the night?'

TWENTY-SEVEN

THE RUNAWAY

LIAM

The Bloodtaker standing below us looks like a blond Captain Jack Sparrow – if Captain Jack traded the pirate look for a Harley-Davidson wardrobe. Leather jacket, leather boots, even leather gloves. It's a lot.

'I must admit, I wasn't expecting to find a Keeper enjoying the delights of this gorgeous hotel and spa.'

Tariq leans over the banister. 'You shouldn't be here, Errett. Take your clan and leave.'

This is the clan leader Tariq was looking for. I expected someone older, though Bloodtakers are immortal, so appearances mean nothing. He could look twenty-five but actually be a hundred.

Errett smirks, showing off sharp, unnervingly white fangs. 'What? No "how have you been?" Perhaps a drink at the bar?' His gaze shifts to me, and his grin widens. 'This one looks... fresh.'

I hope that's just Bloodtaker humour.

Tariq steps in front of me. 'He's a Keeper too. Stay away from him, unless you want the Guild involved.'

Errett's smile doesn't waver. If anything, it grows more sinister. 'Perhaps you'd like to inform your precious Guild that one of their members is a supplier to my clan.'

Tariq stays silent, so I do too.

'Where is he?' Errett demands.

'Who?'

'Don't play games with me, Tariq Ashar. Tell me where Lucas Martindale is, or my children will kill everyone in this hotel.'

The air feels colder. Shadows ripple across the walls as six more Bloodtakers emerge from the dark corners of the lobby, fanning out behind Errett.

Tariq hesitates, his jaw tight. He's weighing his options, but the silence feels dangerous.

'He's gone,' I blurt out. 'He left about an hour ago.'

Tariq turns to me, unimpressed. He shakes his head slightly, like he's trying to rein in his frustration.

Errett laughs, a low, grating sound that's quickly echoed by the others. 'Nice try, Keeper.' He silences his clan with the raise of his hand. 'We can smell the supplier. Now, either my children can continue smashing down doors and feasting on whatever they find, or one of you can go fetch him for me. What's it going to be?'

Tariq grabs my arm and pulls me out of sight behind the banister. 'Go get him.'

'What? You can't seriously be thinking of handing him over to them.'

'If we don't, they'll kill all the guests still here.'

'Then we fight! We've already taken down two of them.'

Tariq shakes his head, his expression grim. 'And there are seven more downstairs, and who knows how many elsewhere. Heather can't fight. Opel's not here. It's just you and me, and I don't like those odds. Do you?'

He's right. If we fight now, we lose. And if we lose, everyone in the hotel will die, and they'll still find Lucas anyway.

'Look, just get him. They'll take him and leave, and when Opel and Nathaniel arrive, we'll figure out a rescue plan.'

At least he's not giving up completely. He's trying to buy time.

'Go,' Tariq says again, and I do.

The corridor above is quiet. I pass several doors, hearing whispers from inside. Families and couples, hiding behind furniture barricades, probably thinking this is some kind of armed robbery or hostage situation.

I finally reach our room and knock. No answer.

Knocking again, I call out softly, 'It's me, Liam.'

There's movement, furniture scraping across the floor. Heather opens the door, her face pale and tense.

'You okay?' The room is empty. 'Where's Lucas?'

Heather nods toward the window. 'Gone. He heard them smashing doors and bolted.'

I rush to the open window. The curtains flutter in the breeze. The roof of the spa is just below, and beyond that, the dark expanse of the lawn. He's climbed down. There's no sign of him now.

'Shit.' Lucas running makes everything worse. His scent will still linger, and the Bloodtakers won't buy that he's gone.

'Find Tariq. He's in the lobby. Tell him to stall the Bloodtakers.'

Heather looks at me, alarmed. 'What are you going to do?'

I hoist myself onto the windowsill, one leg already over. 'Find the supplier.'

Dropping onto the patio, I find the walled garden silent and still. My breath clouds the air in pale bursts as I scan the space. Only one way Lucas could've gone – the iron gate at the far end of the lawn. Beyond it, a narrow path leads straight into the New Forest.

The gate's padlocked, but the chain hangs loose, leaving just enough space for someone with a slimmer frame to slip through. Lucas wouldn't have struggled.

Heat flares within me. Gripping the cold metal, I yank hard, and the chain snaps with a metallic crack, dropping to the ground. The gate creaks open, and my heart thuds faster as I step onto the darkened path.

Please let Tariq keep the Bloodtakers busy long enough.

Beneath the trees, I call out, Lucas's name fading quickly into the stillness. No answer.

Deeper into the woods now, the canopy swallows the moonlight. Shadows twist and shift at the edges of my vision with every step.

'Lucas, I know you're scared. I would be too. But if you don't come back with me, a lot of innocent people will die.'

At first, there's nothing but the rustling of leaves in the breeze. But then, a movement to my right. My muscles tense, and I ready myself for an attack, until Lucas emerges from behind a bush. His face appears neither afraid nor defiant. He's wearing one of my hoodies, one of my favourites, and for some reason, that ticks me off more than anything else.

'Didn't think I'd avoid your keen hearing, Auctus.'

'Lucas, you need to—'

'No.' He's trembling. 'You know what they'll do to me if they get me.'

'And what about everyone else in that hotel? Have you thought about them?'

Lucas looks away, tugging at the hoodie cords. 'So what? You want me to just go back and let them take me?'

'You can't keep running.'

'Some of us don't have superpowers to protect us, Liam.'

'This isn't about powers. It's about doing what's right.'

He shakes his head, tears forming in his eyes. 'I know I'm not likeable. I know I've made mistakes… but I'm nineteen, Liam. I don't want to die.'

For a moment, he's different. Not the arrogant, frustrating boy I've been stuck with before, but a terrified kid, not much older than me, who's been dealt a horrible hand.

'Lucas…'

There's a burst of pain in my side and I'm tackled to the ground. The impact knocks the air from my lungs, and Lucas shouts my name. A Bloodtaker is on top of me, his fangs bared and eyes gleaming with hunger. He grips my hair, yanking my head to the side to expose my neck.

'Wow, you really need to work on your first impressions.' I slam my elbow into his ribs. The Bloodtaker grunts, loosening his grip just enough for me to shove him off.

Another Bloodtaker charges at Lucas. Rushing forward, I catch him by the collar, yanking him back. I give him a powerful shove, and he crashes into the one already sprawled on the ground. Both collapse in a heap, momentarily stunned.

I find Lucas. 'Run!'

'But—'

'Get out of here!'

Lucas hesitates, then bolts into the woods. No time to breathe; the Bloodtakers are recovering. The taller one charges like a freight train. I block two strikes before I spin, landing a solid kick to his chest, sending him stumbling.

The shorter one grabs me from behind, arms locking tight. I jolt my head back. My skull connects with his face, cartilage crunches, and he howls. His grip slackens just long enough for me to flip him over my shoulder and slam him into the ground.

There's a broken section of fence, tangled with barbed wire. The taller Bloodtaker lunges, but I drop and slide, carrying my body low beneath his swinging arms, like something straight out of *The Matrix*.

I reach for the barbed wire, but it's too tangled to pull free.

My legs are yanked from beneath me. The ground scrapes my skin as the shorter Bloodtaker drags his prize toward his waiting fangs.

My hand brushes something, a splintered piece of fence post.

Gripping the wood, I twist and drive it into the Bloodtaker's chest. His eyes widen in shock before his body explodes into ash.

No time to celebrate. The taller one bursts through the settling dust and slams his weight down hard. I'm pinned, my breath knocked out. His snarling face looms inches away, fangs gleaming in the moonlight.

'Screw the Guild. You're mine.' He leans in.

'No!' I thrash beneath his weight.

The Bloodtaker freezes, his nostrils flaring. He sniffs the air, then turns his head. Standing a few metres away is Lucas, a jagged stone in one hand and blood dripping from the other.

The Bloodtaker releases me instantly and lunges toward Lucas.

'Take me to Errett. Your leader won't be happy if you kill me now.'

The Bloodtaker hesitates, his hunger warring with obedience.

He grabs Lucas by the arm and drags him away, toward the hotel.

I pick myself up, brushing off the remnants of the Bloodtaker I killed.

Lucas came back. Did he finally realise the lives that were at stake? Or was it to save me?

Lucas deserves a lot of things, but he doesn't deserve to die.

TWENTY-EIGHT

BIGGER PROBLEMS

TARIQ

E rrett paces the lobby like a caged animal, boots clicking against the wooden floor. His coat snaps with each turn. It's been ten minutes since he sent his Bloodtakers out. Still no sign of them. His pale face stays composed, but the tension in his eyes is rising.

The worn sofa creaks under my weight. Palms pressed to my knees. One leg bouncing, heel thudding against the floor. Liam's out there, searching for Lucas. Errett's Bloodtakers are out there too. And I'm here, waiting, trying not to snap.

The others watch, still and hungry. Like they're deciding whether now's the moment to strike.

Heather shifts beside me, her shoulder brushing mine. 'They're getting restless.'

'You've only just noticed?'

'Not the Bloodtakers. The ghosts. The ones that dwell here. They don't like the immortal ones.'

'They can join the club.'

Heather's gaze flicks warily around the room. Meanwhile, the Bloodtakers tense, their heads snapping toward the entrance like hounds catching a scent. A sound echoes through the grand lobby, the scrape of the heavy front doors. Errett makes a low sound, and gestures to one of his clan to check it out.

The Bloodtaker strides to the door and pulls it open. Lucas stumbles in first, followed by a Bloodtaker who looks like he's been through a fight. The creature shoves Lucas forward, sending him to his knees. Lucas clutches his bleeding hand, blood dripping between his fingers. Every Bloodtaker's attention zeroes in on him, like a pack of wolves scenting prey.

I'm already on my feet, my eyes darting to the doorway, hoping that Liam will step through next. But he doesn't.

'Ah, Lucas.' Errett crouches in front of him, cradling his chin in his clawed hand. 'How wonderful to see you again.'

Lucas doesn't respond. His usual snark is gone, replaced by an emptiness in his eyes. For once, he's defeated, his head bowed, his breathing shallow.

Errett's gaze flicks to the Bloodtaker behind Lucas. 'Where is Barnaby?'

'Gone, sire. The blond Keeper boy killed him.'

A rush of pride floods through me. Liam. But the feeling is fleeting. He's still not here.

Errett straightens, his eyes locking onto me. 'That makes three of my children slain by you Keepers tonight. Should I balance the scales? Perhaps I could start with the ghost whisperer.'

Heather shifts nervously as the Bloodtakers around the room turn their attention to her.

I take her hand. 'You've got what you came for. Take him and go.'

Errett tuts, wagging a finger at me. 'So quick to dismiss such an innocent young man.'

Lucas's eyes meet mine briefly; a flash of something passes between us.

'You're not leaving me much of a choice.'

'True. Although I wonder… what would Charles Martindale say if he knew you did have a choice?' Errett yanks Lucas's head back by his hair, forcing him to focus on him.

Charles would understand, wouldn't he? One life against the many lives at risk in this hotel – it's a simple calculation. And it's Lucas. He's not exactly the family favourite, but… that's harsh. Too harsh. I curse myself for even thinking it.

'My grandfather would side with the Keepers.'

Errett stares down at Lucas, his grin faltering for a fraction of a second. Then he punches Lucas square on the jaw. Lucas crumples to the floor, and for a moment, I almost feel sorry for him.

Errett dusts his hands off and claps them together, the sound sharp in the quiet room. 'Well, I suppose we best be on our way. My children are hungry.' He grabs Lucas by the collar, lifting him as if he weighs nothing.

'You're not taking him anywhere.'

A familiar voice cuts through the room, and every head turns toward the entrance. Relief crashes over me as my eyes land on Liam.

He stands in the doorway, dishevelled and mud-streaked, his chest heaving. He's alive.

'Liam.' Errett drops Lucas unceremoniously to the floor. Lucas lands with a dull thud, groaning as he tries to shift. Errett smirks. 'I hear you've been a busy boy.'

'You mean your Bloodtaker friend? Oh, he's still out there. Just… blowing around in the wind a bit now.'

I resist the urge to applaud Liam's sharp tongue. His words are only going to push Errett over the edge. A fight is the last thing we need. 'Liam, let them pass.'

Liam's gaze flicks to mine. He doesn't move.

'I suggest you do as your fellow Keeper says,' Errett interjects. 'Unless, of course, you'd prefer this lobby to become a bloodbath.'

'Listen to him, Liam. I'm not worth saving.'

Errett grabs Lucas by the collar again, hauling him upright. Lucas writhes in discomfort, but Errett just sneers. 'For once, the supplier speaks some sense.'

I try again. 'Liam!'

The defiance in his eyes softens. He finally steps away, moving to stand beside Heather and me.

I put a reassuring arm around his back, squeezing gently. He catches my eye, and a faint, reluctant smile tugs at the corner of his mouth.

He's struggling with this. I am too. But I've had years to deal with Lucas's endless trouble. Liam's only known him for a few months. This was always going to happen, sooner or later. The Bloodtakers are hungry. Innocent people are at risk here, and Lucas... Lucas made his choices. I can't justify a fight to save someone who gives up his blood willingly, like it's nothing.

Errett dusts off his coat with exaggerated flair. 'Well then, my children, let's leave these Keepers to enjoy what's left of their night.'

The Bloodtakers begin moving toward the door, their eyes still fixed on us. Lucas glances back at Liam, his expression hollow. Liam fidgets beside me.

We'll find a way to save Lucas once we're back in Sarumbourne. If the Bloodtakers let him live that long. Right now, all I care about is getting them as far away from this hotel as possible.

Boom.

A thunderous crash reverberates through the lobby. The Bloodtakers are thrown backward, as if hit by an invisible force. Errett is hurled into the banister of the grand staircase, wood splintering under his weight as he collapses. Lucas hits the floor again, rolling away with a pained grunt. The other Bloodtakers crash into walls, furniture, and paintings, their screeches filling the air.

Opel strides into the room, her hand outstretched, an egotistical smile plastered across her face.

'*Really*, Opel?' I throw my arms up.

Her smile falters. 'What?'

The Bloodtakers stir, groaning as they pull themselves from the wreckage. Errett rises slowly, brushing debris from his coat. His eyes burn with fury, his lips curling back to reveal his fangs. 'Drain them! Drain them all!'

Opel's wide-eyed gaze locks with mine, the gravity of her mistake finally dawning on her.

'Bloodbath time.' My heart pounds as I brace myself for the fight we now can't avoid.

Heather falls back onto the sofa, her eyes fluttering shut.

'Uh, Heather.' Liam shakes her knee. 'Now isn't the time for meditation.'

She doesn't respond, and we don't have time to check on her. The Bloodtakers are already on us.

Liam charges toward two Bloodtakers hovering near Lucas. Opel is surrounded by three, but she can handle herself. One rushes me, its fangs bared and ready to sink into my skin. My hand is already cradling a flame. I let it lunge, and then I release the fire. The Bloodtaker shrieks, consumed by flames, before disintegrating into ash.

Through the haze of its demise, Errett descends the stairs, his gaze zeroing in on Liam. No way I'm letting him get near him. I launch a fireball at Errett, but he's too quick, ducking so it slams into the wall behind him, leaving a scorch mark.

He smirks, wagging a finger mockingly before rushing toward me in a blur. He's faster than the others. Much faster. His hand is around my throat before I can react.

I claw at his arm, struggling to free myself, but his grip is like iron. I summon another ball of fire with my free hand, but he grabs my wrist, his cold fingers smothering the flame before it can grow.

'I've always wanted to taste a Keeper.' His dark eyes glint with hunger as he leans in.

I try to shout, but his grip on my throat crushes my voice. My eyes dart to Liam and Opel, too busy fending off their own attackers to notice.

'Um, excuse me.' Heather's voice startles us both.

Errett pauses, his head snapping toward her. She stands calmly, pointing behind us.

Errett and I both turn to look. An elderly man stands nearby, his grey, sagging skin and short, wiry beard giving him a ghostly appearance. His clothes are outdated, belonging to another era entirely. Wait… it's the man from the painting we saw earlier. John Blackhill. The original owner of the property.

'Get out of my house!' He raises an old, rusted garden shovel.

Before Errett can react, the metal shovel slams into his face with a sickening thud, sending him tumbling across the floor, groaning.

I rub my neck, now free from his grip, and turn to thank the old man, but he shimmers, vanishing into thin air.

Heather beams. 'You're welcome.'

'You did that?'

She nods, grinning smugly. 'Told you. The ghosts here really don't like Bloodtakers.'

'How did you...'

'They just need help corporealising temporarily. I'm a bit rusty, but turns out imminent death is a strong motivator.'

I let out a breathless laugh, gratitude swelling. I want to hug her. But there's no time to celebrate.

Liam manages to take down one of his foes but is still locked in battle with the other. Opel has taken her fight outside, throwing a Bloodtaker through a window with a crash that rattles the entire lobby.

Errett's already recovering from the shovel's impact.

'Help the others,' I say.

Heather rushes off as I grab a large, fallen picture frame from the floor. Before Errett can fully stand, I bring it down on him.

For a brief, ridiculous moment, he's trapped inside the frame. But he tears it apart with a snarl.

I ignite another fireball, ready to throw, when Liam's shout distracts me.

Liam is flung backward, crashing through a cupboard door. The Bloodtaker who threw him follows.

'Jeremiah!' Errett commands. 'Get the supplier and take him away!'

The Bloodtaker halts, turning its attention to Lucas, still unconscious on the floor.

Errett charges at me again, but this time I'm ready. As he reaches for my throat, I grab his arm, twisting it behind him. With his weight off balance, I kick his legs out from under him. He stumbles toward the fireplace but doesn't fall.

He turns, leaping at me with renewed fury. I don't have time to summon flames. We collide, rolling across the floor in a vicious struggle. Somehow, I end up on top. I strike him across the face twice, but he only laughs, throwing me off like I weigh nothing.

I hit the ground hard, but my eyes land on a broken piece of the banister lying nearby. Crawling, I grab it just as Errett lunges again.

I headbutt him, pain exploding in my skull. It stuns him just enough for me to leap on top of him. I drive the jagged wood toward his chest.

Errett grabs the stake before it pierces his heart, his muscles straining as he holds it back.

'The Guild should have vanquished your kind decades ago.' I push down with all my strength.

Errett smirks. 'We Bloodtakers should be the least of the Guild's worries.'

I falter slightly. 'What are you talking about?'

'You Keepers never know. You're always so stupid.'

'Tell me what you mean!'

The stake begins to pierce his skin, and he cries out in pain.

'Witches.'

My strength wavers. Did he just say—

'The Handsel witches.'

'We took care of them.' I force the stake down further.

Errett's sinister smile widens. 'Did you?'

'Sire!' A Bloodtaker calls from the doorway. 'We have the supplier!'

The distraction gives Errett the chance to smack the stake away. He punches me, knocking me off him.

He stands, adjusting his coat and flicking his hair back into place. 'No point in me finishing you off.' His smile sharpens. 'I think I'll leave that to the witch.'

With that, he turns and leaves the hotel.

There's commotion outside before Opel and Heather stumble back into the lobby, looking exhausted. They're joined by Nathaniel, who removes his glasses as he takes in the destruction of the lobby.

'Liam!' I rush to the shattered remains of the cupboard door. Liam stumbles out, coughing and brushing dust off himself. I hold out a hand, and he takes it gratefully.

'They ran off into the woods,' says Opel. 'Cowards.'

'They have Lucas,' Heather adds, gravely.

Liam looks up sharply. 'We have to go after them.'

'No,' I say, quickly. 'I think we've got a bigger problem.'

They all turn to me. Their night is about to get even worse.

TWENTY-NINE

WHAT MAGGIE KNOWS

LIAM

Nathaniel's office is even more disordered than usual. Papers litter the floor, books lean precariously on jumbled shelves, and the chairs are buried under the contents of his desk. Most unsettling of all, the fireplace isn't lit. I can't remember ever being in here when it wasn't. The chill in the room bites at my skin.

'Still no luck in the search for the other Keepers?' Tariq steps carefully around a stack of books as Nathaniel shrugs off his coat and flings it over the back of his chair.

'Nothing.' Nathaniel rifles through a pile of papers, muttering under his breath.

Heather follows us in, closing the door softly behind her.

Before we left the hotel, Opel took off in her car to scout Errett's nest, hoping for a lead on Lucas. The rest of us piled into Nathaniel's tiny Mini to regroup.

A couple of police cars pulled in as we were leaving, lights flashing, no sirens. One officer gave Nathaniel a long look as we rolled past. There were no questions, just a nod, like he knew exactly who we were.

Nathaniel called the Guild en route to the Seven Angels. Told them about the shaken guests still barricaded in their rooms. About the mess in the lobby. When you've got allies in the right places, cleaning up a scene like that gets a whole lot easier.

But not a word about Lucas. I caught the way Nathaniel hesitated, how carefully he chose his words. He didn't want Charles knowing a group of Bloodtakers had his grandson, and that we let them take him.

Rubbing my eyes, I lean against the cold, darkened fireplace for support. My phone screen glows: *3:56 AM*. I should be in bed. Scratch that, I need to be in bed. But instead, we're chasing rumours of witches who may or may not still be alive.

'Are you sure that Bloodtaker was telling the truth?' Nathaniel demands, pulling a dusty book off the shelf.

'Errett had no reason to lie,' Tariq replies.

Nathaniel scowls, flipping through the book before tossing it onto an already crowded chair. 'And you're certain you and Opel checked the remaining witch tree at Grovely?'

'Twice. The night we killed the witch, and again a week later, at your insistence, remember?'

By 'we', he means Jack. Jack killed the witch while the rest of us were tied to trees, helpless. Some Keepers we turned out to be.

'You need to check them again.' Nathaniel pulls another book from the shelf.

'Of course we will, but—'

Heather clears her throat loudly. 'Maggie has something she'd like to say.'

Nathaniel doesn't even look up. 'Heather, this isn't the time.'

'But I think—'

'No.' Nathaniel slams a book shut. 'Unless she has something useful to contribute that isn't a critique of the bar's wine selection, complaints about the modern monstrosity in the training room, or a tally of the grey hairs appearing in my beard, then—'

'She knows the witches!'

The room goes silent. Nathaniel freezes mid-motion, caught somewhere between shock and intrigue. Tariq and I exchange glances, equally stunned. It's hard to say what's more surprising, that Heather's ghost knows something about the witches, or that Heather managed to outshout Nathaniel. Either way, I'm impressed.

'She knows the Handsel sisters?'

'She's been trying to tell me for a while, but I ignored her. None of us were really... listening.'

Tariq steps forward. 'If Maggie's okay with it, maybe you could corporealise her. Like you did at the hotel with John Blackhill. That way, she wouldn't have to speak through you.'

Heather told me about her little stunt. Honestly, it sounded amazing. Her powers are supposed to be fading as she nears the end of her Keeperhood, but they seem to be growing stronger. Nathaniel, hearing this for the first time, watches her closely, his sharp gaze flicking between her and Tariq.

'Well?' Heather asks the empty space beside her. 'Fancy being visible for a while?'

She grins, then sinks cross-legged to the floor, shutting her eyes.

We wait.

At first, nothing happens. Then, like a mirage shimmering into focus, a figure appears. A woman, not much older than

Heather, materialises before us. She wears a long, frumpy blue gown with puffy white sleeves, her brown hair pulled into a loose bun secured by a ribbon. A few strands of hair frame her face.

'Maggie?' I can't believe my eyes.

She nods.

Heather looks up at her ghostly companion with a triumphant grin.

'Heather... I haven't seen you do this in so long. This is remarkable.' Nathaniel stares at Maggie as though she's a priceless artefact.

Maggie narrows her eyes at him. 'I'm not some fossil in a museum.'

Her sharp tone makes Nathaniel flinch.

Tariq glances nervously at Heather. 'Why is she staring at me?'

Heather grins mischievously. 'She thinks you're... how did you put it?'

'Strapping.' Maggie makes some sort of satisfied noise.

'She's got a bit of a thing for you.' Heather jerks her thumb at Maggie.

Tariq looks more nervous now than he did back in the hotel, and I'm sort of enjoying it.

'She follows you around the Seven Angels. It's a whole thing.'

'I like to observe.'

Heather smirks. 'You observe a lot. She goes everywhere.'

Tariq shifts uncomfortably. 'What, the bathroom?'

Maggie shrugs, eyes twinkling. 'Everywhere.'

Tariq groans.

'We can discuss ghostly boundaries later.' Nathaniel rubs his temples. 'Can we please get back to the witches?'

'Yes, please.' Tariq perches on the edge of the desk.

Maggie fans out her skirt, and takes a seat on a small stool in the corner of the room.

'Dorte and Evangeline. Those were the names of the Handsel sisters. I knew them both when I was alive. Dorte used to visit the Seven Angels.'

'Did you know what they were?' Tariq asks.

Maggie shakes her head. 'Not at first. There were whispers, of course. They were... unusual. Foreign sisters who kept to themselves. But things changed when Evangeline fell in love with a young man. A Keeper, like you.'

Nathaniel reacts immediately, snatching a pen and pad from the chaos of his desk. 'Do you remember his name?'

'Samuel Carter.' Maggie's gaze shifts to Tariq. 'He was like you.'

'The Elementa Keeper.'

'They grew close,' Maggie continues. 'Evangeline was happy. That was, until the plague.'

'The smallpox outbreak,' Nathaniel clarifies.

'Many died. Especially the young. I was taken by it too, some weeks later. But I don't believe it was natural.'

'What makes you think that?' I say.

'Dorte talked too freely when she drank. Downstairs in the bar, she'd speak of mass sacrifice. Of bargaining for more power.'

Nathaniel's pen scratches rapidly across the page.

'What about the Keepers?' I ask.

'They weren't spared. The plague wiped them out, all except Samuel. He lived. And by then, the suspicion surrounding the sisters had reached its peak. Desperate to save Evangeline, Samuel went to the Guild. He told them it was Dorte alone who cursed the town, hoping they'd show mercy.'

She pauses, her expression darkening.

'But the Guild didn't trust him. They believed Evangeline had corrupted his mind. He tried to flee with her, but the townspeople got to her first. They executed her in the Market Square. Then they dragged Dorte out and did the same. Samuel watched it all.'

Nathaniel's pen hovers mid-air. 'And their bodies? What happened to them?'

Maggie's mouth tightens. 'The Guild had them buried in Grovely Wood, beneath two beech trees. Beyond that... I don't know. I died.'

Nathaniel lets out a frustrated sigh and tosses his pen onto the desk.

'Opel and I checked Evangeline's tree. The ground's undisturbed. So either the Bloodtakers are lying and Dorte's resurrection spell didn't work... or Evangeline wasn't buried there at all.'

Maggie lifts her ghostly shoulders in a shrug. None of us has the answer.

Nathaniel straightens. 'If Dorte's resurrection spell worked, the other sister would have risen somewhere. What she's doing now... well, that's the question.'

Tariq stands. 'Maggie, do you remember where the sisters lived before they were killed?'

'It was a cottage, just past the Sarum Castle.'

'Old Sarum,' Nathaniel clarifies.

Tariq pulls out his phone and quickly searches for something. He turns the screen toward Maggie, who squints against the glow. 'Is this it?'

She tilts her head, studying the image. 'Yes, I believe so.'

'Hive Cottage. That little one on the roundabout. It's been abandoned for years.'

Nathaniel's face is set with determination. 'Go there. See what you can find.' He turns to Maggie. 'Thank you for your assistance.'

Maggie rises gracefully, casting Tariq a lingering look. 'I'll be seeing you.' She winks before shimmering out of existence.

'I'm never showering here again.' Tariq runs a hand over his face.

Heather stands, dusting off her knees.

'If the witch is out there, why haven't we noticed?' I ask.

'Witches are cunning, Liam,' Nathaniel says, pacing. 'They're not like demons. As dark as their magic is, they're still human. She'll bide her time. Plan.'

'Evangeline will want revenge,' Heather says.

'Mm,' Nathaniel agrees. 'On the town. On the Guild. Starting with... well, starting with the ones who killed her sister.'

A cold dread grips me, and I meet Tariq's gaze. 'Jack.'

'Go,' Tariq says immediately. 'Make sure he's safe. I'll check Hive Cottage.'

'I'll contact the Guild.' Nathaniel's already reaching for his phone.

Heather offers to help, but I don't stick around to hear the rest. I'm out the door, racing down the stairs of the Seven Angels. My best friend might be Evangeline's first target. Not if I can help it.

THIRTY

THE BEEHIVE

TARIQ

My bike squeaks as I brake, swerving around the corner. Hive Cottage is only a twenty-minute ride from the Seven Angels, but after a sleepless night, it feels more like twenty hours. My legs are leaden, every muscle protesting, and the morning sun glaring across the horizon doesn't help. It's too bright, making me squint as I push forward.

Pedalling past Victoria Park, I slow and pull out my phone. Liam thumbs-upped my last message asking him to stay alert for the witch. Maybe I should've added that I hope Jack's safe too. But Liam's my priority.

I tuck my phone back into my jacket pocket and cycle on, the green ramparts of Old Sarum rising in the distance. A coach pulls into the parking bay as I pass; a handful of early-bird tourists spill out with their cameras and sunhats.

It's strange how the Crossing looks so ordinary now, like any other historical site. It's a reminder of everything that happened before Christmas, of Draven, the Dark Friars, and the chaos that nearly destroyed us all.

Draven's death brought some peace, knowing the man who killed Thomas is finally gone. But even now, something still lingers, like a shadow refusing to fade.

I grit my teeth and pedal harder, the burn in my legs distracting me from the churn of my thoughts.

As I crest the hill, Hive Cottage comes into view. It might've once been a charming hideaway tucked in the Sarumbourne countryside, but now it looks tired, out of place beside the roundabout where traffic filters in and out of the city's western side.

It's enclosed by dark, overgrown hedges, its roof hardly visible to passing drivers. For anyone not looking closely, it's just another forgotten relic of the past.

I slow my bike as I approach, scanning the area. The road beside the cottage is quiet, too early for weekend traffic.

After hopping off my bike, I wheel it into a cluster of tall shrubs and lean it against the trunk of a tree, making sure it's hidden.

Adjusting the strap of my satchel, I step toward the hedges surrounding the cottage. The air feels cooler here, shaded by the dense foliage.

I make my way through a broken gate, the iron hinges rusted and brittle. The cottage's stone walls are cracked. Vines creep along the surface, threatening to pull the structure back into the earth. The tiled roof sags in places, a few jagged shards of slate scattered near the base of the walls.

All the windows are boarded up, thick planks of wood nailed haphazardly across them, and of course, graffiti mars the stone, crude symbols sprayed in faded neon colours. A battered sign hangs crookedly on the front door: 'DO NOT ENTER'. The edges curl, the letters barely legible after months of weathering.

Above me, a crow caws sharply, breaking the quiet.

I hesitate, my pulse quickening. A chill seeps into my bones, but it's not from the crisp morning air.

Then, something crunches behind me.

I spin, my hand snapping up as a flame sparks to life in my palm.

'Trespassing is a crime, you know.'

The voice is calm, teasing. I exhale sharply, the fire in my hand flickering out as Opel steps into view. Her smirk is wide, her eyes gleaming as she tucks a strand of black hair behind her ear.

'You were this close to getting toasted.'

Opel shrugs, the sunlight catching on her silver hoop earrings. 'Couldn't help myself.'

'What are you doing here? I thought you were scouting for Lucas and the Bloodtakers.'

'They're gone. The nest's been cleared out, no sign of them.'

Hopefully, that means the Bloodtakers have abandoned Sarumbourne altogether. But knowing our luck, it's more likely they've just relocated. Finding Lucas is going to be a nightmare if they've dragged him somewhere else. Assuming he's even alive.

'That's a later problem.'

'Nathaniel filled me in when I got back. Thought you might need some backup in case you run into Witch 2.0.'

I grab the door handle and twist it, unsurprised to find it locked. 'It's sealed tight.'

'Allow me.'

The door groans, splinters erupting along the frame as the lock snaps. The entire door crashes to the ground, leaving a jagged opening.

'Taking breaking and entering to new extremes, are we?'

Opel grins, gesturing for me to go first. 'After you, flame boy.'

The stale air hits me like a wave. It smells of mildew and damp wood, the scent so thick it clings to the back of my throat. Dust swirls in the faint shaft of light from the open doorway.

The floorboards creak underfoot as I take a cautious step forward. The walls are bare, streaked with grime, and the ceiling sags ominously in the corners. The faint sound of dripping water echoes from somewhere deeper inside.

Opel swipes her finger along a dusty shelf. 'This is not unlike my sister's uni accommodation.'

I scan the room for anything unusual. There's nothing at first glance, just the remnants of a house long forgotten. There's a chill from outside, stronger now, pressing in on me from all sides.

'What exactly are we looking for?' Opel steps up beside me.

I shrug. 'Witchy stuff.'

'That's really helpful.'

'This was the Handsel sisters' home back in the 1700s – you'd think this would be the first place they'd visit.'

'After three hundred years? Really?'

'Do you remember what the witch said back in Grovely Wood? "Familiar places are not the same." She must have come here at some point. Which means her sister probably will have too.'

I continue into what looks like a kitchen, though it is barely recognisable. It's darker now as we move from the doorway. I raise my hand and light a flame. The air grows heavier, thicker, the shadows in the corners seeming to stretch and shift. Something about the cottage feels alive, like it's watching us. Waiting.

Opel nods. Whatever's here, we're not leaving until we find it.

'We should split up. Check the other rooms.'

'Right. Shout if you find a crystal ball or something.'

Opel heads toward the staircase.

As I move around, my boots crunch against the floorboards.

The counters are coated in grime, and an old kettle sits rusting on the stove. A faded calendar hangs on the wall, the dates long irrelevant. I flip it over, revealing a hand-drawn picture of a family: two parents, a little boy, and a dog. It's scrawled in a child's handwriting: 'Our family, 1996'.

I sigh, placing the calendar back.

I move into the next room. It's bare except for a few pieces of rotting furniture: a collapsed sofa, an empty bookshelf, and a shattered mirror hanging crookedly on the wall. The floor is scattered with debris – scraps of paper, old toys, and broken glass.

Opel returns, her steps slow and deliberate. 'Upstairs is a bust. Couple of old bedrooms, nothing witchy. Just... depressing, really.'

'Same down here. Feels like a place people tried to make a home once, but it's all just memories now.'

We stand in silence for a moment.

'Come on, there's another room through here.'

The next space is the emptiest so far, aside from a couple of broken chairs that probably once accompanied a dining table. The shadows from my flame dance around the walls.

Opel peers out of the window, through a gap in the planks of wood that cover the faded glass.

I clear my throat. 'How's Theo?'

Opel looks at me, her face softer than usual. 'He's…
managing.' She leans against the doorframe. 'He mentioned
growing out his hair. Said he wants to cover it up. I told
him he doesn't need to. He's still Theo.'

'Losing an ear isn't something you just… bounce back
from.'

'It's not just that. He's angry. More than I've ever seen
him. At the witches, at the Guild, at himself. And…'
She pauses. 'I haven't told him about Lucas yet.'

'Why not?'

'Because I have no idea how he will react. He'll just want
to run and tell the Guild.'

'It's his brother.'

'And Charles is his grandfather, but Nathaniel's not
telling him.'

I don't press further. Theo's anger makes sense; after
everything he's been through, who wouldn't be angry?

'I'll tell him later.' Opel's voice has softened. 'You're
right, he deserves to know.'

We move toward the back of the cottage, where a
rusted door hangs ajar. The hinges groan as I push it open,
revealing a small, overgrown garden bathed in the pale
morning light.

Stepping outside, I take in the mess of tangled weeds,
collapsed fencing, and broken flowerpots. The garden
might've been beautiful once, but now it's a jungle.

Opel brushes past me, her boots squelching in the
damp earth as she moves toward the centre. 'Nothing
here either.'

Near the edge of the garden, a large patch of earth looks
wrong. The ground is uneven.

'Wait.' I step closer. Opel follows.

The soil is loose, darker than the surrounding ground, and it's split in places, as if something erupted from beneath. A faint, acrid smell wafts up.

Opel kneels, brushing away some of the dirt with her hand. 'What happened here?'

I crouch next to her, staring at the ruptured earth.

'This is it. This is where she was buried. The other sister.' I stand, pulling a hipflask from my pocket. The morning sunlight feels colder now. 'She's out there. Somewhere.'

THIRTY-ONE

BREAKFAST AT THE COOPERS'

LIAM

I react to Tariq's message with a thumbs up. It's automatic, thoughtless. But my focus is Jack, my thumb hovering over his name. I press call again. It's my fifth attempt.

No answer.

What if the witch already has him? What if she's torturing him for what we did to her sister?

The thought ignites something in me, a spark that catches, flaring into the heat of my power. I let it flood my legs, the warmth crawling up through my calves and thighs. A moment later, I'm sprinting, the world blurring around me as I burst up the hill past St Mark's Church.

An elderly man out walking his dog yells something as I dash by, but I don't stop to register it. My lungs burn, my heart pounds, but I push harder, my enhanced speed eating up the pavement beneath me.

When I reach the crest of the hill, I skid to a stop, leaning forward with my hands on my knees to catch my breath. Below me, the Bishopdown housing estate stretches out in neat, orderly rows. Down there is Jack's house. Down there, I hope, is Jack.

My phone buzzes in my pocket, and I snatch it out, answering before even checking the screen.

'Jack?'

'Hey, you,' says a familiar voice, but it's not Jack. It's Lily.

'Lily, this isn't a good time.'

'Oh, come on! You can't leave me hanging. How was your spa night? I want all the naughty details. Did you and Tariq—'

'Lily, stop.' I'm still breathless from running. 'Is Jack at yours?'

There's a pause on the other end. 'What? No. What's—'

'Did you guys have a movie night? Did he stay over?' I pick up my pace, heading down toward Jack's neighbourhood.

'No, Liam. I haven't spoken to him since college yesterday. He said he was going out last night and that he'd message me today. Why? What's going on?'

Shit. Jack went out? He never goes out.

'He's not answering his phone. And after last night—'

'What happened last night?'

I explain everything in quick, breathless bursts: Lucas showing up, the Bloodtaker attack on the hotel, Lucas being taken, Errett warning us about the witches. I even tell her about Maggie and her knowledge of the sisters.

'Where was Maggie when I was doing all my research? Could have used a ghost's help!'

'Lily…'

There's silence.

'Lily? Are you there?'

'I'm here. I was checking to see if he'd messaged me. I'm worried, Liam.'

'Me too.'

I approach Jack's street, the familiar houses coming into view. 'Look, I'm almost at Jack's now. I'll let you know if I find him.'

'What if he's not there? Where do we look?'

'I don't know. Tariq's at the cottage as we speak, maybe he'll find out something there.'

'Can I do anything to help?'

Lily's research. She's done hours of it, combing through old records, piecing together the history of the witches of Grovely Wood. She even won that local history prize for her essay. If anyone might have information, it's her.

'Actually, yeah. Can you pull together everything you have on the witches? Anything you can find about their magic or where they might go.'

'But I thought the Guild didn't want us involved until—'

'Lily, please. Right now, you know more about those sisters than anyone else. Maybe there's something in your research that can help us figure out where she is or what she's planning.'

There's a pause. 'Okay.'

I don't know if she's worried about me, about Jack, or about the curse that hit her the last time she got involved.

'Thank you.' I hang up and break into a jog.

Jack's house comes into view, and I quicken my pace, dread curling in my gut.

When I approach Jack's door, I knock hard, then immediately pull my hand back. I've forgotten how early it is for a Saturday. Jack's mums are lovely, but I doubt they'd appreciate me turning up at this hour, hammering on their door.

Just as I raise my hand to knock a second time, the lock clicks, and the door creaks open. Standing there in a fluffy dressing gown, hair slightly tousled, is Vivian Cooper.

'Liam.' Her initial morning frown melts into a smile. 'Lovely to see you.'

'You too, Mrs Cooper. Is Jack home?' I try to sound casual, though my heart feels like it's about to punch its way out of my chest.

'Um, I think so. I haven't checked on him yet, but...'

'Can I come in?'

Vivian hesitates for a moment but then steps aside. She knows Jack and I have been friends for years, so she waves me in. 'Go on up. Just knock first. Trust me, he's not exactly a pyjamas kind of boy.'

I force a grin, already heading for the stairs.

'Oh, Liam. Do you want some breakfast? Leanne's making scrambled eggs.'

That sounds amazing right now. 'No, thank you, Mrs Cooper.'

I race down the hallway, past all the family photos of him and his mums at various stages in life. When I reach Jack's room, I'm too anxious to heed her warning. I throw the door open, and—

Oh.

Jack's bum is on full display, peeking out from under the duvet. The rest of him, aside from one leg, is covered. He doesn't even stir at my sudden entrance.

I freeze, debating whether to back out and pretend this never happened. But something feels off. This isn't like Jack. He's usually up early, eating cereal, halfway through some ridiculous core workout or head in *World of Warcraft*. I clock his big gaming PC in one corner.

'Jack?' I close the door behind me, still nothing.

For a second, panic grips me. Is he even alive? I rush to his side, relief washing over me as his back rises and falls with each steady breath. He's sprawled face-down, softly snoring, his hair sticking up in every direction.

Taking out my phone, I snap a quick photo of his scrunched-up face and messy bed hair and send it to Lily with the caption: *Safe and sound.*

She replies instantly with a heart emoji and a message: *Please tell me you knocked before going in there.*

I did not, I reply, adding a peach emoji and a facepalm for good measure.

I lower my phone… and nearly jump out of my skin. Jack's eyes are wide open, staring right at me.

'Jack!' I yelp, startled.

He screams.

I scream back.

Still wrapped in his duvet, he thrashes wildly, rolling over and tumbling off the bed in a tangled heap.

'Shhh, Jack! It's me!'

He keeps yelling like I've just tipped a bucket of ice-cold water over him. I grab the nearest pillow and throw it at his face. He finally goes quiet.

Pulling the pillow away, Jack rubs his eyes, squinting at me. 'Liam?'

'Everything okay up there?' Vivian's voice drifts up from downstairs.

Jack and I stare at each other.

'All good, Mum!' he calls back, then fixes me with an incredulous look. 'What the bloody hell are you doing here?'

'I'm sorry! I thought you were dead!'

Jack's mouth opens, then shuts again. Finally, he smirks. 'Aw, that's sweet, mate. Thanks.'

'I'm serious,' I say, launching into a rapid explanation. I tell him everything I told Lily about my night, and morning.

Jack listens, still sitting on the floor, his duvet draped over him like a makeshift toga. When I finish, he frowns, scratching his head. 'So, you're telling me that witch is back after all?'

'Yes. We think so.'

'And you rushed over here because you thought she might be after me?'

'Yes! Because you melted her sister into nothing!'

Jack looks down at himself, taking in the duvet wrapped around his torso and his bare legs sticking out. 'I'm naked,' he announces.

'I know.'

He raises an eyebrow. 'Did you…?'

'See your hairy arse? Yes.'

Jack nods casually. 'What did you think? I've been working on my glutes.'

I smirk. 'Perfectly formed.'

'Thanks, mate.' He grins, then the room falls silent, both of us unsure what to say next.

That is, until the smell of buttery eggs wafts up from the kitchen.

'Your mums are making breakfast,' I say.

'I'm starving,' Jack replies.

'Me too.'

———

As the last piece of warm sourdough toast vanishes, I stretch back in satisfaction. Halfway through breakfast, I'd realised I hadn't eaten in hours, not since the Bloodtakers ruined last night's dinner plans.

Jack is still sluggishly working through his plate, clearly half asleep.

Leanne takes my empty plate with a smile. 'Hungry, then?'

'Like you wouldn't believe,' I say, rubbing my stomach. 'Thanks, Mrs Cooper.'

She heads back to the sink to wash up in their open-plan kitchen, where Vivian is drying dishes and half watching some daytime show on the small TV perched by the fridge.

Jack picks up his phone and scrolls lazily. He pauses. 'Huh.'

'What?' I ask, craning slightly.

He turns the screen to show me. It's the student news team's page. A blurry photo of the football pitch with bold text: *TODAY'S MATCH CANCELLED – WHOLE TEAM OUT WITH STOMACH BUG.*

'Since when does an entire football team go down at once?'

Jack shrugs. 'Classic case of gains before brains. Bet it's some dodgy lean chicken they ate or gone-off oat milk in their shakes.'

Something about it nags at me. Still, I let it go.

Jack drops his phone back on the table with a soft thud, pushing away his plate. His eyes are sunken, and his skin is dull.

I lower my voice. 'You went out last night?'

His face brightens like he's just remembered. 'Yeah. I took Eva to see that *Until Dawn* movie. It was weird.'

'I thought you'd been dying for a movie adaptation ever since you played the game?'

'Not the film; that was bloody good, literally. You absolutely need to see it. I mean Eva was weird.'

I frown. 'Weird how?'

'Well, I took her to the Odeon. I thought she'd appreciate the old Tudor architecture, you know, since she's new here, but when we walked in, she didn't even blink. Like she'd seen it before. But she insisted she hadn't. Then, when we sat down, she looked around all confused and asked me where the people were.'

'What? Why would she say that?'

Jack shrugs, taking a gulp of coffee. 'She thought we were seeing a play or something. I don't always get her, and honestly, I don't think she gets me. But there's just something about her.'

He keeps saying that. The question is, *what* is it about her?

I study him for a moment. He still looks spaced out, like he's in a trance or something. With everything we now know about the witch… leaving him on his own doesn't sit right.

'Maybe we should hang out today.'

'No can do, buddy.' He stretches. 'I've got plans.'

Plans? Jack's never been this busy in his life.

'You're seeing Eva again?'

'Nope. Phoebe.'

I glare at him. 'Jack!' My voice comes out louder than I meant it to. 'You can't string both girls along!'

Jack's about to snap back when Leanne appears beside us, soggy sponge in hand. 'Who's stringing along girls?'

'Err…' I can't exactly say I am.

Jack throws me a look that could kill, but Leanne's already zeroed in. 'Jack Andrew Cooper, is this true?' she demands, arms crossed.

Jack flashes his best innocent grin, the one he thinks will help him charm his way out of a murder trial.

'What's true?' Vivian asks, flicking off the TV and joining the party.

I mouth a silent 'Sorry' to Jack. He rolls his eyes.

'Our son,' Leanne says, like she's delivering breaking news, 'is apparently playing the field.'

'Jack?' Vivian lifts an eyebrow.

'Mums, no, there's no playing with girls in a field!'

He frowns at himself. 'That came out wrong.'

I bite down a laugh. His mums aren't so generous.

'What I mean is... I'm seeing Phoebe today to let her down gently. And tonight, I'm asking Eva to the May Masquerade.'

I blink. 'You are?'

Jack nods, looking oddly... serene. That's new. He usually panics about this stuff.

'Good,' Leanne says, turning back to the sink. 'No son of mine is going to be a womaniser.'

Vivian ruffles his hair. 'Let her down gently, Jack. My little heartbreaker.' She saunters off, looking far too pleased.

Once they're out of earshot, I lean closer. 'Are you seriously not going with Phoebe?'

Jack gives me a look. 'Don't you start. Lily's been on at me about it already.'

'She's just trying to protect her friend.'

He exhales, but it's different this time, less frustration, more... distracted.

'Yeah, well, Eva's... she's just... different. When I'm with her, everything feels... quieter. Like I don't have to think so hard.'

I raise an eyebrow. That doesn't sound like him. Jack overthinks everything.

'And what else?'

He hesitates, glancing toward the window like he's lost track of the conversation. 'Already asked her. She said yes.'

I groan, flopping back in my seat. 'You're hopeless.'

We spend the rest of the morning in Jack's room while he gets ready to meet Phoebe. Regular me would have made my excuses and left by now, but Keeper me? Keeper me can't. If the witch is coming after him, I need to stay close.

Jack disappears into his en suite to get ready, leaving me alone with my reflection in his mirror. I grimace. My hair is greasy, sticking up in all the wrong places. There's a streak of dirt smudged across my cheek, just missing my eye. I must have looked a right state when I turned up earlier.

I lift the hem of my hoodie, wincing at the sight of the large, purple bruise blooming across my side.

Last night's fight wasn't easy. It's stupid, but sometimes I forget that Keepers can still get hurt.

That thought sparks another. I check my fingers again, one by one. Which finger was it? The one I cut yesterday?

There's nothing there now. No sign of an injury, not even the faintest scar.

That Vel girl must really know her first aid. Or maybe... maybe I overreacted. Did I imagine all the blood?

My phone buzzes on Jack's desk. It's Tariq.

All good with Jack, I assume? Heading to the Seven Angels. Meet you there?

I sigh. I just want to sleep.

Jack all good. See you there x

I toss my phone back on the desk, rubbing my eyes. I hate it when Keeper life takes over everything.

All I've been thinking about is our time in the jacuzzi, before everything went sideways last night. We'd finally started talking things out, finding each other again. Things were getting... hot. But now? Now Tariq's back in serious Keeper mode, all business, and it's throwing me off. It makes me feel guilty for not acting the same way, like I should be just as focused.

Maybe if we deal with the witch quickly, we can finally have a moment. Something normal. Something just for us.

'Hey, you good, mate?' Jack's voice cuts through my thoughts. He's standing in the doorway, his mop of brown hair still damp but styled just enough to look effortless.

I nod, shoving the tension out of my head. 'Yeah. I'll walk into town with you.'

Jack raises an eyebrow. 'Liam, I told you, if I see so much as a hint of curses or hexes flying my way, I'll message you. You have more important things to do. You don't have to babysit me.'

'I'm not,' I lie. 'I'm heading that way anyway. We'll part ways when we get there.'

Jack narrows his eyes but doesn't argue. 'Fine, but we're getting the bus. No way do my legs feel like walking all the way into town today.'

'Deal.' Looking in the mirror again, I cringe. 'Hey, Jack... mind if I use your shower?'

He smirks, holding the en-suite door open for me. 'I wasn't gonna say anything, but for a superhero, you're looking a bit like Stark at the end of *Endgame*.'

I peel off my hoodie and chuck it at him. 'Shut up,' I say, closing the door in his face.

THIRTY-TWO

THE DEED

LIAM

Mondays are the worst. Who decided the week should start with this chaos? College corridors are packed, always a tide of people moving the opposite way.

The weekend was quieter, thankfully. Nathaniel and the Guild are scrambling to locate the witch, but honestly, my mind's been drifting. I kept circling back to Lucas.

No one's seen him. Theo's heard nothing. And Nathaniel still refuses to tell Charles his grandson's missing. Says it'll distract from 'the priority'. I get it. But it's wrong. Lucas could be anywhere. Or worse.

I'd meant to ask Tariq about what Lucas told me, but I don't think either of us had the energy for that conversation. I crashed straight through until Sunday afternoon, only waking when Mum knocked to say a roast was waiting for me on the table. I devoured it so quickly I almost threw up.

As I pass the library, a familiar ache twists inside, a phantom pain from where Draven stabbed me. It always flares up around here.

Bad memories flicker. Layla, the Friars, blood, fire, the blade.

I exhale, brushing past a group of workmen outside the library doors. Half the corridor's sealed while they repair the fire damage.

The fire Tariq started to save my life.

Up ahead, Vel's bright red hair bobs through the crowd. She was in my catering class today, and I never got the chance to thank her properly for patching up my finger.

'Hey, Vel!' I shout.

She turns, spots me, and smiles. But before I can say anything else, one of the workmen passing her stumbles over a student's bag.

It happens fast. He falls forward, and the two heavy boxes he's carrying slip from his grasp.

Vel yells. The students around her gasp.

But I'm already moving. Heat surges through me as I close the distance.

I knock one box aside and catch the other. It's heavy, so heavy I almost stagger, but I hold firm. If that had hit Vel, it would've done serious damage.

Vel's eyes widen.

'You good?' I ask, handing the box back to the workman, who's now scrambling to his feet.

She nods, still in shock. 'How did you...'

'Oh, I saw it coming. The boxes, the bag... health and safety nightmare.'

'But you were so far away,' Vel says, disbelief etched on her face.

Sometimes I forget how hard it is to hide what I can do.

'Got lucky, I guess,' I say quickly, changing the subject. 'You heading to lunch?'

Vel hesitates, then nods, though she's still eyeing me like I've just done something impossible.

We make our way into the crowded refectory, where the air is thick with the smell of fried food. It's definitely a burger kind of day.

Vel grabs a sandwich from the fridge and joins me in line.

'Not getting something hot?'

She shrugs, clutching the sandwich like it's already decided. 'Would love to, but I've got to be careful with spending right now.'

I nod, trying not to look awkward. I've never really had to think about money. Mum's always made sure there was enough for lunch, snacks, even the odd takeaway. Though lately she's been hinting about me getting a part-time job. Not that I have a clue how that'd fit in with everything else.

'I can grab you something,' I offer.

Vel gives a tight smile and shakes her head. 'How's your finger?'

She's quick to change the subject, so I let it go.

I hold up my hand. 'Back to normal. It's like it never happened.'

Her face brightens.

There's something about the way she watches my hand, like she's checking her work.

The lunch lady calls me forward. I grab a burger and chips, and we weave through the refectory toward the usual table. Jack's mid-laugh, Eva beside him, one hand resting on his arm like it belongs there. They're practically joined at the hip.

Across from them, Lily looks like she's biting the inside of her cheek hard enough to draw blood. Her expression softens when she sees me.

'Want to join us?' I ask Vel.

She hesitates. Glances toward the table, then down at her sandwich.

'Can't. No classes this afternoon, and I need to get home.'

'Course,' I say gently. 'Enjoy the sandwich.'

She smiles and holds it up, like a salute, before disappearing into the crowd.

I slide into the seat across from Lily.

'She didn't want to eat with us?' she asks.

'Home stuff,' I say, watching Vel thread her way to the exit.

Lily nods, understanding immediately. 'I hope she's settling in better than wifey over there.' She rolls her eyes toward Jack and Eva.

Jack's completely oblivious, his face inches from Eva's as they giggle and fawn over each other. I've never seen him like this before. It's not like him. Not at all. It's all happening so quickly.

Eva checks her watch, her smile brightening as she turns to Jack. 'I've got to get to class.'

Jack catches her wrist as she begins to stand, pulling her back playfully. 'Skip it. Stay here with me.' There's a boyish charm in the way he looks at her.

'Jack!' Eva laughs, swatting at his hand. 'You know I can't.'

'Sure, you can. What's one class compared to spending time with me?'

Eva leans down, placing a quick kiss on Jack's lips. 'I'll see you later,' she says softly, her voice almost musical as she pulls away.

His fingers linger at her wrist for a second too long before he lets go.

'Ugh, get a room,' Lily mutters, stabbing at her pasta.

Jack watches Eva go, his gaze trailing after her. She waves over her shoulder as she slips out of the refectory, and he smiles faintly, like he's waking from a dream.

'What?' Jack says suddenly, blinking at us like we've just appeared.

Lily turns to him, unimpressed. 'Seriously? You turned Phoebe down for someone you've known for five minutes?'

Jack shrugs, but it's stiff. 'Eva's… different.'

He says it like it's a fact. Like there's no room for argument.

Jack second-guesses what to order for lunch, let alone who he wants to date.

'Yeah, well,' Lily says, giving him a look, 'you'd better treat her well. Or the witch won't have time to get you. I will.'

Jack smirks at that, but it's faint. Distant. 'Noted.'

I take a big bite of my burger, and ketchup immediately drips down my hand. Totally worth it. My attempt to lick it off fails and now there's sauce on my nose.

Lily hands me a tissue. 'You're a mess.'

'A satisfied mess,' I mumble through a mouthful as I wipe my face.

She takes a swig from her bottle of water. 'Maybe we should do a movie night tonight. The three of us haven't hung out properly in ages.'

Jack shakes his head. 'Can't. Eva and I have plans tonight. She says she's got a surprise for me.'

'A surprise?' I ask, still trying to scrub ketchup off my fingers.

'Yep.' Jack grins, leaning back in his chair like he's king of the world. 'I bet it's a starlit picnic. Chocolate-covered strawberries. Blanket. The works.'

'Wow, why not throw in a bottle of Lambrini while you're at it...' says Lily.

'Or... sex?' Jack blurts. Then, full panic. 'What if it's sex? I haven't trimmed!'

Lily grimaces. 'Jack. Please. Dial it all the way down.'

But he's already on his feet, slinging his bag over one shoulder.

'See you guys later.'

He strides off without waiting for a reply.

Lily watches him go. 'Does he seem... weird to you?'

'You mean, more than usual? Yes.'

Lily shakes her head and resumes her lunch. 'Well, what about you? Movie night with me? I'll even let you pick the film.'

'Tempting, but I've got training with Tariq tonight. Sorry.'

Lily groans. 'Fine. Hey... are you bringing Tariq to the May Masquerade?'

'Doubtful. He was barely up for the Festive Fling, and he seemed pretty relieved when it was cancelled. Besides...' I shrug. 'I don't even know if I'll be going, with witch number two on the loose.'

Lily leans forward. 'Being a Keeper shouldn't stop you experiencing the fun things in life, you know. You deserve to have fun too.'

I nod. Will I ever have that sort of fun again? What I'd give for one night with Tariq where it's not all doom and gloom.

'Have you found anything else?' I ask. Hoping to steer the conversation away from that out-of-reach dream.

'Actually, yes.' She digs into her bag. 'You said Tariq and Opel found disturbed ground at Hive Cottage.'

'Yeah, that's where they reckon she rose from.'

Lily pulls out her phone. 'Well, I found out who owned that property at the time.' She zooms in on her screen and holds it up to me. It shows a scanned copy of an old property deed.

'Jacob E. Carter,' I read.

'The cottage was owned by the Carter family,' Lily continues. 'They owned a lot of property in Sarumbourne back in the 1700s.'

That name. Carter.

'Maggie,' I whisper, thinking out loud.

Lily frowns.

'The ghost lady I told you Heather conjured,' I clarify, but Lily still seems uncertain. 'The Keeper Maggie mentioned, who was in love with one of the sisters. His name was Samuel Carter.'

Lily quickly scrolls on her phone, then taps. 'Yep. That was one of Jacob's sons.'

'Samuel must have moved her body to Hive Cottage after they were buried at Grovely Wood.'

'But why?'

'Because he loved her. Maybe he thought taking her from that cursed grave in the woods and giving her her own resting place would… bring her back to him.'

Lily continues to flick through her phone, and my attention drifts.

Outside, the clouds thicken, heavy and grey.

Whatever's coming, we're not ready.

THIRTY-THREE

PRIORITIES

TARIQ

'Why are your Keepers not out there searching for him?'

Charles Martindale's voice reverberates through Nathaniel's office. It's sharp, commanding, impossible to ignore. His face is flushed, hands trembling, the sort of fury that could drive a man to jump over a desk. At seventy-something, he'd likely pull a muscle trying, but the look in his eyes says he'd still give it a go.

Theo stands beside him, silent, eyes fixed on the floor.

Opel told him not to breathe a word about Lucas. He did anyway.

She's sitting, arms crossed, mouth a razor-thin line. He won't be getting forgiven anytime soon.

'They should be out there now!' Charles paces like a caged animal. 'How could you have let this happen?'

Nathaniel flinches. Barely, but it's there.

'I didn't *let* anything happen. Lucas knew what he was getting into. And it's not exactly the first time, is it?'

Charles freezes mid-step, face turning an impressive shade of red. 'My grandson may have his problems, but he is still an innocent.'

A snort escapes before I can be stop.

He wheels around. 'Something I said funny, Elementa?'

There is something funny about it. Lucas, innocent? But Nathaniel's glare is sharp enough to draw blood, so I rein it in and shake my head. 'No.'

Charles isn't buying it but turns back to Nathaniel.

'There were innocent people in that hotel,' Nathaniel says, leaning forward. 'And that's why the Keepers let Lucas go. The Bloodtakers would have slaughtered everyone otherwise.'

Charles groans, throwing his hands in the air. 'I do wonder sometimes if your Keepers are doing their job. In the space of a month, Theo loses an ear to a witch…'

He gestures vaguely at his grandson.

Theo flinches. One hand drifts through his white-streaked hair, tugging it lower over the bandaged side. He's already trying to hide the damage.

'…and now the Bloodtakers have Lucas,' Charles says. 'My question, Nathaniel, is what are you going to do about it?'

'Grandad,' Theo says.

The room stills. Everyone stares.

'The Keepers have other priorities…'

'Bah!' Charles dismisses him with a wave. 'The Guild have seen no sign of this witch in Sarumbourne. Since when do we take the word of Bloodtakers at face value?'

The room sinks into a tense silence. Opel shakes her head.

Charles steps closer, planting a hand on Nathaniel's desk. 'I want my grandson returned.'

Nathaniel holds his gaze.

'We've already searched the Bloodtaker nest. Opel found no sign of him.'

Charles pulls away in a huff.

'And we don't have another lead,' Nathaniel continues. 'If we scatter the Keepers now, we lose eyes looking for the witch. We're not talking about one missing boy, Charles. We're talking about hundreds more if we turn our backs on this.'

Charles straightens, jaw clenched, tweed jacket stretching taut across his shoulders.

'Find him,' he says, cold and final, 'or you'll be stripped of your Sentinel role.'

The room holds still. Nathaniel's eyes narrow, but he doesn't rise to the bait.

Opel and I lock eyes. Is he bluffing? Or actually mad enough to follow through?

'You can't do that,' I say.

Charles turns his glare on me, then sweeps out without a word. His footsteps ring down the corridor.

All eyes fall on Theo. His shoulders slump, and he's smaller than I've ever seen him.

'I'm sorry,' he says, quietly.

'Just go,' Opel mutters, not even bothering to look at him.

Theo hesitates like he wants to argue, but thinks better of it and leaves without a word.

He nudges past Liam, who appears just in time to catch the tail end of the drama. He flicks his blond fringe out of his eyes, watching Charles and Theo disappear down the stairs.

My body warms and relaxes.

'Did I miss a meeting?' Liam asks.

'Not a planned one,' I say, forcing a smile. I shoot him a look, the 'I'll explain later' kind.

He reads it instantly and nods.

Nathaniel clears his throat, attempting, and failing, to break the tension still hanging thick in the air.

'Shouldn't you be in class?' he asks Liam, raising an eyebrow.

'Yeah,' Liam replies, completely unfazed. 'History, actually. But I thought I'd skip it to share some history that might actually be useful.'

Opel smirks. 'Such a rebel.'

Nathaniel rubs his beard. 'Go on, then.'

Liam steps forward, launching into an explanation, but I barely catch the words. The way he talks, confident and sharp, it's distracting. The good kind. I snap myself out of it because it's really not the time for swooning.

'So if Samuel Carter's family owned Hive Cottage,' Opel begins, climbing out of the chair, 'that confirms the disturbed ground Tariq and I found would be where Evangeline was buried.'

'Which means the water I took from the garden's legit,' I add, glancing at Nathaniel.

The flask is still stashed under my bed. I wasn't sure it would come to anything, but now we know it will.

Nathaniel nods, but his mind's already spinning ahead. 'We still need to find Evangeline.'

'I think I know where to start,' Liam says, surprising me again.

He's been thinking this through.

'The Carters owned other properties. If Evangeline was involved with Samuel Carter…'

'She might be using one of those properties now,' Nathaniel finishes, already on his feet. 'Where did you get this information?'

Liam hesitates. 'I think we should park that one.'

Lily. He doesn't have to say it. It's all over his face.

Nathaniel must pick up on it too, but he lets it slide, for now. He grabs his jacket from behind the door. 'I'll head to the Guildhall, see if the historians can dig up the Carter property records.'

'What if Charles spots you?' I ask.

He freezes.

'The Guild won't help you if Charles knows your focus isn't on Lucas,' Opel adds.

Nathaniel's shoulders dip.

Then the door creaks open.

'I can help,' Theo says from the threshold.

Opel lifts an eyebrow. 'Decided to come back, then?'

'I can get you into the archives. Or distract my grandad. Either works. I want to help.'

Opel studies him, arms still folded, but her glare softens at the edges. Slightly.

Nathaniel claps his hands once. 'Right. Let's move.'

'I'm coming,' Opel says, already halfway to the door.

'You are?' Theo steps aside, surprised.

'Yeah, just to make sure you don't stab us in the back again.'

So… maybe not fully forgiven.

'I'm not playing couples' therapist all the way to the Guildhall!' Nathaniel calls as they disappear down the corridor.

Liam approaches me, his expression softening as he steps into my space and rests his head against my chest. His warmth is instant and grounding, and for a moment, the chaos of the last half an hour falls away.

'What happened?' he asks.

'I'll explain,' I say, wrapping an arm around him. 'Want to go train?'

'Can we just… stay like this for a bit?' He burrows closer, his body pressing against mine in a way that's both comforting and precarious. I'm seconds away from losing my balance.

'Alright, you.' Without warning, I hoist him up and throw him over my shoulder.

'Tariq!' he protests, laughing as he flails in mock annoyance.

'To the training hall!' I declare, striding toward the door.

Liam groans dramatically, playfully pounding his fists against my back. But the sound of his laughter is infectious, and for the first time today, I'm lighter.

THIRTY-FOUR

TARIQ'S STORY

LIAM

The dull thud of my fist hitting the padded wall echoes through the training room. My arms burn, my knuckles sting, but I'm not about to stop, not with Tariq watching me like a hawk, wearing that infuriating smirk.

'That's not a punch, Liam,' he says, tilting his head like he's trying not to laugh. 'That's… I don't know, some kind of flail.'

I straighten up, rolling my eyes. 'I'm stronger than you, you know. If I land a punch, it'll hurt.'

Tariq steps closer, his hand brushing mine as he grabs my wrist to adjust my stance. 'Strength doesn't matter if you don't know how to swing properly. What are you planning to do, tickle the bad guys into submission?' His grin is maddening, and for a second, I forget what we're even doing.

I yank my arm free, heat creeping up my neck. 'Do you want me to tickle you? Because I *will* do that.'

'Save the dirty talk,' he says, biting his lip, his green eyes still locked on me. 'Watch and learn.'

He moves fluidly, showing me how it's done with an ease that makes it look almost effortless. His fist lands with a satisfying crack against the padded wall, and I hate how impressed I am.

'Show-off,' I mutter, trying to copy his movements.

My next punch lands harder, the sound louder this time.

'There you go,' Tariq says, nodding approvingly. 'See what happens when you actually listen to me?'

'Can I just point out you've been a Keeper for six years?' I shoot back, a smile tugging at my lips. 'I've been one for six months.'

'Point taken.' He smirks again.

We keep at it for a while. The banter fades into comfortable silence, replaced by the steady rhythm of movement training.

Sweat drips down my temple, and my arms feel like lead, but I don't mind.

I lean back against the wall, breathing hard. 'Where's Heather? I haven't seen her since I got here.'

'Here.' He hands me a bottle of water as I slide down to the floor. 'She took off to her room when Charles arrived. She still gets edgy around the Guild.'

I take a sip, and the liquid cools my throat. 'I guess that's what happens when they imprison you for nearly two decades.'

Tariq slumps beside me, just as much of a sweaty mess as I am. 'We don't know what really happened back then. Nathaniel's never really spoken in detail about it. Only that Heather struggled with her powers and the Guild stepped in.'

My mind falls to what Tariq had told me after we left Nathaniel's office earlier. 'Do you think Charles is right? Maybe we should be looking for Lucas—'

'Don't.' He turns away, shaking his head, the playful energy from earlier evaporating. 'Don't start with that.'

'Start with what?'

Tariq's shoulders tense as he picks himself up. The warmth and ease between us vanish in an instant, like someone's snuffed out a flame.

He grabs a towel off the bench and tosses it over his shoulder. 'Why do you have such a soft spot for him?'

I push off the wall, crossing my arms as I follow him. 'Lucas? I don't. I just—'

'Do you have feelings for him?' Tariq spins around, his eyes blazing.

What? Where has that come from? 'No... I don't. I just...'

'Liam, he is dangerous. He puts people in dangerous situations. You don't get it because you haven't seen what he's capable of, but I have.'

'People can change. Lucas has a softer side. He does care, deep down.'

I want to tell Tariq how Lucas saved my life back at the hotel, but judging from the look on his face, he won't want to hear it.

'People like him don't change, Liam. He hurts people...' He trails off, running a hand through his damp hair, then turns toward the glass door. 'Forget it. Training's over.'

'No, it's not.' I step in front of him, blocking his path. 'You don't get to shut me out like this. What's really going on?'

'I already told you—'

'Don't give me that,' I cut in. 'This isn't just about Lucas. Is it?'

Tariq moves to go around me, but I put my hand on his chest to stop him.

'Tell me what happened with you two. Tell me about Leon Strainer.'

Tariq freezes. His eyes flicker to mine, wide with something that looks a lot like panic.

'Don't ignore me again,' I press. 'Lucas wanted me to know, Tariq. Whatever this story is, he wanted me to hear it. Why?'

Tariq exhales sharply. 'It's nothing. Just one of Lucas's games. You shouldn't give it any weight.'

'Don't lie to me.' My voice cracks, but I don't care. 'I told you that you could trust me. Now let me trust you. Just tell me.'

For a moment, he doesn't say anything. His jaw clenches, and his fists curl at his sides like he's trying to keep himself together. Finally, he sighs, the sound heavy and resigned.

'Fine,' he says quietly, not meeting my gaze. 'I'll tell you, but try not to think less of me. For what I did.'

He swallows hard, then sits down on the edge of the bench, his elbows on his knees.

He starts with the same facts Lucas told me at the hotel. How Leon Strainer was a known drunk, responsible for his parents' car accident and Lucas's dad's hit-and-run. How Tariq and Lucas, both grieving and angry, grew close after losing their parents.

'We couldn't let him get away with what he did,' Tariq continues. 'So, Lucas and I made a pact. We'd deliver our own justice.'

I already know where this is going, but I need Tariq to say it, to get it out for his own sake as much as mine.

'One night, we went to the building where Leon worked. We knew he'd be there alone. We'd watched him for days, tracked his movements. He stayed late most nights, drinking instead of going home to his family.'

Disgust flickers across his face. 'I swore I'd never become like that.'

He hesitates, his hands fidgeting with the towel draped over his lap. 'We waited for the last of his colleagues to leave and for him to take his first swig from the bottle. Then we went in. Lucas had brought a can of petrol.'

My breath catches. These are the details I was expecting, but hearing them out loud is entirely different.

'Lucas poured it everywhere. When he was done, he signalled for me to light it.'

He stops, staring at the floor.

'Seeing Leon up close… it made the anger in me boil over. He'd taken everything from me. He deserved to pay. So I did it. The flames left my hands before Leon could even comprehend what was happening.'

'Tariq…'

'I ran outside to join Lucas,' he says quickly. 'We stood there, watching the building go up in flames. Lucas was… beaming. So happy about what we'd done. I thought I'd feel the same. But all I could see were the flames, and all I could think about was the fire from my parents' accident.'

He swallows hard, his eyes shimmering. 'That's when I realised… my parents would be so disappointed in me.'

I reach out, taking his hand in mine, squeezing it gently.

'That's when I decided to go back in,' he continues. 'Lucas screamed at me not to, but I didn't care. I pushed through the flames, and that's when I found Leon. He was on the ground, unconscious but alive. The fire hadn't reached him yet, and he still had the bottle in his hand.'

I blink. 'You saved him?'

'I dragged him outside and laid him on the forecourt. Lucas was already gone. He left me there. Then the sirens came, and I ran.'

'But you did the right thing,' I say quickly. 'He survived, didn't he?'

Tariq shakes his head, a single tear rolling down his cheek as he finally looks at me. 'A few weeks later, I saw the headline in the *Sarumbourne Journal*. He... he took his own life.'

Leon Strainer killed himself? Was it because of what Tariq and Lucas had done? Or the guilt over the lives he'd destroyed? Or maybe it was just the drink.

'He had a wife. Kids. And I took him away from them. Just like he took my parents. Like Lucas's dad.'

'You don't know what was going through his head, Tariq,' I say gently. 'You can't blame yourself for his actions.'

'Can't I?'

'No. Look at me.' He does. 'You're a good person. You were angry and scared, and... Lucas probably spurred you on.'

At the mention of Lucas's name, Tariq shakes his head. 'Do you know what I never understood?'

'What?'

'Leon's suicide... it was unexplained. And then his family suddenly moved into this big house over in Winterslow. But Leon had nothing – no business assets, no life insurance because of his drinking. I looked into it. It didn't make sense.' He pauses, his jaw tightening. 'Until it did.'

The realisation hits me like a punch to the gut. 'You think the Guild helped them?'

He nods.

'But why would they...' The pieces click into place. 'Lucas.'

Tariq shrugs, his expression resigned. 'I could never prove it. But yeah. Charles was protecting his grandson.

And when I didn't go through with the plan, Lucas cut me off. We barely spoke after that.'

'Tariq, I...' I don't know what to say. The weight of his story, his pain, hangs heavy between us. But I do know one thing. 'I don't think less of you,' I say softly. 'You were a kid who'd just lost everything. What you did wasn't right, but it wasn't all your fault.'

Tariq exhales shakily, his gaze dropping to where our hands are still joined. His thumb brushes over mine, tentative and unsure.

'Do you... still want to be with me? After hearing all of this?'

I don't even need to think about it. 'Of course I do.'

His head jerks up, and I catch the flicker of disbelief in his eyes.

'Tariq, you've been through hell, and yeah, you've made mistakes, but none of that changes the person you are now. You care so much, even if you don't always show it. And I...'

I pause, my heart pounding. Is this the right moment?

'What is it?' he asks, his brows knitting together in confusion.

I pull my hand back just enough to steady myself.

'The May Masquerade at college,' I say, trying to keep my voice even. 'It's this Friday. Come with me.'

'A masquerade?' He blinks, clearly caught off guard.

'Yeah, you know... masks, questionable punch bowls, and cheesy music,' I say, holding his gaze. 'I want us to do something normal. Even if things aren't normal right now. Or might never be.'

He doesn't respond. His lips part like he wants to say something, but the words won't come.

'You're more than just a Keeper, you know.'

Tariq looks away, his jaw tightening.

'Besides,' I add, nudging him gently, 'you still owe me for bailing on the Festive Fling.'

A flicker of guilt crosses his face. 'That got cancelled because of a gas leak, not my fault.'

I smirk. 'Really? Because I got your "sorry, can't" text the day before the gas leak announcement.'

'Okay, I panicked,' he says, rubbing the back of his neck. 'I don't exactly thrive in rooms full of people and paper snowflakes.'

'I'm not asking you to dance or anything,' I say, lifting an eyebrow. 'Just to show up.'

His shoulders sag as he exhales slowly. After a moment, he lifts his eyes to mine, and there's something quieter there. Hope? Maybe. Fear? Definitely.

'You really want me to go?' he asks.

I smile, keeping it light. 'Tariq, I'm not going to beg. But yeah. I want you to go. Preferably with me.'

His lips twitch into the faintest smile, and he lets out a quiet laugh.

'Okay,' he says at last, voice low. 'I'll go.'

Relief washes over me, and before I can stop myself, I lean in and kiss him.

The buzz of my phone shatters the moment like a glass dropped on concrete.

I fumble for it, my heart sinking when Lily's name flashes on the screen. Her timing is, as always, terrible.

'Lily?' I say, swiping to answer. 'What's up?'

'Liam. Can you hear me?' she bursts out, frantic and breathless. 'It's Jack. He's in trouble.'

'What do you mean? What's happened?'

'I… I don't even know how to explain,' she stammers, her words tumbling over each other. 'He called me, but he wasn't himself. He sounded… out of it. Nothing he said made any sense. Liam, something's really wrong. I called his house, but his mum said he was out. I'm heading into town now.'

Tariq's expression hardens when he sees my face.

'Did he say anything at all that you understood?' I ask, forcing my voice to stay steady.

'Bits and pieces,' she says, though her hesitation makes my pulse quicken. 'I don't know.'

I press the phone tighter against my ear, trying to focus past the static in my brain.

'Lily, listen to me,' I say firmly. 'Come to the Seven Angels. Tariq and I are here.'

'Liam… the witch.'

'I know,' I say, swallowing hard. 'Just get to us, okay? We'll figure it out.'

I hang up and look at Tariq. His jaw is tight, his shoulders rigid, but his eyes are sharp and focused.

'What's going on?' he asks.

'It's Jack,' I say, already moving toward the door. 'Lily thinks he's in trouble. He was supposed to be with Eva tonight.'

'Eva?' Tariq's brow furrows. 'Who's Eva?'

'This girl he's been seeing,' I explain quickly. 'She's a new student.'

But the moment the words leave my mouth, something clicks in my head. New student. Tariq's already a step ahead.

'How new?' he asks.

'Shit.'

'Eva,' he says slowly, his eyes narrowing, 'as in…
Evangeline?'

'Double shit.'

We don't waste another second. We're out the door in
an instant.

THIRTY-FIVE

PASSWORD REQUIRED

TARIQ

Liam paces the length of the Seven Angels bar. His hands keep flexing at his sides like he's trying to stop them shaking. He hasn't spoken since Lily's call, not even when we got changed upstairs. He's just kept moving, like stillness might make it worse.

The bar is closed for the night, which helps, as he'd be drawing stares right about now.

I've got Opel on the phone; her voice is crackling in my ear.

'Nothing yet,' she says. 'Nathaniel's digging through the Carter family registries, but it's slow going.'

I pinch the bridge of my nose.

'I can't believe I didn't see it,' Liam blurts, still moving. 'Eva sounds just like her sister. They even look similar!'

'Liam, relax.' I attempt to break his pacing. 'Okay, keep me updated.' Opel cuts off.

The moment I lower the phone, the door flies open, and Lily bursts in. Her face is pale, but her eyes are sharp and fierce, darting between me and Liam. Without hesitating, she crosses the room and wraps Liam in a tight hug.

'Any news?' she asks.

Liam's hands hover awkwardly on her shoulders before she pulls back. 'Nothing yet.'

She exhales, sharp and frustrated, before glancing at me with a half-apologetic look. Not that I blame her. The clock's ticking, and Jack's out there somewhere.

'Opel says Nathaniel's still digging,' I say, answering Liam's unspoken question. 'But so far, nothing useful.'

Liam's jaw tightens as his pacing slows. 'We need to figure out where Jack could've gone. Lily, did he say anything else on the call? Anything we can work with?'

She hesitates, frowning as she tries to piece it together. 'He… he mentioned something about a river.'

'A river?' I echo, exchanging a glance with Liam.

'I'll let Opel know. Maybe it'll help them narrow the search.' I pick up my phone and type: *Jack mentioned a river. Check records near waterways.*

Liam stops pacing entirely. 'Lily, you know what I'm thinking about Eva, right?'

'That she's Evangeline?' Lily doesn't even blink. 'Yeah, clue's in the name, I guess. She registered as just Eva at college, otherwise I'd have picked up on it.'

'Wait,' he says, his expression shifting like a lightbulb just went off. 'If Eva had to register as a student, she'd have had to put an address, right?'

'Yeah,' Lily says slowly, her gaze narrowing.

'I have an idea, but it's going to involve some breaking and entering.'

I raise an eyebrow. 'Where?'

'The college.'

The college rises ahead, its Georgian brickwork etched in shadow. Moonlight bleeds through the trees beyond Craythorn Forest, casting the building in a pale glow. Everything feels unnaturally still.

I tap out a quick message to Opel: *We've got a lead. Heading to the college. Will update.*

Our footsteps echo softly as we head up the tarmac drive.

'Are you sure this is a good idea?' Lily whispers, clutching her coat tighter.

'No,' Liam says, looking around. 'But if you've got a better idea how to find Jack, I'm listening.'

We reach the steps. The entrance doors are shut, the glass catching our reflections as we approach.

Liam exhales through his nose. 'So... now what?'

I smirk. 'This was your plan.'

'Right, but does that mean I have to do *everything*?'

Lily's already eyeing the frame. 'Can't you just, I don't know... use your super-strength?'

'You mean smash it in?'

'No,' she says, deadpan. 'Let's not lean too hard on the breaking and entering part. I meant pry them open.'

I wedge myself between them and give it a go.

Nothing. 'Yeah, this one's on you.'

Liam rolls his eyes, steps up, and digs his fingers between the panels.

A voice slices through the quiet behind us. 'And what, exactly, do you think you're doing?'

We freeze.

A figure steps out of the shadows, her face immediately familiar. I've seen her at more Guild meetings than I can count. Her greying blond hair is pulled back so tightly that her sharp features seem sculpted into place. She's wrapped in a suit jacket, arms crossed against the chill.

Her gaze locks onto me first, then Liam, then Lily, her expression softening ever so slightly.

'Principal Gellar!' Lily exclaims.

'Lily Boynes. Liam O'Connor,' she says, her voice slipping into that condescending, overly concerned tone adults use when they think they're being clever. 'It's awfully late for you to be skulking around the college grounds. Care to explain?'

Liam straightens. 'Jack Cooper's in danger,' he says bluntly, cutting straight through the pretence. 'We need to access the college system. Now.'

Gellar blinks, clearly taken aback. She's probably not used to talking Keeper stuff outside of the Guild, especially not in the presence of an outsider to it all.

'Liam, what are you doing?' Lily says.

'Danger?' Principal Gellar asks, composing herself. 'What are you talking about?'

Liam looks at me for approval, but I'm not giving it. It's too late now.

'We think he's been captured by the Handsel witch,' he continues.

Her eyes narrow. She knows who we are. She saw both of us sworn in as Keepers of the Crossing.

'You shouldn't be talking about this so openly,' she snaps. 'And last I checked, the Guild is focused on the missing Martindale boy. Not playing rescue for your friend.'

Liam glances at me, desperate.

Principal Gellar huffs out a breath. Then, after a pause, her lips curl into something almost amused. 'However,

I never liked Charles's youngest grandson. Between us, he's a complete tit.'

Maybe I would have actually attempted college if there were more principals like her.

Lily steps forward. 'Principal Gellar, please. If you don't help us, Jack might not make it through the night.'

For a long moment, Gellar just watches her. Then, with an exaggerated sigh, she reaches into her pocket and pulls out a key. 'Fine. But if anyone asks, I didn't see you.'

She leads us inside, her heels clicking against the polished floor as we move through the dimly lit reception.

The admin office is behind the welcome desk. It's cold and sterile, filled with humming computers and the faint scent of cleaning products. Gellar flips on the light, making us all squint.

'Do what you need to do. Quickly,' she says, leaning against the doorframe.

Lily wastes no time, pulling out a chair at the nearest computer station. Liam and I stand on either side of her. She taps at the keyboard.

'Anything?' I ask, my voice low.

'I need a password to access the system,' Lily mutters, her shoulders dropping.

Gellar leans over and types quickly. A beep. They're in.

'Thanks,' Lily says, then clicks through various tabs.

As I wait, my gaze drifts to a poster on the wall. It's a fundraising plea for the renovation of the college library. The one I destroyed last year.

Principal Gellar follows my gaze, her expression unreadable.

I grin, as innocently as I can. 'Sorry about that.' I gesture toward the poster.

Gellar folds her arms. We both know I did it, but she can't exactly report me for arson. Besides, I was saving Liam's life.

'Got it,' Lily says after what feels like an eternity. She points to the screen. 'There's an address tied to Eva Carter. It's on Castle Street.'

'She's using Samuel's surname to hide her identity,' Liam says.

Gellar steps forward. 'Are you telling me one of our new students is the witch?'

'Afraid so,' Lily says awkwardly.

'I can't believe it. Although the admissions team did say she was unusual… a bit "older than her years".' Gellar bends down, studying the photo on the screen.

'They weren't wrong, try nearly three hundred years older!' I say, pulling out my phone.

I message Opel: *We've got an address – 113 Castle Street. Is it linked to the Carter family? Confirm?*

'Are you all done?' Gellar asks. 'I'd quite like to get home sometime this evening.'

'Yeah,' Lily says, and we file back into reception as Gellar locks everything down.

My phone pings. Opel: *Confirmed. Carter owned. Be careful.*

'It's a match,' I say.

'We're going,' Liam announces.

'I'm coming with you,' Lily says firmly.

I protest but Liam's already there.

'No, you're not.' Liam's voice is sharp. 'It's dangerous, Lily. Let us handle this.'

'What?' Her eyes are blazing. 'You're not shutting me out of this. I'm coming whether you like it or not.'

'No!' Liam raises his voice to a level I haven't heard before, and it catches both me and Lily by surprise.

'Sorry... I...' He hesitates, choosing his next words carefully. 'Lily, the last time you got mixed up in all this you nearly died.'

Lily nods, but she appears not swayed. 'I can help. You said it yourself I know more about these witches than anyone, remember?'

Liam sighs, giving up.

'It's Jack,' Lily says.

'Lily...'

She stares me down.

'You won't win,' Liam says. 'She's more stubborn than me.'

'Fine,' I say. 'But you do exactly what we say. No arguments.'

'Deal,' she says.

Gellar shoos us outside, keying in the security alarm.

'Thanks, Principal Gellar,' Liam says. 'And if I could suggest one thing? Maybe work on your recruitment process. A Dark Friar history teacher and a student who happens to be a murderous witch? It's not a great look.'

Gellar folds her arms. 'Thank you, Mr O'Connor. Is there anything else you'd like to address, or would you prefer to discuss it in my office first thing tomorrow morning?'

Liam wisely shuts up.

'We're going to need some backup on this,' I say, already scrolling my recent contacts.

THIRTY-SIX

NO REST FOR THE WICKED

LIAM

The house stands mid-terrace on what is usually a busy street in the middle of the city. But it's late, and traffic is low. It's shorter than the other houses in the row, its front door narrow and painted deep grey, almost black. A small wooden sign beside it bears the number 113. Above, two windows glimmer faintly, reflecting the glow of the streetlamp, but the curtains inside are drawn tight. Another window juts out from the slanted roof, a dormer with a crooked frame, like a watchful eye peering down at us.

Lily shivers beside me, checking her phone again for any word from Jack.

Heather, who joined us about ten minutes ago, rubs Lily's back. 'Cold, m'dear?'

Lily nods, clicking off her phone, the blue light fading from her face.

'We'll find him,' Heather says.

We met Heather at the bottom of the street, and Tariq filled her in on what's happened.

Tariq moves toward the nearest window, peering inside. After a moment, he turns back, shaking his head. 'Think you can hear anything?'

I press my ear to the door, closing my eyes, letting my hearing stretch beyond the barrier. The world sharpens. Heather's breathing, steady and measured. Lily's, shallower. Tariq shifting his weight beside me.

Inside the house?

Nothing.

No movement. No breathing. No heartbeat.

I open my eyes and step back. 'Either she's out... or playing a really good game of sleeping lions.'

Lily tilts her head. 'So, are you going to kick this one in?'

I grimace. 'Well, we don't have a key.' A car whizzes by. 'Get close. Cover me.'

The others crowd around, shielding me from view. I grip the handle, positioning my fingers just right, and twist. There's a sharp crack and the lock snaps. The handle breaks clean off. The door nudges open.

We wait.

No sound.

No movement.

Tariq steps in first, moving cautiously. I follow.

Inside, the air is stale, carrying a faint scent of old wood and something... herbal.

The living room is not what I expected. It's clean. Contemporary.

I recognise the same Ikea armchair as Mum and I have in the flat, tucked into the corner. A coffee table sits in the middle, covered in papers. A map of the city. It's new, unfolded. Candles. Jars of dried herbs. Strange little trinkets that feel more like charms than decorations.

Lily picks up a college prospectus that was wedged between two books.

Heather fingers the spine of a thick hardback. 'She's been catching up on history.' She tilts the book toward me. *The Changing Face of England: 1700 to Present Day.* Another beside it is labelled *Industrial Revolution and Its Social Impact.*

'She's trying to blend in,' Tariq says, flipping through the map. 'Learning how the world works now. How people live. Probably covering centuries of lost time.'

Heather wanders into the kitchen, and Lily glances toward the staircase. 'I'm going to check upstairs.'

'Not alone you're not,' Tariq says.

'I'll go with you,' I say.

Lily rolls her eyes but waits for me to follow.

The stairs creak under our weight.

We reach the landing and something is wrong.

The air is thick with rot. The stench makes my eyes water, and Lily and I cover our noses. A door is closed at the end of the hallway.

'Wait here,' I say.

And, for once, Lily listens.

I open the door and step inside.

And stop.

There's a bed, neatly made. A wardrobe, slightly ajar.

And two bodies.

A man and a woman, naked, lying on the floor, hands folded over their chests, their eyes closed. At first glance, they could be sleeping. But there's symbols drawn across their skin in something dark. Blood. The symbols are similar to the one carved on the witch tree at Grovely Wood.

Burnt-out candles surround them in a half-circle.

The more I stare, the more I don't want to. Their flesh is peeling. Their features are sunken. They're decomposing.

I step back into the hallway, gripping the doorframe.

Lily steadies me. 'What is it?'

I don't speak. I just look at her.

Tariq and Heather arrive moments later. Lily's breath catches. She nudges past me and into the room.

Heather kneels between the bodies, her hands in her lap. 'Some sort of ritual,' she says to Tariq, who looks just as sickened by the scene as the rest of us. 'I don't know what kind. Nathaniel might.'

Tariq moves closer. 'Can you see them? Are they… here?'

Heather stands, checking her surroundings. 'No. They've moved on already.'

Lily, on the other side of the room, scans an open book. It's old and worn, different from the others downstairs.

'It's a restoration ritual,' she says, handing the book to Heather. 'Eva had to find a way to restore her body when she rose from her grave. Just like Dorte did to me.'

'Lily's right,' Heather says, turning a page. 'This couple must have been living here, and she used their life force to restore hers.'

Silence falls between us.

We don't know these people. We never will. But that doesn't make it any easier.

They were innocent.

And now they're gone.

'What now?' I say.

'Well, normally I'd call the clean-up crew at the Guild,' Tariq says. 'But they can't know we're on this. Not when Charles wants us to be searching for Lucas.'

Heather moves to the window, peering outside.

'We still have no idea where Jack is,' Lily mutters.

'This is not good,' Heather says.

'Lily, we'll find him. We just need to—'

'Not good.'

Tariq joins Heather. 'What is it?'

They both look startled, their eyes fixed on something outside. I move between them.

A young woman walks toward the house from across the street.

Blond hair. A sauntering, self-assured stride.

Eva.

'That's a problem,' Tariq says.

'Who is it?' Lily asks, panicked.

'Jack's not-so-better half.' I move away.

Tariq reacts instantly. 'Everyone, hide.' He pulls the curtains shut. 'Lily, stick with me.'

'I'll get the lights,' I say, already moving. Down the stairs in a blur, switching off every lamp and overhead bulb on the way. Above, hurried footsteps scatter as the others scramble to hide.

No time to join them.

A cupboard under the stairs catches my eye. I dive in, and the door clicks shut just as the front door creaks open. Something underfoot nearly trips me, but I freeze, holding my breath.

The broken front door will alert her to something, but maybe not us if we can stay hidden.

Back pressed tight against the wood, every muscle locks into place. The living room light flicks on. Footsteps cross the floor. Slow. Deliberate.

Through a crack in the door, Eva's shadow moves.

I stay perfectly still, barely breathing.

Eva's hair is pulled back into a loose ponytail, her black coat trailing behind her as she crosses the room. She drops something onto the floor, something dark and crumpled.

It's Jack's bag.

She flicks on the lamp beside the sofa, bathing the room in a dull, yellow glow, then moves toward the wall. A small calendar hangs beside a bookshelf, neat little marks scored through each passing day. She picks up a pen and drags a line through today's date.

Then she stops.

Her head tilts.

I tense, pressing myself back against the cupboard wall.

Eva turns slightly, eyes scanning the room, a slow smile spreading across her face.

'I know you're hiding, Keeper,' she says, her muddled accent dripping with amusement. 'Come forth.'

My heart hammers. She knows I'm here. There's no point pretending otherwise.

I could stay put; maybe she's bluffing. But she has Jack. And she just confirmed what I already feared. She knows what I am.

I let out a slow breath and push open the cupboard door.

Eva watches me step out with an almost pleased expression, like she was expecting me. She folds her arms, raising a single eyebrow. 'Liam. I see neither of us have been entirely honest.'

I say nothing, my fists clenching at my sides.

She gestures vaguely at the room. 'What do you think? I have adjusted quite well, all things considered.'

The bookshelves, the modern furniture, the city map still spread out on the table. Then my gaze drifts upstairs, to the room where the bodies lie, slowly decomposing.

'Yeah,' I say. 'You're really fitting in. Where is Jack?'

Eva's smirk remains. 'You would be surprised how easy it is to slip back into a world that forgot you ever existed.' She briefly catches her reflection in a mirror to my side. 'Of course, it helps when you wear the right face.'

'Did the bodies upstairs help with that?'

Her smile doesn't fade, but her eyes sharpen. 'They were necessary.'

'You think that justifies it?'

'Justifies?' Her laugh is empty. 'Oh, Keeper. What justifies betrayal?' She takes a step closer, voice lowering. 'My sister warned me. She told me not to love him. But I didn't listen.'

A chill passes through me. 'Samuel Carter.'

She nods once. 'He made promises. That he would keep me safe. But when the whispers turned to suspicion, when the Guild began to watch us, he chose fear over me.'

'He told them it was only Dorte.'

'I told him the Guild wouldn't believe that,' she says, bitterly. 'And they didn't. They thought he was corrupt. Said I'd bewitched him.'

Just like she's bewitched Jack. I want to say it, but I also want her to keep talking. I need to know where Jack is.

'And when the crowd came... Sam just watched.' Her voice cracks then. But the moment's gone before it lands. She straightens, cold fury settling over her like a veil. 'The Guild dragged us into the square like criminals. Dorte begged for my life.' Her eyes flick to mine. 'I died with his name on my lips.'

Silence stretches between us.

'And now this is revenge?' I ask.

'This is justice,' she says. 'The Keepers stole my heart. The Guild stole our lives. This town, its people, they stole our power. And then they buried us like a secret. But the earth does not keep secrets forever.'

'So how does Jack fit into your justice?'

'Well, he murdered my sister, of course,' she says, more gleefully than I expected.

'You don't exactly seem cut up about it.'

'She brought me back, and for that, I will forever be grateful. But Dorte was weak. She never saw the bigger picture. Your friend will pay for what he has done to her, but his death will serve something greater.'

I grit my teeth. 'Where is he?'

Eva tilts her head, feigning curiosity. 'Poor lad. Ever so quick to bend, ever so eager to please. He slipped into my hands as if fate willed it so.'

A floorboard above us creaks. Her eyes dart to the sound, just briefly, but it's enough. I move.

But Eva is quick to react.

She throws up her hand, muttering something under her breath, and an invisible force slams into me like a brick wall. I'm thrown backward, crashing against the armchair, knocking it sideways.

Pain jolts through my ribs.

Eva laughs. 'Do you truly think you can stand against me?'

I push myself up, ready to go again.

But someone rushes in front of me.

Tariq crashes into Eva and she stumbles backward.

I get to my feet, but Tariq doesn't waste a second. He swings a fist, flames sparking at his knuckles.

Eva throws up another spell, blocking the hit, but Tariq presses forward, forcing her back.

'So you're the Elementa of today. You're different from the one I once knew.'

Tariq holds firm. I take the opening, speeding toward her. She dodges, but not fast enough. I grab her arm, wrenching it behind her. She snarls, twisting, her free hand sparking with energy as she throws another spell. A pulse of purple energy erupts from her palm.

Tariq and I are hurled in opposite directions as the air crackles with heat.

I crash into the coffee table, its legs shattering beneath me.

Tariq is already up, but the flames licking at his hands are gone. Instead, he reaches for something in his jacket pocket.

It shimmers in the light.

A hip flask.

Eva takes a step back, eyes darting between us, then scowls.

Tariq unscrews the cap and thrusts the flask forward.

Water lashes at Eva's face.

She screams and shouts, flailing around.

But nothing happens. No reaction, no smoke, no melting.

Eva continues to scream, although now it sounds as though she's mocking us.

Tariq frowns and tosses again, but the water has no effect.

'Do you really think I'd fall for the same trick as my sister?' Eva says, now still, and smirking.

'But Hive Cottage was your home…' Tariq begins.

Eva laughs. 'Indeed it was. I knew it would only be a matter of time before you Keepers began snooping around there.'

'You dug up the garden,' I say, now realising we're the ones who have been tricked.

Tariq looks at me. He can't believe he got it wrong.

'You shall never find my grave,' she says. And with that, she raises her hands, and suddenly, the floor trembles. Her eyes find mine. 'And you won't save your friend.'

The light overhead flickers violently.

Then, smoke engulfs the room, and she's gone.

Silence. The only sound is my own heavy breathing.

Tariq curses under his breath. 'Literally gone in a puff of smoke. Come on.'

The smoke dissipates. I cough sharply, running a hand through my hair. 'Yeah, she really Wicked Witch-ed her way out of that one.'

Tariq helps me up.

Footsteps pound down the stairs. Lily and Heather appear in the doorway.

'I asked you guys to stay put,' Tariq says.

'What happened?' Lily asks, scanning the room.

'She got away,' I say.

I grab Jack's bag, gripping the fabric tightly before holding it out to Lily.

Her face crumples. She snatches it from my hands, clutching it to her chest.

'We'll find him,' I promise.

She nods, but there is fear in her eyes.

A sudden, sharp knock on the door makes us all jump.

Tariq's eyes snap to mine.

'Excuse me?' A muffled voice calls from outside. 'Could you please keep it down? Some of us have work in the morning!'

We exchange looks. Tariq presses his lips together, exhaling through his nose.

'Sorry!' I call back, shrugging to the others.

Silence. Then, a loud huff and retreating footsteps, followed by a door slamming.

I let out a breath, glancing at the others.

Tariq shakes his head. 'We need to get out of here.'

Lily wipes her eyes. 'And we need to find Jack. Now.'

Tariq nods. 'I'll call Opel for an update.'

And with that, we leave the house behind.

THIRTY-SEVEN
UNDER THE MILL

TARIQ

The Market Square is silent as we cross it. Rain mists the air, slicking the stone beneath our feet, turning the pavement glassy. The scent of wet concrete clings, and the streetlights throw restless shadows from the trees lining the path.

Up ahead, the Guildhall rises from the dark, tall and imposing against the night.

Opel and Theo are already there on the steps.

Theo stands with his arms folded. Opel paces like she's too charged to stay still, her hair whipped loose by the wind.

The second she spots us, her gaze snaps to Lily and sharpens. 'What's *she* doing here?' Opel says.

'Excuse me?' Lily bites.

'She's helping,' Liam says, stepping in front of his friend and matching Opel's stare.

Opel turns her glare on me, unimpressed. 'Are we taking on work experience now or something?'

'She helped us find the witch's address,' I remind her. 'And she's worried about her friend.'

Opel looks like she wants to argue. She's always been blunt, never one to sugarcoat things, but even she knows we don't have time to stand around debating this.

'You said on the phone to Tariq just now that you had something,' Liam prompts. 'What is it?'

Opel's gaze flicks back to me before settling on Liam. 'Your friend Jack mentioned a river, right? The Carters used to own the Bishops Mill. It's right on the river.'

I frown. 'That's a pub. It's hardly a secret lair for a witch.'

Opel tilts her head, unfazed. 'It's also a historic watermill with underground chambers.'

A flicker of unease twists in my gut.

'Yeah, that sounds about right,' I say, though I don't like it.

'It's the only property Nathaniel's been able to locate that's near any sort of water,' Theo adds.

'Then we need to go,' Liam says. He turns to Lily. 'You need to stay this time.'

Lily tenses immediately. 'I'm coming with you.'

'No,' Liam says. 'It's too dangerous. You know what happened back at the house.'

Lily scoffs, ready to argue.

'Lily, please,' Liam continues. 'We don't know what we're walking into.' He takes her hand. 'All I want is you and Jack safe. In the space of a month, you were cursed by a witch and Jack's been captured by her crazy sister. I'm not risking it again.'

Lily glares at him, her grip on his hand tightening. But something shifts in her eyes, fear, maybe, or reluctant understanding. She sighs. 'Fine.'

'I'll find him,' Liam promises.

I step beside Liam, turning to Heather.

'Can you take Lily to the Seven Angels?' I ask.

'Of course,' Heather says.

Opel turns to Theo next. 'Stay with Nathaniel.'

'Ask him to look into other possible resting places for Evangeline,' I say.

Opel quizzes me with her eyes.

'She played us,' I say, throwing my hands up. 'The garden at the Hive was never her grave. The water had no effect on her.'

'So, we're heading off to fight a witch with no way of stopping her?' Opel's eyes widen.

'Yeah,' Liam and I say in unison.

'I'm in.' Opel joins me at my side.

'Be careful,' Theo says, before heading back inside.

Opel doesn't answer; she's already moving. Liam squeezes Lily's hand one last time before letting go.

I've spent plenty of nights at the Bishops Mill, but none quite like this.

The building is a strange blend of past and present. Weathered brick and timber beams soaked in centuries of history, yet neon signs flicker in the windows, promising warmth, laughter, and a steady flow of drinks. Right now, I want to be inside, not outside in the cold rain.

The river rushes beneath us as we step onto a footbridge. The water is black and restless, reflecting the pub's lights in fractured ribbons. The wood creaks underfoot, damp with the drizzle. The closer we get, the louder the hum of conversation becomes, bursts of laughter breaking through the night from inside the pub. To the side, the outdoor seating area is abandoned, save for a few empty glasses and chairs shoved back in a hurry.

Opel stops, glancing at me. 'What's the plan? We kindly ask the manager if we can have a look in the cellar?'

'Yeah, because that'll go down well.' I scan the building, searching for another way in. 'Eva wouldn't just stroll through the front door. She must have her own way in.'

'Over here,' Liam calls, from further along the bridge.

We join him, following his gaze down beneath the mill. A powerful cascade of water spills out into the river, churning white and furious. I squint, and there, halfway up the stone wall, is a hatch. Barely visible unless you knew where to look.

'You see it?' Liam asks.

'Yeah,' I murmur. 'But I don't see a way to reach it.'

'I think that's our way in,' Liam says.

'Kid, we don't even know if Jack is—' Opel starts, but Liam suddenly holds up a hand. His whole body goes still.

'What is it?' I ask.

Liam doesn't answer right away. Then his eyes widen, his breath catching. 'Someone's in pain. They're crying out.'

Before I can react, Liam bolts, shoving open a side gate that leads down to the river.

'Liam!' I call after him, but he's already stripping off his hoodie.

I grab his arm. 'We should think about this.'

'Yeah, outdoor swimming was not on my to-do list today,' Opel mutters.

'Guys, this is our only way in,' Liam insists, pointing at the rushing water. 'Jack's in there. I'm not waiting.' And with that, he jumps.

Water splashes up, drenching my jeans.

Opel throws up her hands. 'Seriously?'

I sigh, already unzipping my jacket. 'Come on.'

She gives me a look as I peel off my jeans.

'What? These are my Levi's.'

With just my boxers and T-shirt on, I take a breath and jump. The second I hit the water, the cold slams into me like a thousand knives. I suck in a sharp breath. It's shallower than I expected. I can stand, but the river still pulls at me, waist-high and unforgiving.

A splash behind me. Opel surfaces, cursing, pushing soaked hair from her face. Her mascara runs down her cheeks, but judging by her expression, that's the least of her concerns.

'I swear,' she shivers, 'if his friend isn't in there, I'll kill him myself.'

Liam is already at the cascade, trying to climb.

'Liam, wait!' I wade toward him.

Too late. His foot slips, and he crashes back down, hitting the water with a loud splash.

'Didn't think this through, did ya?' Opel smirks.

Liam spits out water. 'We need to reach that hatch.' He gestures up at it.

I follow his gaze, watching how the water crashes down over the ledges. The current is strong; the rocks are slick. Even if we made it halfway, one wrong move would send us tumbling back.

'Let me,' I say.

Closing my eyes, I focus. The power stirs inside me, the familiar heat rushing through my veins. I step onto the first ledge, using one hand to steady myself. With the other, I reach out to the water.

It bends.

The cascade shifts, parting slightly, just enough to create a dry path up the rock face. Like water flowing around an invisible obstacle.

'Hey, waterbender,' Opel shouts over the roar of the river, 'we don't all have fancy powers, you know.'

'Follow me,' I call back. 'Stay behind me. I don't know how long I can hold this.'

Liam scrambles up first, Opel close behind. I keep moving, stepping carefully. The ground beneath us is slippery, algae-covered stone. The second I let my guard drop, the water will come crashing back.

The further we climb, the darker it gets. The streetlights fade behind us, and shadows stretch beneath the mill's wooden beams. The air is damp, thick with the scent of river water and old stone.

I'm almost at the hatch.

A groan. Low and pained.

Someone is in there. Beyond the walls.

From the look on Liam's face, he's heard it too.

I grab the rusted handle of the hatch and pull. Nothing. It doesn't budge.

'Liam,' I say, shifting so he can take my place. My free hand falters, and the water rushes against us again before I can steady it.

'Sorry,' I mutter.

Liam grabs the handle, yanking hard. It snaps clean off.

'Fuck it,' he growls. He grips the edge of the hatch instead, plants his feet, and heaves.

With a resounding crack, the entire thing breaks free from the wall. He hurls it behind him. It clatters down the cascade, vanishing into the river.

'Well, that's one way to do it,' Opel says.

Liam climbs inside first. Opel moves around me and follows.

I take one last breath, release my hold on the water, and slip inside after them.

My bare feet land on cold concrete. My underwear clings to my skin, soaked through, and a violent shiver racks my body.

'What is that?' Opel whispers.

The roar of the river outside fades, replaced by a deep, rhythmic cranking.

I flick my fingers, summoning a small flame. The dim glow flickers against damp stone walls, revealing the tight, square chamber we've entered. It also brings a warmth I've been craving.

The sound is coming from the mill wheel, its wooden beams groaning as it turns.

Nathaniel once told me it doesn't serve a purpose anymore, just an old mechanism left to move with the current.

An iron barrier separates us from another pool of water beneath the wheel, the surface churning.

'There,' Liam says, moving toward a metal ladder bolted to the wall. It leads up to a hatch in the ceiling.

He's already halfway up when I grab his arm. 'Wait. Do you hear anything?'

Liam freezes, closing his eyes. A moment of silence.

'No. Nothing.'

That should be a relief. It isn't.

I nod, and he keeps climbing. Opel follows, then me, my limbs aching from the cold. Liam reaches the hatch first, tests it, then pushes. It creaks open, revealing a dimly lit space above. One by one, we climb through.

The room we step into is bigger than I expected. Circular, with wooden beams forming a low, slanted ceiling. Dim lanterns flicker against the walls, casting long shadows.

In the centre of the room stands a large, round table.

Carved deep into its surface is the witch symbol. The lines are crude, jagged, scraped into the wood with something sharp.

Suspended above the table by thick ropes, stripped to their underwear, are three people.

Jack is one of them.

Liam gasps and sprints forward. 'Jack!'

Jack's body hangs limp. Shallow cuts mark his arms and chest, thin streams of blood trailing down his skin, dripping onto the table below. His head bobs to one side and he groans.

'He's alive!' Liam scrambles onto the table, fumbling at the knots. 'Jack. Jack, it's me. Liam.'

Beside him hangs another boy. A chain necklace dangles from him.

Liam hesitates, his breath catching. 'I know him.' He swallows. 'He's one of the new guys from college.'

I step closer. The boy's head droops forward, his face slack.

Opel reaches up, pressing two fingers to his neck. A long pause. Then, slowly, she shakes her head.

Liam sucks in a sharp breath.

'Liam?' A weak voice croaks from across the table.

All of us turn.

The third person, a girl, lifts her head slightly. Her dishevelled red hair hangs low.

'Vel?' Liam stumbles across the table toward her.

Unlike Jack and the other boy, the girl isn't bleeding. She's bruised, shivering, but untouched by whatever is happening here.

Opel is already untying the dead boy. She gestures to Jack. 'Burn the rope, get him down.'

I step onto the table as Liam grips the girl's arms, whispering reassurances. The ropes are thick and coarse, but with a single fiery grip, one snaps, then the next. Jack's body slumps forward. I catch him as best I can, but he's dead weight, barely conscious.

Liam turns, eyes full of desperation. 'Is he…'

'He's breathing,' I say quickly. 'But we need to get out of here. Now.'

Opel lowers the dead boy onto the table, then moves to help Liam with the girl.

Jack's blood has pooled inside the carved symbol on the table.

It soaks into the grooves.

Liam grips the girl, holding her upright as she sways. She could pass out at any moment.

'Eva…' The girl's breath is shallow.

Liam's expression hardens.

'She… she's taking our blood. One by one.' Her gaze flickers to the dead boy on the table. 'She started with him.' She swallows; her voice is raspy. 'Then Jack. I was… I was next, but she… stopped.'

Opel glances at the carved symbol, still slick with Jack's blood. 'We need to get out of here.'

'Why?' Liam says.

The girl's eyes roll slightly, her body sagging. 'I don't… I don't know. She said it wasn't enough. That she needed more.'

Her knees buckle. Opel catches her, steadying her. 'We can't stay here,' Opel says. 'She needs a bed. And Jack's losing blood by the second.'

A sound echoes from below. A rustling at first, then the slow creak of shifting wood.

The girl's eyes snap open, wide with terror. Her fingers dig into Liam's arm. 'She's coming back,' she whispers, trembling.

A heavy bang rattles the hatch.

My eyes sweep the room. There's a door on the far side. 'That's our way out. Liam, you carry Jack. I'll cover the rear.'

Liam hesitates, then nods, draping Jack's limp arm over his shoulder. Opel tightens her grip on Vel.

I clock the table. Solid wood. If we're lucky, it'll buy us time. I shove hard, the legs screeching against the floor. The moment it tips, I push it over the hatch with a thud. Dust rises into the air.

Something below slams into it, making the wood jump.

'Move!' I snap.

We rush through the side door, and I slam it shut behind us.

A metal staircase winds up ahead, dimly lit and rusted in places. We take it fast, feet pounding against steel. At the top, another door. I push through, and we stumble into a large room, more modern than the ones below. The walls are lined with wooden crates stacked high, some splintered, others marked with faded labels.

'Pub cellar,' Opel says, breathless.

I don't waste time. I grab a heavy crate and shove it against the door.

Another bang sounds from the other side. Then a slow, dragging noise.

And then, a voice.

'Keepers.' It's twisted. Warped. It's Eva. But it's different now. Distorted. The voice is hollow, stretched. Wrong.

'Run,' I breathe.

Opel scans the room. 'There!' She points to a staircase leading up.

No hesitation. Liam grips Jack tighter, Opel pulls Vel forward, and we race up the steps.

I reach the door first. No time to think. I throw my shoulder against it, forcing it open.

Light. Neon glare. The scent of beer and sweat. The hum of conversation.

For a second, no one moves.

People turn and the laughter dies. The music, some lively folk tune, cuts off mid-verse.

We must look like hell. Damp, half dressed, breathless. Jack, bloodied and pale, slumped against Liam's shoulder. Vel swaying, bruised and weak.

No one speaks.

'Rough night?' The bartender blinks.

Then, below us. A door bursts open.

I swallow hard, clear my throat, and force a grin. I gesture vaguely at our state.

A screech rises from the basement.

I shut the door behind us. 'You could say that,' I reply, half smiling. 'Go!' I say to the others.

We bolt. Out into the night. Barefoot, half-naked.

The cold bites harder when you've left your favourite jeans behind.

We don't stop running. Not until the mill is far, far behind.

THIRTY-EIGHT

THE DEFENSOR

LIAM

Jack lies still on the bed, his face pale, his chest barely rising and falling. Nathaniel kneels beside him, carefully tending to the deep gashes on his chest. The dried blood makes me queasy.

Lily sits on the edge of the mattress, gripping Jack's hand so tight her knuckles have gone white. 'He should be in a hospital.'

Opel, standing with her arms crossed near the foot of the bed, exhales sharply. 'And what exactly do you think a hospital's going to say when we bring him in looking like that?' She gestures to the carvings still visible on Jack's skin.

'They'll have questions.' Nathaniel doesn't look up from his work. 'And we won't have answers they'll believe.'

'The Guild could handle that,' Tariq says.

Opel scoffs. 'You think they'd help after we went after the witch when we weren't supposed to?'

No one answers.

Heather appears at Vel's side, pressing an ice pack into her hand. Vel, curled up in the armchair beside the bed, takes it with a quiet thanks and presses it against her bruised cheek. She's wearing Heather's dressing gown.

It's floral, a little too long in the sleeves, but it looks warm. Cosy, even.

'I'm not sure my medical skills will be enough,' Nathaniel says.

'Vel, you're good with this sort of thing, right? I mean, you fixed my finger almost perfectly.'

Vel gives me a small, tired smile. 'That was just instinctive. I didn't really know what I was doing.'

Why is she talking herself down? I hold up my finger. 'Look, whatever you did was like…' I'm still struck by how there isn't even a scar. 'Magic.'

Vel avoids my eyes.

'Am I missing something here?' Tariq asks.

The room goes silent.

Since I met Vel, she's had this energy, like I'm connected to her, and I didn't know why, until now.

'Liam?' Nathaniel prompts.

'Nathaniel, you've been looking into the two missing Keepers, right?' I ask, my eyes still on Vel, who is burying her face in the ice pack. 'The Tempus and the…'

'Defensor,' Nathaniel finishes, standing and removing his glasses.

'Liam.' Tariq steps up beside me. 'What are you getting at?'

Vel finally meets my gaze, and there's something different in her eyes. A knowing look.

'Nathaniel told me, in one of my training sessions, that the Defensor Keeper has the ability to heal.' I look to Nathaniel for confirmation. 'Right?'

Nathaniel hesitates. 'Correct, it's their primary ability.'

I crouch down so I'm eye level with Vel. 'You healed my finger, didn't you?'

Vel looks around the room but doesn't say a word. Then, slowly, she nods.

'You're one of us,' I say, smiling despite everything. 'We can help you.'

She's unsure, but right now I need her to be thinking about Jack, not herself. As scary as this all is.

'I know this all sounds really weird. But I know you know what you can do, and right now, I need you to help my friend.'

Vel straightens, staring into me. 'I've never done anything this serious before,' she whispers.

I don't care. 'Please. Just try.'

Everyone is silent, but I can almost hear the cogs turning in Nathaniel's brain. We've found a new Keeper, just when we need one most.

Vel hesitates. Then, with a deep breath, she nods. 'I'll try.'

I slowly pull Lily away from the bed, and she lets go of Jack's hand.

Nathaniel coughs, then eyes my pendant.

'Oh. Right.' I remove my pendant and place it around Vel.

'You don't have to bribe me. I said I'd try.'

'It's just in case any Wretches show up,' Tariq says.

'What?'

'Ignore him.' She doesn't need to know about demons that feed on power just yet. 'That's for another day.'

Vel leans over Jack, placing a trembling hand on his chest. The room stills. Every breath, every rustle stops.

Last time she did this, I wasn't really watching. But this time is different.

She exhales slowly and closes her eyes.

Then her whole body tightens, muscles locking in place.

The air thickens, charged, electric. Like the moment before a storm breaks.

A soft glow pulses beneath her hand. Not bright, not showy, just a faint shimmer, like heat on tarmac.

And then, Jack's wounds begin to close.

Not all at once, and not neatly. It starts deep, like something under his skin is stitching itself back together. The worst of the gashes slowly draw shut, skin knitting at the edges. Bruises fade, swelling recedes.

The blood on his chest stays where it is, dry and congealed. But the damage beneath it disappears.

Lily gasps beside me. 'Oh my god.'

Vel's face is pinched with effort. Her hand trembles. She doesn't stop.

The energy in the room keeps building, like everything is being pulled toward the space between them. It's not just healing. It's restoration.

Then, all at once, Vel's hand drops. The glow vanishes.

She sways, eyelids fluttering. 'Easy-peasy,' she says, before her legs buckle and she slumps sideways.

I lunge forward, catching her before she can hit the floor. She's burning up, her breath shallow against my neck.

Nathaniel kneels beside me, his expression a mix of intrigue and concern. 'Take her to Tariq's room. She needs rest.'

Lily doesn't look away from Jack, still unconscious but no longer covered in wounds. 'I'll stay with him,' she says softly.

I nod and scoop Vel into my arms, her head lolling against my shoulder. Opel, Heather, Nathaniel, and Tariq follow as I carry her out of the room.

I place my pendant back around my neck, tucking it under my T-shirt.

Vel lies unconscious on the bed, her breathing steady but shallow. She's smaller like this, curled on her side, her red curls spilling across the pillow.

Nathaniel rubs his temples, still staring at Vel like she might vanish if he blinks. 'I can't believe it,' he mutters. 'All this time… all the searching… and she was right here in Sarumbourne.'

He watches me like I've got all the answers. I don't, but I tell him what I can. That her name is Velora and she's new at college, born here in Sarumbourne, moved away when she was small. Came back recently with her mum, who's not well.

Opel, arms folded, leans against the doorframe. 'We think we can trust her?'

'You were there, Opel,' Tariq says. 'We all saw what she did for Jack.'

'She saved his life,' I say.

Nathaniel exhales, adjusting his glasses. 'She's the Defensor, no doubt about that. But this isn't exactly great timing for a new Keeper to emerge, given everything else going on.'

'Will you tell the Guild?' Tariq says.

'Not yet. Let's deal with one thing at a time.' Nathaniel sinks into the armchair by the fire. 'What do we know about the witch?'

I scrape a hand through my hair, trying to piece it all together. 'It's not just revenge. She sees this as justice, for what was done to her and her sister.'

'But it's also about power.' Tariq cuts in. 'She wants the energy from the Crossing. That's why they came to Sarumbourne in the first place.'

'You were unable to vanquish her in your confrontation?' Nathaniel asks.

Tariq shifts beside me. 'The water I took from Hive Cottage did nothing. That means Samuel never buried her there.'

I nod slowly. 'She said we'd never find her grave.'

Nathaniel frowns. 'So she's not acting on impulse. She's playing a long game.'

'She was in love with him,' I say, quieter this time. 'Samuel Carter. He promised to protect her. But when suspicion started swirling, he turned. Claimed it was only Dorte doing magic. Tried to save her by outing her sister to the Guild.'

Tariq mutters, 'Didn't work.'

A silence settles between us. I don't fill it.

Eva's voice when she said Samuel's name, how it cracked just for a second before she buried it under all that rage.

He loved her. Enough to betray his own. Enough to lie to the Guild. But not enough to save her in the end.

Tariq is staring into the fire. Maybe he's thinking the same thing I am, that for all their power, the Keepers couldn't protect the people they loved. That loving someone like us, someone wrapped up in this ancient mess of secrets and duty… it comes with a cost.

Nathaniel leans forward, steepling his fingers.

Heather, who's been quiet until now, suddenly stiffens. She touches her ear like she's listening to someone.

Opel rolls her eyes. 'Here we go.'

Heather ignores her. 'Maggie's saying something.'

'What is it?' I say, eyeing Tariq and secretly hoping Maggie divulges more shower-snooping stories that make him go all shy and cute.

Heather hesitates, then turns to Tariq. 'She says... if Samuel truly loved her, he wouldn't have buried her any old place.'

Tariq frowns. 'Then where?'

'Where all wealthy families were buried at the time,' Lily says.

Everyone looks to the hallway, where Lily now stands.

'Sorry,' she says, a deer in headlights. 'Jack's still resting and... well, I overheard you talking.'

'Keeper business,' Opel snaps.

Tariq shoots her a look before I can.

'You were saying?' Nathaniel says.

'The graveyard of St Thomas's Church,' Lily continues. 'All the Carter family were buried there at the time, including Samuel.'

I blink. 'You mean, literally out the back? Behind the courtyard?'

Nathaniel exhales sharply. 'Of course. It makes sense. Samuel would want her buried with him. Tariq, Opel, Heather, go check out the grave.'

Heather hesitates but nods. She, Opel, and Tariq head for the door.

Nathaniel turns to Lily. 'Would you stay here with Vel? She'll need someone when she wakes up.'

Lily nods.

'Liam, come with me.'

Nathaniel pulls a thick, leather-bound book from the stack beside him, flipping through the brittle pages. The Seven Angels' library is cold and musty. Out the rear window, there's no sign of Tariq, Opel, or Heather in the cemetery beyond the courtyard. Darkness swallows everything.

Nathaniel stops on a page and turns the book toward me. 'I've done some research. This isn't just any old witch mark. It's a symbol used for a particular spell.'

A circle with a series of interlocking lines and curves, shaped like leaves or petals.

It's the one we saw carved into the table at the mill. The one Tariq saw above the door at Hive Cottage. And the one that had been burned into the bark of the witch tree in Grovely Wood.

'What does it mean?'

Nathaniel presses his lips together before answering. 'It's called an Industria Vocare – loosely translated, it means "energy summon".' He adjusts his glasses. 'It's used as part of an extraction spell, one that draws out great power or energy.'

A chill runs through me. 'The Crossing.'

Nathaniel nods. 'Exactly. Many of these spells require sacrifices, blood of the innocent, to be successful.'

'Innocents like Jack and Vel?' I say, my throat tightening. 'But Vel said the witch didn't have enough,' I remind him. 'Like Jack, her, and that other boy weren't enough for what she had planned.'

Nathaniel considers for a moment. 'Perhaps she miscalculated how much blood would be required for a spell of this scale. If it's something she and her sister began in the 1700s, Sarumbourne was much smaller then, both in geographical size and population. The Crossing's energy would have been much smaller as well.'

I swallow hard. 'So now that the city's bigger, the Crossing's power has spread and grown. She'd need more sacrifices?'

'Hundreds, possibly,' Nathaniel says grimly.

I shake my head. 'But how would she do that? It took her weeks to gain Jack's trust. Same with Vel and the other boy.'

'I don't know,' Nathaniel interrupts. 'But she lost two tonight, and if she's realising how many more she'll need… she may turn to more drastic measures.' He closes the book. 'And that worries me.'

Before I can respond, the lights flicker.

Nathaniel frowns, glancing up. 'Strange. The wiring here is usually…'

But I don't hear the rest.

The air shifts. A deep, sickening dread coils around my chest.

She's here.

I move, bolting for the door. Nathaniel is right behind me.

I hit the stairs fast, nearly tripping over my own feet as I reach the first floor. The lights still drifting in and out. Lily is in the hallway, looking around in confusion.

'What's going on?' she asks.

'Get back in the room and stay there,' Nathaniel says.

'Liam…' Lily begins.

'Do as he says!' I shout, not stopping.

She doesn't argue. The door clicks shut behind me as I take the stairs two at a time, my pulse hammering.

The second I hit the ground floor, I stop.

The bar is a mess. Chairs overturned, glasses shattered. A low groan comes from behind the counter. My eyes dart to the bartender. He's slumped across the bar, barely moving, his body twisted unnaturally. He's alive, but barely.

Eva.

She's sitting in one of the chairs in the middle of the room, sipping from a large glass of ale like she owns the place.

Her eyes flick to me, and her lips curl into a slow, wicked smile. She lifts her fingers in a lazy wave.

'Hello, Keeper.'

THIRTY-NINE

YOU'RE INVITED

TARIQ

The grave is smaller than I expected.

Samuel Carter, 1718–1738.

Only twenty years old.

I fold my arms, breath fogging in the cold night air. 'He was my age,' I murmur.

'Yeah, well, we Keepers do tend to have an expiry date,' Opel says, dry as ever.

Heather stays quiet, watching the grave, one hand resting against the rusted iron fence that borders this part of the churchyard.

I crouch down, brushing my fingers over the turf. 'The grass is so thick around here. There's no way to tell if his grave was disturbed.'

Opel raises an eyebrow. 'Better grab a shovel.'

'You want me to dig up the grave?'

'Well, how else are we gonna find out?'

'Do you know how long that'd take?' I stand. 'It's been nearly three centuries. We'd be lucky to find anything besides mulch.'

Opel turns to Heather. 'Alright then, resident ghost-pert. You're up.'

Heather examines the other nearby gravestones. 'Ghosts don't just hang about for fun, y'know. Not unless something's holding them here. Unfinished business, a curse, really bad FOMO.'

Opel throws up her hands.

'What about the Everlasting?' I ask.

'No chance,' she says quickly.

'Heather, come on, you did it when Liam went looking for Katie.'

'That was different. Katie had only just passed. Do you know how long it could take to reach someone who's been gone for three hundred years?'

'We have to be sure this was Eva's final resting place,' I say. 'The water here could be the key to stopping her. Please, Heather.'

She sighs. 'Okay, say I do zap all my energy and deal with a migraine that lasts a week, I still don't have anything of Samuel's to use as a guide.'

Opel strides over to the headstone and presents it like she's on a game show. 'We have this. Will it work?'

Heather studies the stone. 'Maybe.'

'Then try,' I say. 'We need answers.'

Heather ties her hair back, kneels, and presses her bare hand to the stone. Her eyes flutter shut. Her breathing slows.

Then she gasps, and her head falls back.

She's gone. Not physically – she's still kneeling, hand to the stone – but I recognise that hollow stillness. Liam had the same look when he travelled to the Everlasting.

'I'm so glad I got the telekinesis package,' Opel mutters. 'This whole astral-spirit stuff gives me the creeps.'

'I just hope she finds him fast.'

'How long did it take Liam to find Katie?'

'In the Everlasting? A minute or two.'

'And for you?' Opel puts her hands on her hips.

'Six hours.'

'Tar! What the f—'

'What are you kids doing out here?' A voice slices through the air.

We both turn. An elderly man stands in the side doorway of the church, coat pulled tight against the breeze, his face shadowed by the porch light.

'Who's he calling *kid*?' Opel mutters.

'We're just paying respects,' I say quickly, nodding toward the grave. 'An ancestor.'

The man eyes us, then the grave. 'Strange hour for it.'

'We're night owls,' Opel adds, flashing a thin smile.

'Samuel!' Heather cries out, still deep in her trance.

The man flinches. 'Is your friend alright?'

'Yes,' Opel and I say at the same time.

'She's just… mourning,' Opel adds. 'Very family oriented.'

'She was close to… Great-Uncle Samuel,' I say, forcing a grin. 'Spiritually.'

The man frowns, stepping closer. 'That one's been trouble lately. Had to refill the grave a month ago. Someone dug it up. Grave robbers, most likely. Nothing left but bones and an empty hole.' He shudders. 'Damn disrespectful, if you ask me.'

'Wait, someone opened the grave?' I ask.

'Wide open,' he says grimly. 'We had to handle it fast, before anyone noticed. Can't have stories getting around.'

Opel raises her eyebrows. 'Yeah. Imagine that.'

'Luckily, the fresh seed I put down has taken well. Like magic, you could say.'

Opel and I fake a laugh.

He gives us one last look. 'Five minutes. Then be on your way.'

He disappears back into the church. The door clicks shut behind him.

'Well,' Opel says. 'Guess that confirms it. Looks like this is where Eva clawed her way out.'

'And then probably did a little cover-up job on the ground.'

Opel nods.

Heather still hasn't moved.

I kneel again, pressing my palm to the turf. A jolt of energy flows through me, and a moment later, water begins to puddle around my hand.

'Opel, the bottle.'

She hands it over. I coax the water from the earth, pulling it gently into the air, then guiding it into the container. The cold makes it harder to focus. My fingers shake, but I manage.

'Tariq.' Opel's voice is tense. 'What's happening?'

The Seven Angels' windows flicker. Light pulses behind the glass, bright, dim, then bright again.

Something's wrong.

Heather's still rooted to the spot. But her spirit's elsewhere, her eyes closed, brow pinched in concentration.

'Stay with her,' I say, sealing the bottle.

'Tar!' Opel calls after me.

I'm already running.

I sprint through the courtyard, boots hammering wet stone. Cold air scratches at my face.

The Seven Angels looms ahead, its lights flickering wildly, then suddenly cutting out.

I hit the back door and wrench it open.

Inside, the bar's a wreck. Chairs overturned. Glass shattered. The sharp tang of alcohol thick in the air. Behind the counter, the barman is slumped over, too still.

The front door stands wide open. Wind stirs napkins across the floor.

Near the window, Liam and Nathaniel face each other in silence.

No sign of the witch.

No one else here.

'Are you okay?' I ask, breath catching. 'We saw the lights from the yard.'

Nathaniel doesn't look at me right away. His eyes are sharp, fixed on nothing. When he finally speaks: 'She was here.'

I tense. 'The witch?'

He nods. 'Didn't attack us. Just wanted us to know she could.' He glances to the bar. 'Kevin might need an ambulance, though.'

Liam hasn't moved. Still pale. Still gripping something in his hand like it's the only thing keeping him upright.

'Where are Heather and Opel?'

Now's probably not the time to tell Nathaniel that Heather's in the Everlasting, and she doesn't even need to be.

'Long story,' I say. 'But I think we got our answer.'

Nathaniel turns to me. 'Did you get it?'

I reach into my pocket, pull out the bottle. 'Fresh from her grave.'

He takes it, inspecting the murky liquid inside, but his focus is already drifting, calculating whatever's next.

Liam still hasn't said a word.

I move closer. Rest a hand on his shoulder. 'Liam?'

Nothing.

'Did she do something?'

He just shakes his head, then slowly lifts his hand and holds something out.

A thick, glossy piece of paper.

I take it, fingers brushing his.

You are cordially invited to the Sarumbourne College May Masquerade.

The college crest is embossed at the top, and beneath it, in loopy gold lettering, is the date and time, followed by a dress code I'm pretty sure translates to 'wear a ridiculous mask and try not to sweat through your suit'.

A shaky breath escapes me. 'Liam, I already said I'd go with you.'

'It's not from me,' he says.

Dread blooms inside me.

The witch symbol is burned into the bottom of the invitation.

Eva.

Liam's room is dim, the glow from a single bedside lamp stretching shadows across the walls. I lean against the chest of drawers, arms folded, watching him with Jack and Lily. I wasn't sure about them at first. It's hard to imagine anyone outside the Keepers really getting it. But seeing the way they orbit him, steady, unfazed, I'm starting to understand. They remind me a little of Opel and Thomas, back when things felt simpler. When I had people to lean on. Maybe Liam has that too.

The door creaks open, and Opel slips in beside me. She nudges my arm.

'Got your message,' she says, lifting her phone.

'Is Heather—?'

'Back in the real world. Headachy. She's with Vel.'

'Did she find Samuel?'

She shakes her head.

On the bed, Jack perks up. 'Nice to have visitors,' he says brightly. He's propped against the headboard, pale but conscious, his hair sticking up like he's been electrocuted. Lily's cross-legged beside him, and Liam's on the other side, quiet but close.

'You sure you're okay?' Lily asks.

Jack stretches, groaning. 'I feel absolutely fine. Just a little bit achy. What exactly happened again?'

Liam rakes a hand through his hair. 'Eva had you under some kind of charm. You were part of whatever she's planning... a ritual.'

'But we don't think there was enough blood,' says Lily.

Jack pulls a face. 'Great. So, I was only *nearly* sacrificed? That's just embarrassing.'

'Told you to stick with Phoebe,' Lily says, bumping his shoulder. 'Worst case would've been a slow dance.'

Jack groans louder. 'Ugh. So much worse.'

Liam lets out a quiet laugh, and for a second, the room softens. The three of them fall into that easy rhythm that only comes with years of shared history. Liam smiles, and that jealousy I once felt seems to melt away.

Of course, Nathaniel's not built for softness.

He clears his throat like he's trying to reset the room. 'Touching, really. But we need to focus.' He's standing in the corner, arms crossed. He's been silent since the paramedics took the barman away a while ago.

Liam's smile fades.

Nathaniel nods toward Lily and Jack. 'If you're feeling better, you should both go home.'

Liam straightens. 'No. They stay. They need to know what we're up against.'

Nathaniel frowns. 'They shouldn't be dragged into this.'

I push off from the drawers. 'They already are. Whether we like it or not.'

To my surprise, Opel backs me up. 'If Eva's planning something at the masquerade, they'll be there too. They deserve to know what they're walking into.'

Nathaniel presses his lips together. Clearly not thrilled, but he doesn't argue.

'We'll be sensible,' Lily says. 'We'll do what Liam says.'

Liam tilts his head at her, amused.

She rolls her eyes. 'Within reason.'

Nathaniel exhales. 'Fine. Then let's talk about the invitation.'

'It has to be a trap,' I say. 'Eva doesn't just want to gloat. She wants us there. All of us.'

'She's targeting the Crossing,' Liam says slowly. 'That's where our Keeper power is drawn from, right? If she's sacrificing people in order to extract power from it, we'd amplify it just by being close.'

Nathaniel nods. 'She wants you on site. It's bait.'

Jack claps his hands. 'Cool. So we're accessories to our own murder. Great. Now what? Do we roast her? Drown her? Crown her May Queen?'

Everyone stares at him.

'What?'

Lily swats him. 'Shame Vel couldn't grow you a new brain while she was healing you.'

She turns serious. 'Should we cancel the masquerade? I'm on the student council, I can talk to Principal Gellar, now that she knows I know. We can shut it down.'

Nathaniel narrows his eyes. 'And how, exactly, does Principal Gellar know that you are aware of all this?'

Lily glances at Liam. He shrugs helplessly.

Nathaniel sighs. 'You know what? Forget I asked.'

I step forward. 'We can't cancel it. If Eva's planning to strike there, we need eyes on her. Cancel the event, and we lose our only shot at stopping this before it starts.'

'So how do we stop her?' Liam asks.

Jack leans back, hands behind his head. 'Pfft. I've already taken out one witch. I'm basically a professional.'

I raise an eyebrow. 'Such humility.'

Jack winks.

'We think we've got the right anti-witch detergent this time,' Opel adds.

'Yeah, but she'll expect us to use it,' I say. 'We have to be smart. Unpredictable.'

Nathaniel folds his arms. 'She's been around Keepers back when she was alive. She'll anticipate your strengths, your weaknesses.'

Everyone falls quiet.

'What about Vel?' Liam asks.

Nathaniel doesn't hesitate. 'No. We don't bring her in.'

'She's one of us now,' Liam says, frowning.

'Exactly. This is all too new to her. You remember what that's like.'

Liam nods reluctantly. The silence that follows is heavy, storm-front heavy.

'We've got two days to prepare,' Nathaniel says. 'That's not much time.'

Lily looks at me, something shifting in her expression. 'I might have an idea. About how we outplay her.'

I meet her gaze. 'Right now, we're open to anything.'

Jack lifts both hands. 'Okay, but before we go full witch-hunter... we've got more pressing matters to deal with.'

We all glance around.

'What?' Liam asks.

'The masquerade,' Jack says. 'We need masks.'

Everyone groans.

I shake my head. For all his chaos, Jack's not wrong.

Witch or not, this'll be my first real party. It's going to be formal, chaotic, and dangerous.

And I'm going with the most handsome boy I know.

Two goals for the masquerade:

Stop Eva from turning the place into a supernatural bloodbath...

And look good enough to make Liam go wild.

FORTY

THE MAY MASQUERADE

LIAM

I don't often think of myself as good-looking. Never, actually. I've spent most of my life blending into the background, thinking there were people far more interesting than me. But damn, put me in a suit, and suddenly, I'm… sharp. Refined. Maybe even a little bit powerful.

I smooth my hands down the fabric, eyeing my reflection in the bathroom mirror. The black jacket fits well, though it's a little tighter. It's been over a year since I wore this suit to my grandad's funeral. I don't think I've grown much since then, but the Keeper training must be making a difference. The fabric tugs slightly around my upper arms and thighs. Have I actually put on muscle? That's new.

Not that I'm suddenly built like Tariq. I enjoy food way too much for that to ever happen.

I'm excited to see what he's wearing. Tariq doesn't own a suit, so Opel is lending him one of Theo's. They're about the same height, but Tariq's broader, thicker; where Theo is lean, Tariq is solid. That jacket is going to be fighting for its life, but I have no doubt he'll still look incredible. Tariq looks good in anything. And out of anything, for that matter.

The warmth of the jacuzzi back at the hotel, the way the water caught on his skin, the way he looked at me, like he actually wanted me. Maybe, if we hadn't been interrupted, I'd have let him have me. All of me.

But then Lucas showed up and the whole night turned into an *Underworld* movie.

I swallow hard, fixing my tie.

It's been days since the hotel, and I still don't know how to feel. Lucas saved my life that night. He made a choice, and that choice was me. But that doesn't erase everything else, what Tariq went through with him, the lies, the manipulation.

I believed he was someone worth saving, but maybe I was just fooling myself.

Now we have no idea where he is, if the Bloodtakers have even kept him alive. Does he deserve it? That's what is niggling at me.

Tonight is more important.

I straighten my tie and reach for my mask. The soft fabric is streaked with blue, green, and white. Lily said she based the colours on my pendant stone. She'd been thrilled to rope in her mum's sewing club for the job, probably bossing them around like a tiny factory supervisor.

I tie the mask at the back of my head, take one last look in the mirror, and step out of the bathroom.

The moment Mum sees me, she lets out a dramatic squeal. 'Oh, my boy!'

Before I can react, she rushes forward and clutches my face like I'm five years old. 'You look so handsome!'

Then she hugs me, violently.

I barely manage to gasp, 'Thanks, Mum,' before she squeezes the air out of my lungs. My shirt untucks slightly in the struggle.

She finally releases me, and Jack and Lily appear behind her. They must have arrived while I was in the shower.

Jack grins, giving me an approving once-over before dusting off my shoulder. 'Scrub up well, mate.'

'Not bad yourself,' I say, taking in his outfit. His maroon suit is crisp, paired with a teal bow tie that somehow works. It's very Jack.

He flashes his jacket open with a proud flourish. 'Cost a fair bit. I'm just glad I finally get to wear it after the Festive Fling was cancelled.'

Lily stands, and my brain short-circuits for a second.

She twirls, sending the soft lace of her pink dress fanning around her. The colour is perfect on her, her blond curls falling in perfect spirals past her shoulders.

'And me?' she asks expectantly.

'Beautiful,' I say, meaning it.

She beams as I pull her into a hug.

Mum sniffles dramatically, clasping her hands together. 'You all look so grown up.'

'Mum, this isn't graduation. Save the waterworks for then, please.'

She's about to protest when there's a knock at the door.

Everyone who's supposed to be here is here.

'I'll get it,' I say, moving past her.

As I pull the door open, the air leaves my lungs.

Tariq.

He stands there, a grin stretched across his face so wide that even his sharp jawline seems to struggle with it.

'Surprise,' he says.

I need a second. Maybe several.

His three-piece emerald suit fits like it was tailored just for him, the deep green making his warm brown skin glow under the light. The matching waistcoat hugs his torso, and his black shirt, worn open, only makes the colour pop more. My gaze lingers on the chain of his pendant resting against his chest. I swallow.

'You look incredible,' I murmur.

He grins again, his confidence faltering just slightly as he tries to blow a curl of black hair from his eyes. It doesn't budge.

'Don't,' I say, catching his wrist before he can move it himself. 'I like it.'

His fingers curl around mine, warm and sure. He traces the edge of my mask with his other hand. 'Is that you in there?' he asks, voice quieter now.

I nod.

'Good,' he whispers.

Then he kisses me.

It's soft, brief, but the warmth of it spreads through my entire body.

Jack coughs loudly enough to bring be back to the present.

We both pull apart and I clear my throat.

'Hi, Marie,' Tariq says as he steps in, giving my mum a small, awkward wave. 'Guys.' He nods to Jack and Lily.

Mum beams, eyeing him up and down. 'Very dapper, Tariq.'

He glances down at himself again, like he's still not entirely convinced he isn't being pranked. 'Thanks.'

I shut the door behind him. 'What are you doing here? I thought we were meeting there?'

Tariq hesitates, his hand tightening briefly around mine before he meets my eyes. 'I wanted this to feel like a normal night. So… I'm picking you up. As my date.'

My insides melt.

Somewhere behind me, someone lets out a squeal. Could be Lily or Mum.

'Wait, you're driving?' I search his hands for keys.

Tariq laughs. 'No, I won't put you through that again. I've got a taxi waiting outside.'

Jack strides over, clapping Tariq on the back. 'Good man. We were going to have to walk.'

He heads out the door, Lily trailing behind, beaming at both of us as she passes.

Tariq sighs. 'I was sort of hoping…'

'I know,' I say, understanding immediately. 'And I appreciate the gesture.'

I squeeze his hand before stepping over to Mum and kissing her cheek. 'Bye, Mum.'

She cups my face, eyes shimmering with emotion. 'Take care of him,' she says, directing the words to Tariq this time.

Tariq nods, his grip on my hand tightening. 'Always.'

And with that, we step outside, together.

The moment we step out of the taxi, Tariq stretches his arms out with an exaggerated groan. 'That was tight.'

Jack nudges his shoulder. 'Cosy, mate. We're basically family now.' He waggles his eyebrows, earning a laugh from Lily and an unimpressed look from Tariq.

The cool evening air hits my skin as I take in the college forecourt. It's packed. Students – in elegant dresses, snappy suits, and all kinds of masks – gather in clusters, their conversations a buzz of excitement. The warm glow of the hanging lanterns overhead reflects in sequins, silk, and polished shoes. Everyone looks their best, transformed by the mystery of the masquerade.

'Oh! Wait, wait!' Lily gasps suddenly, patting at the clutch purse on her wrist. 'Our masks!'

She scrambles to open it, pulling out three neatly wrapped cloth bundles. 'I knew I was forgetting something.'

'I have mine,' I say, with a thumbs up.

Jack takes his first, unfolding the fabric to reveal a deep blue mask patterned with silver. He tilts it to the light. It's got the Avengers logo stitched into the design.

'Lily, you legend,' he says, beaming. He ties it over his face immediately, striking a dramatic pose. 'Captain Jack, assembled.'

Lily rolls her eyes before handing the next one to Tariq. 'And this one's for you.'

Tariq unravels it slowly. His expression shifts, curiosity giving way to something softer, more appreciative. The mask is deep red and black, flecked with golden flames that shimmer as he moves it.

'It's not fireproof, though,' Lily adds, smirking.

Tariq lets out a short laugh, shaking his head. 'Lily, this is amazing, thank you.'

'You're welcome. But really the thanks go to my mum and the Sarum Sewing Club.' She beams, before unfolding her own. It's soft pink, with intricate floral embroidery, tiny petals and leaves curling outward from the edges. She ties it in place.

We move toward the entrance, following the neatly positioned lanterns. The sound of laughter and chatter grows louder. The flow of students guides us down the side of the college, toward the sports hall where the main event is happening.

'There's a lot of people here,' Tariq murmurs, eyes scanning the crowd.

'Well, yeah,' Jack says. 'It's Noir Spire. Everyone wants to see them.'

I blink. 'Wait. Lily, you actually managed to book them?'

She grins like she's been waiting for me to realise.

'Of course,' she says, practically bouncing on her heels. 'Becky wanted Just Billy, but when the rest of the student council found out she was dating him, they all voted with me.'

'Good to know democracy still works.'

As we reach the entrance to the sports hall, a black and white balloon arch welcomes us. Standing just in front of it, beside Principal Gellar, is Nathaniel.

Principal Gellar gives us a knowing smile. 'We're delighted that Nathaniel has agreed to chaperone tonight.'

Nathaniel dips his head slightly. 'Opel and Theo are already inside,' he informs us.

'Any sign of Eva?' I ask.

He shakes his head. 'Not yet.'

The music swells from inside, drowning out my thoughts before I can spiral. I take a steadying breath, pushing it aside. Whatever's coming, it's not happening yet.

Right now, this is just a party.

We step through the doors, and I'm hit with a wave of warmth and noise.

I haven't been inside the sports hall since my first induction day, and I barely recognise it. The usual fluorescent lights have been supplanted by strings of golden fairy lights draped from the ceiling, casting everything in a soft, dreamy glow.

Clusters of balloons in black, white, and silver bob along the edges of the dance floor, and at the far end, a raised stage is set up, where Noir Spire is playing, their music thrumming through the speakers. The band's lead singer, dressed in an all-black suit with a feathered mask, grips the microphone, belting out a song I vaguely recognise from Lily's sixteenth birthday party.

Students move in waves across the floor, some dancing, others gathered around the edges, sipping soft drinks from the makeshift bar. The scent of punch and something sweet, candy floss maybe, lingers in the air.

It's surreal.

Tariq is beside me. His gaze shifts around the room, like he's mentally mapping the exits.

'Okay,' Jack says, adjusting his mask. 'This is actually sick.'

I nod, letting the energy of the place wash over me. For a moment, it's easy to believe this is just a normal night. A night of music, dancing, and minging punch. A night where nothing bad could possibly happen.

I let that thought settle, just for a second.

FORTY-ONE

SPECIAL GUEST

TARIQ

The crowd is dense, a sea of students in their glittering masks, moving like a living organism beneath the thumping bass of Noir Spire's set. I take in the room, my eyes scanning over each mask, each silhouette, searching for any sign of Eva.

I'm not sure what I expected from tonight, but I didn't think it would feel like this. Like a normal party. Like nothing's waiting just beneath the surface, threatening to ruin everything.

I catch sight of Theo and Opel near the edge of the dance floor. Theo's in full charm mode, tie loosened, hair a little messy, smiling like he's finally able to breathe again.

Opel, beside him, is actually dancing. Not just swaying or hovering awkwardly at the edge... actually dancing.

Then she notices me.

The smile vanishes. Her steps slow.

She cuts through the crowd and heads my way.

'Nice moves, where'd they come from?'

Opel smirks. 'Well, you don't know everything about me, Tariq Ashar.'

I let out a short laugh. 'Yeah, clearly.'

Theo's voice cuts through the brief silence. 'Didn't know Opel could move like that.'

He's still watching her, the admiration on his face a little too obvious.

A sly grin tugs at my lips. 'Yeah, didn't realise your hips were that loose.'

Her eyes snap to me, and the playfulness vanishes, replaced with a cool, sharp edge. 'Zip it.'

She looks back at Theo, who's already regretting his comment, shifting awkwardly on his feet.

'So, do you think the plan will work?' Opel's voice drops a little. 'If witchy doesn't show up, this whole thing's been for nothing.'

In the distance, Liam laughs with Lily and Jack.

'She'll show,' I say firmly. 'It's too good an opportunity for her not to.'

Opel narrows her eyes, clearly still unconvinced, but nods.

'We should split up,' I suggest, scanning the room again. 'Keep an eye out, in case she sneaks in.'

Liam's at my side. 'Don't I get a dance first?'

'Later, if we get through this.'

He turns to Lily and Jack. 'You guys stay close to me,' he says, and the three of them start to move off toward the side of the hall.

'Nathaniel's still outside, in case she makes her way in that way,' I say quietly. 'He's got a pretty good view from there.'

Opel snorts. 'You really think she's going to walk in like any other student?'

I shrug, keeping my voice low but confident. 'She's been pretending to be a student the entire time. Why stop now?'

Opel looks at me, then nods. 'I'll take the area near the band. She might try to blend in with the crowd there.'

'Good plan,' I say, glancing around again. 'I'm going to roam around a bit, see if I can spot anything.'

We split up, the music swallowing me again as I push deeper into the crowd.

The bass pulses through the floor, every beat a reminder to keep moving, keep watching. I weave my way toward the bar in the corner, where strings of fairy lights flicker above neat stacks of plastic cups.

The punch fountain is spewing glittery orange liquid in perfect arcs.

'Hi. Want a drink?'

Heather holds out a plastic cup.

She's not supposed to be here. She's meant to be keeping an eye on Vel, making sure she didn't get involved in this.

'Vel's here,' Heather says, as if reading my thoughts.

'She shouldn't be.'

'She's a seventeen-year-old girl at her first college party. She's not exactly going to stay home. You should have seen me at seventeen. I was a wild child.'

Nathaniel was clear about Vel staying out of this. 'Where is she?'

Heather points. 'Over there. On the dance floor.'

I follow her gaze... and freeze.

Vel's dancing with someone. A tall blond girl. She moves like she owns the space, every step smooth, every gesture precise.

She looks just like Eva.

The crowd blurs around me as I move, keeping my focus locked on the girl. I need to stay calm, to not draw attention, but my legs are already carrying me faster than I mean them to.

Vel notices me first. 'Tariq? What are you...'

I reach them and tug off the blond girl's mask in one swift motion.

She gasps, eyes wide and startled, blinking up at me. Nothing about her face is familiar.

She isn't Eva.

My hand drops to my side, the mask still clutched in it. 'Sorry,' I mumble, already stepping away as she snatches the mask back.

She stares after me; the heat in my face is driving me straight into the crowd, head low.

Vel is behind me, following.

'You shouldn't be here.' I stop and turn to face her. 'This is too dangerous.'

'I could be helpful.' Her expression is a mixture of defiance and resolve. 'Besides, what makes my life more valuable than anyone else's here?'

She reminds me of Liam, the same fire in her eyes, the same stubbornness. It must be some Keeper trait they don't tell us about.

I take a deep breath, trying to rein in my frustration. 'Fine. But you stay in sight of me. I don't want...'

I narrow my eyes, trying to focus past the flashing lights. The floor is marked with the usual painted lines for basketball and badminton, but beneath the chaos of the dancing students, the shapes look... wrong. The angles too sharp, the patterns too deliberate.

'What's wrong?' Vel's voice snaps me out of it.

I barely register her at first, still fixated on the floor. 'The lines,' I mutter. 'They don't look right.'

Vel frowns, following my gaze. 'It's just the sports court markings.'

No. It's more than that.

The pieces start fitting together, and I curse under my breath.

'Stay with Heather,' I tell Vel, stepping back.

'What? Why?'

'I need to check something.'

Without waiting for her response, I weave through the crowd, pushing past a group taking selfies. I reach the far end of the hall and shove open a set of double doors, finding a stairwell leading up.

The balcony overlooks the entire hall, rows of empty seats stretching out before me. I move to the railing, gripping it tightly as I scan the mass below. The change in perspective makes it clear. Laid out in crisp white paint beneath the dancers, twisting between the real sports markings, is the witch's symbol.

The same one we've kept seeing. The one Nathaniel explained to us.

The witch is here. Somewhere.

'What are you doing up here?'

A girl stands by the doorway, clutching a clipboard like it's a weapon. Her face is masked up like everyone else's. She's wearing a badge that reads *Becky Whittaker, Student Council Chair.*

'I just needed a second to chill. Too much dancing,' I say, gesturing as if I'm much hotter than I actually am.

She eyes me suspiciously. 'I don't recognise you as a student.'

'I'm here with my boyfriend, Liam O'Connor.'

Her expression shifts. 'Oh, you're Lily's friend?'

I nod, hoping that's enough to make her drop it, but she folds her arms. 'Where is Lily, anyway? She hasn't been very helpful today. It's like she's been completely preoccupied with something else.' Becky shrugs. 'I had to enlist the help of a newbie to set everything up.'

A strange prickle runs down my spine. 'A newbie?'

'Yeah, Eva Carter.'

Every muscle in my body tenses. 'Where is she?'

Becky sighs, looking around. 'That's what I'm trying to figure out. I thought she was up here.'

I scan the crowd with renewed urgency, but there's no sign of Eva. She could be anywhere. Watching. Waiting. Our plan won't work if she's not here.

Becky shifts her weight, eyeing me again. 'No one's supposed to be up here except the student council team. If you need a breather, you should go outside.'

I force a nod, backing away from the railing. 'Right. Yeah. I was just heading out.'

I leave quickly, my pulse still racing. I need to find Nathaniel. He needs to know about the symbol on the floor.

Once back downstairs, I push my way through the crowd.

The gym is a blur of movement, students laughing, dancing, completely unaware of the danger. My heart pounds as I scan the space.

Heather and Vel are near the edge of the dance floor. Vel is saying something animatedly, but at the sight of me, she stops.

'Heather,' I say, going up to them. 'Have you seen Nathaniel?'

She shakes her head. 'No. I assume he is still outside.'

I clock the entrance, determined to get to him. I rush forward.

Slam.

The doors to the hall swing shut with a deafening finality.

The entire room shifts.

The lights dim, casting eerie shadows along the walls. The music cuts off mid-beat, leaving behind an abrupt, echoing silence. A murmur ripples through the crowd, confused voices, uneasy laughter. People turn to each other, whispering, asking what's going on.

Then, across the hall, the students begin to part.

Like someone, something, is making their way through.

I follow the movement, my pulse hammering as the band step back from their instruments, clearing a path to the microphone at the front of the stage.

Draped in flowing black fabric, a figure moves with slow, deliberate steps. A heavy veil obscures their face, trailing down over their shoulders, blending seamlessly with the dark ballgown that pools at their feet.

Something in my gut twists.

The figure stops at the microphone.

For a beat, nothing happens. Then, with an almost theatrical grace, they raise a hand, grasping the veil between their fingers, and lift it away.

Thick blond curls spill down over a dark masquerade mask, framing her face.

Eva.

FORTY-TWO

INDUSTRIA VOCARE

LIAM

Laughter and music swirl around us as we move with the beat, the pulse of the bass thrumming under my skin. Lily twirls beside me, grinning, while Jack is caught between busting out his ridiculous dance moves and trying not to trip over his own feet.

For a moment, I let myself enjoy it. The normality. The idea that we could just be regular students at a college masquerade, having fun.

But my eyes keep darting over the crowd. Searching.

For Eva.

For Tariq.

I haven't seen him since we split up. He can handle himself, but that doesn't stop the worry I have.

'Phoebe!' Lily suddenly exclaims, pulling me back to the present as she throws her arms around the girl who's just appeared beside us.

Phoebe hugs her back, her thick brown hair partially getting caught in Lily's mask. They laugh, but her gaze quickly flickers to Jack. Jack, who instantly stiffens like he's just remembered he has a body and doesn't know what to do with it.

Right.

Well, this is awkward. Jack was meant to be coming to the dance with Phoebe, before Eva cast whatever love-hold she had on him. But now we know about Eva, Jack is here alone, and Phoebe is probably wondering why.

But instead of giving him the cold shoulder, Phoebe smiles.

'Want to dance?' she asks.

Jack goes completely, utterly, hopelessly giddy.

Lily gives him a shove toward Phoebe before he can overthink it.

'Go,' she says.

Jack barely spares us a glance before disappearing into the crowd with Phoebe, leaving Lily and me in his wake.

'Stay close!' I shout after him.

Lily sighs. 'Relax.' Then, quieter, she adds, 'You definitely have it on you?'

I nod, reaching into my pocket and pulling out the tiny glass bottle. The grave water sloshes inside, our best shot at stopping Eva.

Lily exhales. 'Hold on tight. We don't know when she'll…'

The lights cut out.

The music dies.

A strange hush falls over the hall.

And then… a voice.

Smooth. Confident. Unhurried.

'Good evening, everyone.'

All eyes turn to the stage, where a figure stands at the microphone. The black ball gown. The mask. The thick blond curls.

Eva.

I take a step forward, but before I can move any further, a hand clamps onto my shoulder, holding me back.

'Wait,' Opel murmurs.

On stage, the lead singer of Noir Spire steps forward. 'Hey, no speeches until after the set—'

He chokes.

His hands fly to his throat, eyes bulging as he gasps for breath. An invisible force tightens around him, and a ripple of panic moves through the audience.

I tense.

I'm about to charge forward when Eva casually flicks her fingers, releasing the singer. He crumples to the floor, coughing, but alive.

She turns back to the microphone.

'This world has changed,' she says. 'And not for the better. You go about your days in this city, completely unaware of the power upon which it sits. Well...' She tilts her head, her lips curling into a smile. 'That power is mine. And you are going to be my key to unlocking it.'

A chill runs down my spine.

Then she begins to chant.

The words slip from her lips in a fluid, eerie language, each syllable laced with something unnatural. The sound slithers through the air, curling around us like smoke.

Confusion ripples through the crowd, some people shift uncomfortably, others whisper nervously. A few laugh, assuming this is all part of the performance.

'Tariq,' Opel says.

He's pushing toward us.

'She's started,' he says. 'Look at the floor.'

Beneath our feet, the witch's mark glows, stark and white against the darkened hall floor. The same symbol we've seen before.

The glow pulses brighter, stretching outward like cracks of lightning across the floor. The air thickens, buzzing with energy.

The first cough.

It's sharp, wet.

Then another.

A girl nearby clutches her throat. Blood trickles from her nose. Someone else stumbles, catching themselves against a row of chairs, coughing so hard their entire body shakes. Murmurs of confusion turn into whispers of fear, and then, screams.

Eva keeps chanting.

Vel and Heather rush over, Vel's face pale as she glances around at the people collapsing, clutching at their faces, at their chests.

'I can't heal all of them,' Vel says, voice tight with urgency.

Tariq shakes his head. 'It won't make a difference. We need to get people out, away from the witch's mark.'

He turns to Vel and Heather. 'Get to the exits. Get them open. Move as many people as you can.'

Heather doesn't hesitate, grabbing Vel's wrist as they both disappear into the crowd, shoving people toward the doors.

Tariq lifts his vial of water and turns to Lily and Jack. 'We good?'

Lily nods.

'Operation Rainfall can begin,' says Jack.

'That's not what we're calling it,' I say, and raise my own vial.

'Then you guys have done your part,' Tariq says. 'Go help Vel and Heather get people out.'

But Lily's not listening. She sways slightly, pressing a hand to her nose. Blood.

I rush to Lily's side.

'I feel weird,' she says, breathless.

The spell is getting to her, too.

Jack catches her elbow, steadying her.

'Go,' I say. 'Take her away from here.'

Jack nods and drags Lily toward the doors.

'Opel, you're up,' Tariq says. 'Let's get this thing going.'

Opel moves toward the stage, pulling a tiny vial from beneath her dress. She lifts her hand. The vial hovers, suspended in mid-air, and then she hurls it over the crowd and straight at Eva's face.

The moment stretches.

The glass inches toward its target.

Eva's eyes snap open mid-chant.

The bottle stops. It freezes in the air.

A heartbeat later, the glass cracks. Then shatters.

The water spills uselessly to the floor.

Eva smirks. 'Nice try.'

'Glad I could get your attention,' Opel says.

Eva hisses something, low and sharp, and Opel is flung backward, slamming into the ground at our feet.

'You okay?' I ask, helping her up.

'Bitch!' Opel blurts. 'Two can play at that game.'

Tariq grabs my shoulders. 'You and Opel need to keep the witch distracted – she can't finish the spell.'

I squeeze his arm, nodding.

Opel cracks her knuckles. 'On it.'

My pulse kicks up. I tighten my grip around my vial and head straight for Eva.

I break into a sprint, as chaos erupts around me. Students shove toward the exits, some staggering, some barely conscious. Blood splashes onto the floor. The pounding of my own heartbeat, the sharp breaths of those around me, and above it all, Eva's voice. Chanting.

Opel moves faster, and the crowd parts before us like an invisible force has cut through it. She doesn't hesitate, just throws out her hands, sending a wave of energy straight toward Eva.

It slams into an invisible wall. A shimmer in the air.

Eva lowers her gaze to us, her lips curling. 'And so the Keepers strike again. How quaint.'

I don't give her time to gloat.

With a burst of strength, I launch forward. The stage blurs beneath my feet. The vial gripped between my fingers. All I have to do is land it.

I hurl the vial straight at her chest.

Eva doesn't even flinch. Just tilts her head. The vial stops mid-air, spinning in place. The liquid inside turns black.

Then it explodes.

Glass erupts like shrapnel. I shield my face.

A pressure wave slams into my chest. Like a truck, full speed.

I hit the stage hard, crash-rolling until I slam against a speaker stack. Pain flares across my ribs, hot and sharp. I grit my teeth.

'Hey, witch bitch.'

Eva turns to Opel. 'Motus,' she muses.

Opel snarls and throws both hands forward.

The room answers her.

Chairs, cups, even the mic stand, everything not bolted down around her, rips free and flies toward Eva like a storm.

Eva takes some hits, her dress shredding at the base.

But the whole barrage freezes.

Then, it turns. Straight back at us.

I dive sideways as the mic stand punches into the stage next to me. A chair smashes into Opel's shoulder, sending her skidding back.

Eva steps forward, palm raised.

'Hey, Eva!'

Jack stands at the foot of the stage, wild-eyed and panting.

'So... I've been thinking. We never would've worked out. You're a little high-maintenance, and I'm just not into girls who commit magical homicide. Bit of a red flag.'

Eva blinks.

He's distracting her.

'Oh, darling Jack. You were barely worth the effort.'

A crackle of violet energy surges from her fingers.

Opel rushes to Jack.

I'm up again, ribs screaming, and I charge.

Eva spins.

Her hand locks around my throat.

Agony. Like acid burning beneath my skin. My limbs seize. My vision pulses white at the edges.

Someone shouts. 'Liam!'

I can't breathe. Can't think. Her grip tightens.

She leans in. Her eyes are darker now, veins throbbing in their sockets. 'The Crossing is mine.'

The ritual symbol beneath us glows brighter, lines of white-hot energy pulsing out across the floor. Feeding her.

She's drawing power from the Crossing itself.

'Eva,' I choke. Her grip loosens, slightly.

'You don't have to do this,' I rasp. 'Samuel... he didn't betray you. He moved your body from Grovely Wood. Had you buried with him.'

She frowns, just a flicker.

I push on. 'He loved you, even after the Guild marked you.'

Something shifts in her eyes.

'I know what happened,' I say, steadier now. 'He'd never want this. He'd never want you to become this.'

For a moment, her eyes brighten. She looks away.

'Maybe you're right,' she says softly. 'Maybe... I once believed in love.'

I take a breath.

Then she looks back, and her smile is pure venom.

'But belief is for fools.'

Her hand slams into my chest. I'm thrown backward, again, this time straight off the stage.

I crash hard, tasting blood.

'You think I loved Samuel? He was a means to an end. The Guild had already made up their minds. I had to give them a reason to show me mercy.'

Opel joins me at my side. 'You manipulated him... just like you manipulated Jack.'

Eva sneers. 'The Guild, the Keepers, even my sister. Yes, I cursed the town knowing my sister would be blamed.'

'You wanted the power to yourself,' I say, getting to my feet. 'Only the Guild turned on you too.'

'I bewitched Samuel into burying me in his family plot. I needed a grave I could claw my way back out of. And now, after three centuries, I will finish what I began.'

She lifts both hands, and the light from the symbol surges. Magic crackles around her, distorting the air.

She's winning.

We're losing.

Everyone in this hall is going to die.

FORTY-THREE

OPERATION RAINFALL

TARIQ

The hall is a warzone.

Students are collapsing all around me, writhing on the floor, blood seeping from their noses, eyes, ears. Some are coughing up red, their bodies convulsing, their breath shallow. The air stinks of sweat and iron, and I push forward, forcing myself not to look too closely.

I can't help them.

Not yet.

I lift my gaze, looking toward the high beams criss-crossing the ceiling. That's my target.

Then, movement from the balcony.

Nathaniel.

And behind him, Principal Gellar.

Nathaniel meets my eye, then tilts his head toward the ceiling.

I nod. That's the signal.

Lily's plan better work!

I flex my hand, and heat rushes to my fingers. Flames burst to life in both palms, flickering wildly. I take a steadying breath, then launch them upward.

Twin streaks of fire rocket into the air, illuminating the darkened space in a flash of orange.

But I don't stop there.

I move through the hall, sending flames shooting up like fireworks, spinning, dancing across the ceiling. A Catherine wheel of fire. The heat rises, smoke curling upward. One of the wooden beams catches.

The fire spreads, crawling across the old timber.

An alarm wails into life.

A piercing, high-pitched scream that rattles through my bones.

For a second, I lose focus. My eyes are drawn to the stage.

Liam.

Eva has him, her hand clamped around his throat, his heels lifted slightly off the ground. His mask is gone. His face is twisted in pain.

My whole body jolts forward before I can stop myself.

I can't let her hurt him.

But I'm not here to save him. That's not my role tonight. We have a plan. If I break from it now, if I give in to this instinct, I could jeopardise everything.

He's strong. He can hold her off, just a little longer.

I drag my eyes away, forcing my hands back into motion. Heat gathers at my fingertips as I launch another burst of fire at the rafters. The beams groan above me, but not enough to make what I need to happen, happen.

My attention snaps back to the stage. Opel floats a nearby speaker off the ground, then tosses it at Eva, slamming it into her side. She stumbles back, releasing Liam in the process.

And Liam is already moving again.

He lunges, grabs her by the arms, and throws her off the stage.

Damn. That was cool.

She crashes to the gym floor, right into the centre of the glowing witch symbol.

Eva pushes herself up, now just a few feet from me, face twisted in fury.

'You can't stop me, Keepers,' she snarls. 'Your water is gone. The Crossing's power is mine.'

A wicked, rasping cackle escapes her.

Then, a deep, metallic grind from above. Followed by a sharp squeak.

Eva hesitates, looking up.

And the sprinkler system erupts. A torrent of water pours from the ceiling, drenching everything in sight.

Eva stiffens.

She tilts her head, blinking as droplets splatter against her skin. 'What new contraption is this?' she hisses.

She screams.

It starts slow, her skin bubbling, like boiling wax. Then it spreads. The pale flesh of her arms melts, peeling back to reveal dark, oozing sinew beneath. Her fingers stretch, distort, disintegrate.

I take the opportunity to produce my own vial. I remove the cap, take Eva by the hair, pulling back her head. I empty the contents into her foaming mouth.

She thrashes, clawing at herself, at the air, at us.

The symbol beneath her pulses violently, one last attempt to give her power. But it's no use. The lines dim, flicker, and then die out completely.

Eva collapses to her knees, hands outstretched, her body sloughing away in thick, steaming chunks. Her mouth opens, lips curling into a final, desperate curse.

Then, she is nothing but a puddle of ooze and steam.

The last of the students evacuate, the sirens still wailing in the background.

I exhale, my entire body shaking.

Liam stumbles toward me, collapsing into my arms. Opel into Theo's.

Nathaniel and Principal Gellar join us, followed by Jack and Lily, Heather and Vel.

We all just stand there.

Taking it in.

Taking a breath.

It's over.

Lily staggers in Jack's arms, wiping her bloody nose with her sleeve.

'You alright?' Liam asks her.

'Better now, thanks to you guys.'

'Actually, I think that thanks goes to you,' I say. 'This was your plan, after all.'

'Indeed,' Nathaniel says.

It's genius really. Lily had me draw more water from Eva's grave, enough to fill a barrel, and – with the help of Principal Gellar – she, Jack, and Nathaniel got it into the sprinkler system. Eva would have never seen it coming. There was nothing like that in the 1700s.

Jack claps his hands together. 'Ding, dong, the witch is…'

'Don't ruin the moment, Jack,' Liam says.

And somehow, despite everything, we all laugh.

FORTY-FOUR

THE FIGURE IN THE DARK

LIAM

Mum has already left for her hospital shift by the time Tariq and I get back to mine. The house is quiet. Too quiet, after everything that went down at the masquerade.

It still doesn't feel real.

The witch is dead.

We won.

Nathaniel confirmed it before we left. Ambulance crews had arrived soon after, treating the students who had suffered the most, though many were already beginning to recover. Principal Gellar wasted no time assembling a team to scrub the witch's mark from the hall floor. By morning, there'll be no sign of what happened there tonight – at least, not physically.

I'm proud of Lily and Jack. They helped us stop the witch. But now they know everything. About me. About Sarumbourne. About the parts I was never supposed to share. There's a strange relief in that – finally being seen, completely. But the Guild won't care about how I feel.

Jack and Lily know too much now. And that kind of knowledge? It doesn't come without consequences.

Charles will probably go ballistic; even more so when he realises our focus has been on the witch, not Lucas. But maybe, just maybe, knowing we have a new Keeper on our side, Vel, will soften the blow.

I pass a glass of water to Tariq, and he downs it in one go.

Neither of us have changed. We're both still damp from the sprinklers, our clothes clinging to our skin. Tariq's suit is a darker shade of green now, heavy with water. His curls, usually so controlled, are wild, frizzy, and falling into his face.

And yet, he's still so handsome.

'You were amazing tonight.'

He lets out a soft laugh. 'Me? I just lit some fires. You fought a witch.'

'I was pretty badass at the end there, wasn't I?'

Tariq smirks and steps toward me, a mischievous glint in his eyes.

I gulp, swallowing hard.

The space between us shrinks.

His emerald eyes bore into mine, and my entire body hums.

Then his lips crash into mine.

They're cold from the water, but I don't care. I don't want it to stop.

When he pulls away, he catches the end of my tie between his fingers, playing with it dreamily.

'We didn't get to dance.'

Tariq tuts, running his fingers up my tie, over my collar, tracing the edge of my jaw. 'Shame.'

His hand lingers on my skin, a teasing touch that leaves warmth in its wake.

I push it away playfully, grinning.

He chuckles, eyes darkening as he grips my hips and pulls me closer. 'How can I make it up to you?'

I meet his gaze, heart pounding.

Tariq has always been able to read me.

His lips find mine again, softer this time, slower, lingering. The kind of kiss that steals my breath, that sets a fire low in my stomach. My hands slide up his chest, his shirt damp beneath my fingertips.

We fall into each other, staggering, barely breaking the kiss as we move down the hall toward my room.

Tariq kicks my door shut as I yank off his sodden jacket, letting it fall to the floor beside mine. His fingers move to my shirt, unbuttoning it slowly, fingertips grazing my skin with each undone button.

I shiver, though whether it's from the lingering dampness or something else entirely, I don't know.

I kiss him again, swallowing the quiet hitch in my breath as more layers drop between us. My trousers are next. I step out of them. Only my foot is caught.

I yank it free, and my elbow shoots out, smacking Tariq square in the jaw.

He stumbles back.

'Oh, shit! I'm so sorry!'

He rubs his jaw, then lets out a laugh. 'It's okay.' He takes the offending trousers from my hands and tosses them aside. Now, we're both standing there, stripped down to just our underwear, our pendants hanging between us.

His arms circle my waist as he presses against me again, his lips finding mine. He's warmer now, heat radiating through the cold fabric of our boxers. I kiss him back, letting myself melt into it, but my body keeps trembling.

He slows, his forehead resting against mine. 'You okay?'

I swallow hard. 'Yeah, just… this is my first time.'

Tariq lifts his hand, brushing his thumb against my lower lip. 'Do you want to stop?'

No. I want this more than anything else right now.

I shake my head.

He pulls me closer, pressing into me fully, and we tumble back onto the bed. His pendant stone rubs against mine, warm between us. He kisses me again, deeper, harder, his fingers tracing slow, wandering lines over my skin. My entire body tenses.

I pull back, suddenly breathless. 'Do you have, er…?'

Tariq blinks at me. Realisation hits. 'A condom?' His cheeks flush. 'No. Sorry.'

'I don't either.'

He runs a hand through my hair. 'It's okay.' His other hand skims down my side, fingers hooking into the waistband of my boxers. 'There's plenty of other stuff we can do.'

I laugh softly, my nerves loosening a little. 'Yeah?'

His smirk returns. 'Oh yeah.'

Then he sinks into me again, his weight grounding me, his warmth chasing away any lingering hesitation.

I let him take the lead, and just like during our first kiss, my senses go into overdrive. His touch feels electric, like nothing I've ever known. I'm flying.

The rest of the night is a blur of breathless laughter, and of a passion I never imagined possible.

And I don't ever want it to end.

The night is still, but something wakes me.

A pull. A presence.

I stir, my senses sharpening even before my eyes fully open.

Beside me, Tariq is there, his breathing slow, steady. The faint glow of the moonlight catches on his skin, casting soft shadows over his face. A warmth washes over me. I'm safe.

But only for as long as I'm looking at him.

The moment I turn away, the feeling vanishes.

Something calls to me. A whisper, just on the edge of hearing.

I sit up, heart thudding, and listen.

Silence.

Yet the pull remains, stronger now.

I slip out of bed, reaching clumsily for my boxers and tugging them on. The carpet is soft beneath my feet as I step carefully across the room, trying not to wake Tariq. He shifts slightly but doesn't stir.

Through the flat, the hush feels unnatural.

When I reach the window, the road below is dark and quiet, except for the flickering streetlight, sputtering in and out like a failing heartbeat.

Then, another whisper. The words are faint. But my name might be in there, stretched and distorted by the night.

A chill crawls up my spine.

The light outside flickers again, then dies completely.

I inhale sharply, my breath caught in my throat.

A figure stands on the pavement, just beyond the reach of the shadows.

At first, it's just a shape, tall, still, watching. But my eyes adjust, and details emerge.

The face is familiar.

But it's wrong.

His eyes. Something about him is different. Changed.

Then, his lips part, and it's clear this time.

'Liam.'

The whisper is louder now, no longer distant.

Because now, in the darkness, he's there. His gaze locked on mine.

Lucas.

ACKNOWLEDGEMENTS

First and foremost, thank you to you, the reader. Thank you for spending time in Sarumbourne with this cast of characters. The response to The Dark Friars from readers around the world has been extraordinary. I hope this next instalment continues to bring you enjoyment, surprises, and some escape from reality.

To my editor, Hannah McCall, thank you for returning to this world with me. Your insight and encouragement have been vital. Finding Tariq's voice was no small task, and I'm so grateful for your help in bringing him fully to life.

Huge thanks to Jamie Flack, who once again designed a cover straight out of my dreams. It's gloriously wicked! The detail work is out of this world and it truly brings this story to life. Thank you also to our brilliant character models: Toby Cooper, Delacey-James Foster, Paige Hanson, Ronnie Marshall and Vanessa Sell.

To my proofreader, fundraising guru, and dearest friend, Becca Moore. Thank you for your time and support, this book would not have happened without you. You helped me cross that finish line!

Thank you, Duncan Potter, at Chalk Stream Books for once again getting this book print-ready and for answering all my many questions along the way.

To my family: the Clan, the Squad, the Crew, and my friends, you all know who you are, thank you for your continued love and support.

Bellamy, your insistence on daily forest walks got me out from behind the desk, and that was often exactly what I needed to think, reset, and imagine.

And to my partner, Rich, thank you for proofing the first and final draft. Thank you for being my biggest fan, and for believing in me and this world I've created. Love you, always.

Thank you to all those who gave to my Kickstarter campaign – you helped make this book happen. In particular, *The Handsel Witches* would not have been possible without the generous support of the following individuals:

Georgina Cooper, Jim Cooper, Gillian Hamshaw, Eugene Harrington, Breda Hennessy, Becca Moore, Lindsey Moore, Mike Moore, Oliver Pointer-Jones, Joel Rochester, Linda Smith, Anthony Sweeney.

I never imagined having books (plural!) out in the world. Being able to continue this series is something I don't take for granted.

Writing *The Handsel Witches* has given me joy and immense comfort in a year that's brought sadness and loss. Returning to the world of the Keepers gave me exactly what I needed: space to process, and to dream.

About the Author

The Handsel Witches is Ryan's second novel, following the release of his debut, *The Dark Friars*, in November 2024.

Ryan works full-time for an arts and education charity and writes fiction in his spare time. When he's not working or writing, he enjoys reading, going to the cinema, playing badminton, pottering in the garden, and exploring the countryside with his dog.

He lives in Wiltshire, England, with his husband, Richard, and their energetic springador, Bellamy.

You can follow Ryan on Instagram, Threads, and TikTok at @ryanjhamshaw and subscribe to his newsletter at ryanjhamshaw.co.uk

www.ingramcontent.com/pod-product-compliance
Lightning Source LLC
Chambersburg PA
CBHW030644260626
47157CB00007B/2477